USA *Today* Bestselling Author

TRILINA
PUCCI

synopsis

Me: Ask me what happens in Vegas...

Samantha: What happens in Vegas?

Me: Let me tell you.

WHAT HAPPENS IS THAT YOU GET "MAKE OUT WITH STRANGERS AND PEE IN A PARKING LOT" DRUNK.

TIE THE KNOT WITH A GUY YOU JUST MET.

THEN *ALLEGEDLY* PARTICIPATE IN DEPRAVED GROUP ACTIVITIES WITH HIM AND HIS FRIENDS IN THE HONEYMOON SUITE OF A FIVE-STAR HOTEL.

BUT THAT'S NOT EVEN THE WORST PART.

BECAUSE AFTER AN EPIC WALK OF SHAME, YOU FIND OUT HE'S SOME INSANELY FAMOUS BAD-BOY QUARTERBACK WHO'S IN THE MIDST OF CLEANING UP HIS ACT.

SO NOW, YOU HAVE TO PRETEND TO LIKE HIM...*SOBER*...UNTIL YOU CAN SKIP TOWN WITH AN ANNULMENT AND A SHIRT THAT READS, *"I'D HIT THAT."*

EXCEPT FOR BAM—TINY HICCUP. HIS PERSONALITY CANCELS OUT HIS HOT AF FACE.

AND LET'S NOT MENTION HOW YOU *DEFINITELY* TOOK A TRIP TO POUND TOWN WITH HIS FRIENDS.

SO, YEAH. THAT'S WHAT HAPPENS IN VEGAS.

YOU GET *KNOT SO LUCKY* EVEN WHEN YOU THINK YOU HIT THE JACKPOT.

playlist

1. Last Night (Beer Fear)—Lucy Spraggan
2. Raise Your Glass—P!nk
3. Brightside—The Killers
4. I Want You To Want Me—Cheap Trick
5. Cool For The Summer (Sped up) Nightcore)—Demi Lovato, Speed Radio
6. Misery Business—Paramore
7. Paper Rings—Taylor Swift
8. Chemical—Post Malone
9. Waking Up In Vegas—Katy Perry
10. SunKissing—Hailee Steinfeld
11. 1-800-Bad-Bxtch—Saucy Santana
12. Pieces Of Me—Ashlee Simpson
13. Oh My Gawd—Diplo (feat. Nicki Minaj & K4mo)
14. Karma—Taylor Swift
15. Nonsense (Remix)—Sabrina Carpenter, Coi Leray
16. Get Low—Lil Jon

dedication

Here's to live, laugh, coming our way through a bad bish summer.

dear reader,

I wrote this book with the intention of giving an "every woman" experience. That means the heroine isn't described. I did this on purpose. To allow anyone reading the chance to picture themselves or someone who looks like them. I strived to keep her as vague as possible. So enjoy, because this one's for you and you and you and YOU!

Xoxoxo, Trilina

prologue

. . .

"About last night."

eleanor

Samantha: ELLE!!!! WHERE ARE YOU? WTF WAS THAT ON YOUR INSTA LAST NIGHT?

Samantha: Eleanor. I'm serious. It looked like you were at a chapel in Vegas.

Samantha: Tell me I'm wrong.

Samantha: Oh. My. God. I will strangle you when I see you if you don't answer me stat.

Me: ...

Me: ...

Samantha: Eleanor Margaret Thomas. I can see the bubbles.

Me: All caps...seriously? My head hurts, and you're yelling? Have some respect for the hangover.

Me: You're a menace. Why couldn't I have been an only child?

Samantha: SHUT UP. We're texting. And how am I supposed to know you have a hangover?

Me: Because I'm in Vegas. Duh.

Me: Stop being stupid on purpose. Also, how dare you call me by my full name.

Me: There is trauma in my initials. One monogrammed hand towel, and suddenly I'm calling for help.

Samantha: You'll need an EMT if you don't answer my questions.

Me: Fine... Jesus Nagatha Christie... Fuck. So yeah, about last night...

one

. . .

"Marrying some rando you just fucked is like a rite of passage in Vegas."

eleanor

She's yelling. My older sister, Samantha, is actually yelling at me.

I don't think she's done that since we were kids.

Admittedly, I just texted her that I got piss drunk in Las Vegas and married a total stranger. So, yeah, this sudden call and her head-splitting tone aren't exactly a shocker. But still, I didn't anticipate *how* mad she'd be.

Because it's loud, mad. Her voice is slicing my brain open. She's too loud for the delicate balance I'm barely holding on to. That balance between wanting to puke my guts up or just giving up and finding a bench to sleep this hangover off, hobo-style.

I pull my cell away from my ear as I navigate through people with fanny packs and cheap tropical shirts. All of them milling about in the middle of the busy casino floor like forgotten Sims players.

"Excuse me," I breathe to some random dude holding a three-foot-tall drink before— *Oh. My. God.*

My eyes blink quickly, my mouth falling open as I try to

12

ignore the glance I just got of myself in the reflective side of the slot machine.

"Excuse what?" my sister rants, thinking I'm talking to her. "Excuse you for making the single stupidest decision of your life?"

"Give me a break. Marrying some rando you just fucked is like a rite of passage in Vegas. There are movies made about it. I'm not the first, and I won't be the last. But holy shit...Sami. If you could see what I see right now—"

I can't even finish my sentence because I'm chuckling. Jesus Christ. I look like a clown who's been fucked three ways from Sunday. My shoulder meets my ear, sandwiching my phone and also freeing my hand so I can lick the pad of my finger and attempt to rub the black spread of mascara from underneath my eyes.

"Listen to me. I'm a mess—I've been walking through this whole-ass casino in a white bodycon button-front dress short enough to show off my liver. And most of the buttons in the middle are missing. *Don't ask.* I'm having to hold it closed, otherwise, my entire stomach will show—I'm a poster child for that Katy Perry song 'Waking Up in Vegas.'"

She doesn't let me finish, cutting me off.

"Be serious, Eleanor. For the love of god, why are you making jokes?"

I roll my eyes as last night's faux red bottom heels click a bit faster on the shiny floors.

"Sami, stop overreacting. It's not that serious because—"

She still doesn't shut the fuck up.

"How did this happen? Please tell me this wasn't your idea." Her voice switches to panic. "Wait, were you drugged? Oh my god."

"Are you crazy?" I laugh.

"Are *you*?" she huffs. "You married some guy you just met in Las Vegas. What do you expect me to think?"

"Not that I'm involved in some secret scheme to drug girls

into marriage. Because we all know guys are just desperate to get to the altar. Stop watching those crime shows, weirdo."

I can't help but laugh because she's about to go from lecture to holy shit, from big sister to a co-conspirator, in about two seconds when I say what's sitting on the tip of my tongue.

"Whatever," she breathes.

So I hit her with the real tea.

"Plus, it'll be fine because he's not just *some guy*, Sami... He's Crew Matthews—the quarterback for the fucking Las Vegas Raiders."

This bomb is particularly hilarious for two reasons: one, our father is a die-hard 49ers fan, so my pussy committed treason last night, and two, my sister is in a poly relationship, and one of her boyfriends is a Hall of Fame quarterback.

"I mean, what are the chances? This is wild, right?" I add, grinning ear to ear over the ridiculousness of the whole situation.

I hold my breath, waiting for her to explode. I can already picture her face. Shock and awe plastered all over it.

The silence feels like forever.

But then her voice thunders over the line, louder than all the slot machines I'm surrounded by.

"Shut the fuck up. Lies. Holy fuck. Dad's going to kill you. You'll need to change your name to Julia Roberts because your ass is sleeping with the enemy."

"I know," I squeal, laughing harder as I pass a wall of mirrors and get the full picture of my appearance.

Jesus. The back of my head is matted and sticking up like a broken-ass version of a bouffant. I can't even look at my outfit because it's worse than it feels. I knew it had to be bad, but I look crazy.

And my mouth... *God, why did I wear red lipstick?* The remnants left staining my face should be renamed *blow job* instead of *starlet*. It's fucking smudged all over my mouth.

My eyebrows raise because if this wasn't real life, it would be the opening of a very funny movie.

I swipe my thumb around my mouth, only able to remove some of the smeared red before I give up and keep walking.

"Oh my god. The back of my hair looks like when you made me go to that wacky goat yoga class, and we did that pose called plow. I'm that—minus the hay." My voice drops to a low whisper. "And remember how one of those little furry assholes rammed me in the ass? I'm pretty sure that happened again last night too...multiple times."

I squint, trying to remember the hazy parts of last night. Damn. There was too much alcohol.

"I *think* I may have fucked his friends. My memory's not my friend right now. I can't tell if it was a dirty dream or reality. I need coffee and a nap. And maybe an STD screening."

Another chuckle brims as I run my fingers through the matted mess I call hair. But my sister isn't laughing. My brows draw together just as her words are cracked like a whip.

"Bangs."

I gasp, immediately stopping my trek through the casino. A full fucking stop just to answer her insult. Because that's exactly what that word is.

"Bitch," I hiss. "This is not *bangs*. How dare you call me a copycat. I didn't even know you got bangs when I got bangs."

She almost chokes her words out.

"The fuck you didn't. I sent you a picture of myself, and then you went out and did it too."

"Whatever. Maybe that's true," I huff, completely unwilling to own any of that, like a true little sister. "But dicks aren't bangs. I didn't copy you because I only fucked three dudes...*allegedly*. I breathe too, or have you trademarked that as well?"

She mockingly repeats my words as if I sound like a thirteen-year-old boy, making me grin harder. But I keep going.

"Don't be sour because you can't add. You're fucking four dudes simultaneously—I *allegedly* did three. And I married one. Not the same. Way to be down for the sisterhood, ho... I would've thought getting double-dipped on the reg by your boyfriends would lead to a looser hole...but you're still soooo tight."

"You're such a little twat." She laughs.

I slide past a group of middle-aged guys with jerseys, all staring at me like cartoon wolves staring at a steak. *Gross.* So, I ignore them, continuing with my sister.

"I'm starting to think we must have some crazy-ass genetic disposition. They say kinks are inherited. That means Mom's probably doing the whole cul-de-sac. This is an epidemic. So you need to get it together, narcissist, because not everything's about you. It's about me."

She howls, and I follow suit as she throws out, "You're a dummy. And disgusting. And I'm telling Mom you said that."

"I'll hold you underwater like that scene in *Basic Instinct.* I'll be like, 'Shhh, go to sleep.'"

"Psychopath," she jokes.

I look up at the directional signs, turning around, trying to figure out where I'm going as I counter.

"Nah, sociopath...I'll feel no regret," I breathe out absent-mindedly, looking around, adding, "Damn, these casinos are like mazes. How the hell do I get out of here?"

Sami's talking, but I can't hear her past the whirl of the machines and some people celebrating. *What the fuck? Where is the exit?* I turn another hundred and eighty degrees, looking for divine intervention, but nothing.

"Fantastic," I huff. "I'll be stuck here forever with all this lipstick around my mouth that makes me look like I did when I was nine and wouldn't stop licking a circle around it. Remember that? The skin chapped into a big red ring. I looked like I had an asshole on my face every time I puckered...I'll be Eleanor Assmouth again."

I chuckle to myself, pulled from my thoughts as Sami play-fully snarks, "I'm so glad you're enjoying yourself. Jesus Christ, this shit only happens to you."

I'm nodding, even though she can't see me.

"I am the epitome of a walk of shame. I expect a trophy. If getting railed and smelling like sex was an Olympic sport, I'd get gold. Because there is no amount of cigarette smoke in this casino that could rid me of the smell of whore and unwanted pregnancy."

"You didn't use protection?" she shrieks.

The fake sound of coins spilling into a metal bucket rings out. The combination makes my head pound again.

"Sami," I breathe out with a groan. "That tone makes me hate your whole face. Make your voice go away. It was a joke, dummy. Of course, I used protection...I think." Before she can say anything, I add, "No, we did. I distinctly remember buying condoms that looked like poker chips. Because when they rolled them on, I yelled *jackpot*."

"Liar. I can't believe you raw dogged it."

I laugh. "Shut up, lunatic. We exchanged records on our phones like normal people in the 21st century. But poker chips sound amazing, I should trademark that."

My eyes tick up, finally seeing the exit sign just as the crowd in front of me parts. I swear to god I hear angels sing because— doors. Big, beautiful glass doors. I let out a relieved breath.

Samantha chimes in again.

"B.T. Dubs. Where the fuck is Millie? I thought you guys went out there together?"

"Ah yes, the bestie. Best guess? She's tonsil-deep on a DJ's turntable...if you get my meaning. He's a douche, but she likes him. Plus, our room is a hep B containment center."

I take a few quick steps, attempting to slide out between the massive doors, but a bald, potbellied dude gets in the way and doesn't move fast enough, so they close.

I look down at myself. *Shit.*

Improvisation is required between holding my dress with one hand and squeezing my phone between my face and shoulder. The debate in my head only lasts seconds before I spin around and use my bottom to push it open. My heels dig into the concrete, making an awful scuffing sound as I get through. I spin off the glass, stumbling a few steps before righting myself.

"What are you doing?" my sister asks as I huff breathlessly before I answer, "Persevering."

"Holy shit," I gasp, causing eyes to dart in my direction, but I ignore them as the door closes behind me, taking with it the glorious air-conditioning. "Why is it so hot at six in the morning? It's freaking scorching my skin, and I'm under the porte cochere." I squirm where I'm standing, feeling like I'm already sweating. "This place is hell. It's probably why it's so fun."

"Well, you might want to try to acclimate," Samantha snarks. "We both know you were always headed there."

I look up and down the valet area for the Uber pickup, squinting as I say, "Too bright. Need glasses. Jesus, this is assault. The sun should be charged with first-degree battery."

I drop my head, eyes locked on my fist—the one clutched around the fabric of my dress.

Fuck it. Be free.

My entire stomach springs into view as I let go before fumbling through my bag for my sunglasses and slap them on my face.

"Sooo," Sam breathes. "What's the plan? I mean...you're getting this shit annulled, right? Even if he is Crew Matthews."

"Duh? Like I care who he is," I shoot out incredulously. "I don't even know anything about football. You know that. I left him all my info. When he wakes up, we can take care of it. The great thing about Vegas is you can get married and divorced on the same day. Everyone knows that."

She ignores the important part, blurting out, "Hold up. You snuck out? Whyyyy?"

"Shut up."

No way. I'm not talking about it. She's just going to probe me for information until I admit I woke up in a T-shirt that said *I'd hit that.* That my kitty requires an ice pack as well as underwear

—*which I still don't have*—and that there's still enough red on my cheeks to force an admission of blushing.

My nose scrunches as I lift my hair off the back of my neck.

"Sami, I can feel the hot air in the back of my throat every time I speak. It's like I'm swallowing the sun." I'm trying to sound serious but failing as I add, "I just can't answer any more questions right now."

A loud and far-too-enthusiastic "*Eleanor*" makes my shoulders jump. She's like a fucking dog with a bone. Shit.

"Eleanor! You cannot drop tiny little bombs like that. I want to know everything. Literally, from the beginning. Why is my *not-even-remotely-shy* sister suddenly shy? Dish. Do you have a crush on your future ex-husband? And if you don't tell me, I'll call your ex and tell him you slept with his twin…before you guys broke up…and on purpose."

I suck in all the fucking hot air, gasping again. Because while Sami's grasping at straws, she's unknowingly right on target. *Sometimes you gotta run a little product comparison.*

And those twins were definitely not identical. Unless it's measured in the ability to find my clit because then, they were the blind leading the fucking blind.

"You are a demon spawn," I spit, playing along. "And one day, I'll find your real family and have you returned."

She chuckles like the witch she is. But we both know that eventually I was going to tell her everything. Because that's us. Not all sisters can be this cool, but someone has to set the standard.

"Fine," I hiss, giving in as I look at the valet, mouthing, *Uber pickup.*

He points to an empty line sectioned off by red velvet ropes. So, I traipse over as I speak, seeing my ride pull up.

"I have to start from the beginning. So don't interrupt. Pretend you're choking on dick…we both know you're an expert at that."

two

. . .

"Let's get slutty, buddy."

eleanor, yesterday

"It's open," I yell over my shoulder, zipping the last item into my suitcase.

The door swings open as Millie bursts into my apartment. She's feral, holding up a bottle of pink champagne in one hand and a stack of ones in the other.

"Vegas, baby," she shouts, shaking her hips.

"Whooooo," I yell back, arms lifting in the air as I do a little dance.

We deserve this. We've both been busting our asses at the salon we work at, each of us taking on extra clients, working with zero days off to save for our future salon and spa. But even boss bitches need a weekend off. And there's nothing better than a trip to Sin fucking City.

Laughter spills out from both of us as she sashays toward me, holding out the bottle.

"Pre-party is now commencing, bitch. Get the cups."

She doesn't have to ask me twice. I'm already moving quickly, walking into the kitchen of my apartment before I grab two glasses and tossing my words over my shoulder.

"The Uber will be here in fifteen minutes, so we're shooting the champs and then maintaining until we get off the plane. Because I am not missing the best fucking weekend we're ever having because we're too drunk to drive a rental car."

"Deal." She laughs.

I set the mismatched glasses in front of me on the counter. She's smiling, manhandling the cork as I scrunch my face, anticipating the thing that makes me squeal.

The pop sounds, my shoulders jump, and Millie laughs as the bubbles cascade over the rim.

"Oh shit," I breathe out, tossing her a kitchen towel.

"For you…" she silly sings, filling my cup, uncaring of the mess before she adds, "And for me."

We lock eyes as she places the Moët bottle on the counter and picks up her glass for a toast. But I go first.

"To meeting famous DJs who fly you out for lavish Fourth of July weekends and let you bring a plus-one."

There are wingmen, and then there's my Millie Boobie Brown, as I affectionately call her. She always seems to stumble into the pot of gold at the end of a rainbow—aka a hot dude—every single time she tries to ensure I get lucky.

Millie winks and raises her glass even higher, adding her own toast.

"Here's to the best weekend of our lives, Eleanor Roosevelt. Because what happens in Vegas stays in Vegas. Let's get slutty, buddy."

WE'RE STANDING ON THE CRACKED PAVEMENT BETWEEN THE STRIP and downtown in front of a shitty pink motel with a half-lit no vacancy sign and neon palm tree. And apparently, whose biggest flex is that a celebrity from the fifties slept there once.

The minute we drove up in the rental car, we both knew this

had to be a mistake. And after meeting the smarmy check-in manager in the claustrophobia-inducing lobby, we were further validated.

I blink twice more, staring over at a green half-filled pool before my head turns. My eyes locked on Millie's profile.

"This doesn't look like the pictures."

She bites her lip, her brows almost touching her forehead.

"That's an understatement."

"Millie Rock...this place—" My duffel lifts in the air as I swing my arm, motioning toward the fucking Bates Motel. "This is not a hotel with an *H*. It's a motel with a fucking *M* for murder. I'm pretty sure, based on the smell, there's a fucking dead body in one of these rooms."

"Yeah," she breathes out as she turns to look at me, chewing the inside of her cheek. "I should message the girl I booked it with. This can't be right—"

My eyes pop open as I cut her off. "You booked through a travel agent? Amazing. Call them. They can fix this."

A car horn honks, drawing my attention to the street, the one we're literally standing next to on the sidewalk that's littered with last night's bottles and old cigarettes.

A guy leans out his car's window and yells, "Ten bucks," as he makes lewd gestures with his tongue.

"Okay," I press, looking back at her, and add with sarcasm, "Call like, right now. As much as getting eaten out by a guy with no teeth sounds like the perfect Vegas adventure...I'm gonna pass on catching dry rot. Plus, a tenny seems steep for his sample skill set." I hook a thumb over my shoulder. "Can we get the fuck out of here, please?"

She winces, then shakes her head.

"Why are you doing that? *Millie*, why is your face doing that?"

She lets out a whoosh of breath before she rushes her words out in a long, rambled stream of consciousness.

"It's Fourth of July weekend. We're never finding a room.

Everything was booked weeks ago when I called...even this place. I was stoked when we got this room. And I can't call her because she's not an agent. I met her on TikTok. She's more like a travel blogger, *kind of*. Basically, she made a video that was like hotels to stay at based on your astrological sign... You know I'm a Sagittarius, and we love adventure, so I thought off the Strip would be fun. And the pictures I saw online looked nostalgic, not hazardous—"

Oh. My. God.

I'm already looking down at my phone for available hotel rooms as she adds, "When's the last time you had a tetanus shot?"

My eyes search the screen, coming up empty left, right, and center. Fuck. But still, I lift my head, a grin on my face.

"You sure you don't want to take Hey Mr. DJ up on his offer to stay with him and the other groupies?" I breathe out, staring back at her, a row of red *sold-out* labels littering my phone screen.

"Umm, pass. Plus, where would you go? My blow-job skills aren't that impressive. There's no way I am carrying the weight for both of us. I'm more of a pretend blow job while I actually jerk you off kind of girl."

I laugh. Fair point.

"Well then." I shrug. "We better hope the guy who runs this place doesn't have a creepy guy who stabs us in the shower. Because it's us, possible murder, and the cockroaches tonight. Which one of our signs is best suited for that?"

She chuckles and winks as she wiggles the hotel key card between her fingers.

"Yours. Geminis are basically sociopaths."

The lock clicks just before the door swings open, and Millie and I let out matching whooshes of breath.

Our eyes meet, and we nod at the same time as I say, "We should start drinking again."

BASS. DEEP VIBRATING BASS SHAKES MY FUCKING SOUL AS MY HEAD whips side to side. I'm tipsy and sweaty, dancing on top of a speaker in the balmy summer Vegas weather.

It's exactly how I pictured this weekend, which is a perfect upgrade of the day.

People are singing at the top of their lungs, bodies moving in rhythm, some too close because there's no room and others because the night's taken an even better turn for them.

"Elle," Millie screams up at me, motioning to the bar.

I smile and nod as I squat to a seat and slide off the speaker.

"Shots?" she yells again.

So, I yell back, "Fuck yes."

We make our way, arm in arm, laughing and talking too loud toward the bar at the far end of the outdoor area. Our bodies are still warm from the last time we were here downing shots. But that's the fun of Vegas. Getting drunk and in the best kind of trouble.

I'm fanning myself as Millie bellies up to the wooden top, leaning halfway over and calling the bartender's attention. The music's lower over here, so I can hear her better.

"Are we hanging with Tito or his friend Jacky D?" she throws out, looking back at me, smiling brightly.

I chuckle. "Tito's. Jack makes me feisty. You know that."

Millie shrugs, but as her shoulders relax, I watch her eyes widen. My brows draw together, lips parting as I'm about to ask her what's wrong, but my words catch in my throat because a deep masculine voice rumbles quietly in my ear, exploding goose bumps up my neck.

"I vote for Jack. I bet feisty looks good on you."

The smell of hot fucking dude infiltrates my nose. Whoever's behind me is wearing the kind of cologne that pisses you off when the face doesn't match the scent.

I start to turn around, biting my lip as I think, *Please be pretty, please be fucking pretty.* But I barely get my face sideways before his lips meet my cheek, giving me a small peck.

Oh, hello.

I should be offended. But maybe it's the liquor because I'm the opposite. I'm grinning, especially since he says something cute.

"Excuse you," he whispers as if aghast, before drawing his head back. "If you want me to kiss you, you have to ask. What kind of guy do you take me for? I'm a good boy."

Oh, his charm game's competing at elite level.

I'm about to turn around to get a good look at Mr. Adorable when I feel someone on my other side slip their very large hand into mine.

What the fuck?

My head immediately snaps in that direction, but the grin I'm wearing turns into a smile. Because staring back at me are sexy brown eyes attached to a face that most definitely coaxes panties off with only a smirk and a suggestion.

He's only wearing the smirk now, but I can see the suggestion hanging in the air.

Tall, dark, and handsome winks, and like the fucking audacious big dick he clearly is, he lifts my hand before softly biting my fucking knuckle and says, "Your lips are pretty."

Millie blows out a small whistle, making me chuckle. Because yeah. *DAMN.* I stare up at my hand before I look back at stranger danger.

"Didn't you ever learn to keep your hands to yourself?" I tease.

He unlocks his fingers from mine, still owning me with that smirk as I turn to look between both of my Friday night suitors.

"What in the threesome—" I whisper to myself and Millie, feeling her hand me my shot from over my shoulder. I raise my hand, accepting it as I stare between the two handsome giants.

"Is this the part where I choose which one of you is my favorite version of a one-night stand?"

They look at each other, smiling before they look back at me and shake their heads. Mr. Adorable offers a different option with a wink.

"Who said you have to choose?"

Millie clinks her shot to mine, whispering, "Jackpot," before we down them, and the night gets just a little bit more interesting.

three

• • •

"You two look like there's gonna be a tiger in the bathroom."

crew

"**W**ake up, dick."

My eyes struggle to open. No, fuck that. They straight up refuse as rough-ass hands rock my shoulder back and forth, trying to jolt me from sleep. But I grumble because my head is pounding.

"Jesus Christ, he sleeps like he's in a coma."

I don't have to open my eyes to know it's TJ, my best friend. His barely there Southern drawl gave him away.

A hoarse voice from my other side says, "Then shake him harder. Punch him in the fucking face if you have to. Desperate times, motherfucker."

Nate—aka the one with all the bad ideas. He completes our trio of idiocy we call a crew.

"Fuck off," I groan, shoving TJ's hand off me before trying to pull the blanket over my head, but he yanks it back down, so I growl out, "It feels way too fucking early. And I feel way too fucking drunk. So eat a dick. Let me sleep."

"Let's put him in the shower. Fuck it," Nate groans.

I shake my head. But my eyes are still closed as I flip him off, barking, "I'll break your jaw if you try to get me outta this bed."

My hand smacks down on a pillow next to me before I drag it over my face.

"Nooo," TJ spits. "Nope. You gotta wake up."

He jerks the pillow off and starts slapping my cheek. Hard.

For fuck's sake.

"I'm up," I bellow, smacking his hand as my eyes finally open. "Damn. All right. I'm up." I rub a hand against the stubble on my jaw roughly, grinding out my words, "What the fuck is so important that you're in here making me hate you?"

I blink up at them, suddenly grinning because they're staring down at me, looking haggard, like in a scene straight out of *The Hangover*.

"You two look like there's gonna be a tiger in the bathroom."

Nate's wearing his boxer briefs and last night's shirt, despite missing all the buttons. But TJ takes the cake because he's wearing an Elvis jumpsuit. Except it's only half on, hanging at his waist with stains on the legs...pizza, maybe?

"What happened last night?" I say with a yawn, hearing them chuckle. I'm still half asleep, wiping my watery eyes, but even all teared up, I catch something.

Something on my left fucking hand.

Hold up.

I shoot to sitting like I've been jolted with a thousand volts. But as I do, the whole debaucherously insane night plays out at hyper speed through my mind until I land on the most important part.

"Holy shit. I got married..." My eyes lock with theirs. "And you two fucked my wife."

"Yep. There it is," TJ rushes out, clapping and looking at Nate. "He's with us now. Welcome back, buddy. And the tiger ain't in the bathroom. She's in the fucking living room. You gotta get up. Claire's here."

Shit. Claire. A five-foot-three austere trainer from hell who prides herself in making grown men cry...in the NFL.

My head swings toward the nightstand as I tap my phone for the time. It's 7:00 a.m. I'm late...but that's not what's got my attention. It's the stained, scribbled-on bar napkin.

I swipe it up, unable to hide my smirk as I read it, seeing the wildest girl I've ever met left her number and hotel info.

Dear hubby,
I'd like a divorce. Since you're rich and famous, you're paying for the lawyer.
And since I'm not a gold digger, there's no fee for the memories.
Love, your future ex-wifey
Hit me up when you rise and shine, sleeping beauty.
I'm at The Palm Tree Motel, rm #17
408-242-8381

"Dude. Focus on the immediate issue," Nate blurts out, lowering a hand to cup his junk as I toss the note back. "Claire's pissed, and her aim is as good as yours. She threw a fucking paperweight at me and told me she was aiming for my dick before she hit it."

TJ touches the back of his head like he's traumatized, cutting in and talking over Nate. "I'm pretty sure she punched me in the back of the head to wake me up... she's so mean. I'm probably gonna have to do concussion protocol now. That means no television. The season finale of *Love Is Blind* is this week. And shit is messy."

Nate motions to TJ, nodding at me like it's the most reasonable thing ever said.

These fucking two. But the way TJ's voice broke at the end, like not watching his fucking show is a tragedy, paired with the fact that he's six two and a hundred and ninety pounds...with a beard...almost makes me laugh.

Almost. Because this is actually a crisis. Claire will make me train until I vomit multiple times today. *Fuck.* My stomach turns over at the thought, and my head pounds as I swing my legs over the edge of the bed, keeping my lap covered with the blanket and holding up my hand.

"Okay. One of you tell her I'll be right out. I've gotta call my lawyer and my fucking agent—"

"Shit," they say together, but Nate adds, "How bad did we fuck up?"

Calling my lawyer, Josh, is one thing. Calling his sister Barrett, my agent, is another. Now's not the time for what I did last night. But I've learned that shit's not a problem until it is. So I'm not going to overreact...yet. But before I can answer, my bedroom door flies open, and the tyrant of the hour barges inside.

"Shit," TJ shoots, throwing up his hand as Nate covers his dick, whispering, "Here we go."

Claire holds up her cell, stalking toward my bed.

"What time is it, Crew? Because last I checked, it's my time... and that's important."

I bring my hand to my head, trying to add some more sound-proofing. But she keeps going.

"Your coaches will not be happy. This is rookie behavior. Arrogant, irresponsible bullshit. I thought you were past this kind of shit. What was so important that you had to miss the morning training?"

I grin. I can't help it. Because answering "pussy" isn't an option, even though that's my answer. Damn, that girl was something else. And the shit her mouth did. Fuck. I've never had better. The thought makes blood rush in the wrong direction, so I look up, clearing my throat.

And thank god I do because the guys provide the perfect entertainment for my cock to behave itself.

TJ half raises his hand like he has to ask permission to speak. But Nate smacks his shoulder, making him add, "My bad.

Right. That was rhetorical. Got it... Don't hit me again, mommy."

Claire shoves her phone back into her pocket, snapping, "Shut up, TJ."

Jesus. I know she's pissed, but...one day isn't the end of the world. I'm well aware of my reputation. Shit, some of it is well-earned. But I haven't missed a single day during the off-season, so Claire needs to fucking relax.

I run my hand through my hair as I lock eyes with her.

"I have to make a few calls. We can pick up the afternoon session. I look forward to the torture."

She huffs. Overstepping.

"Yeah? Great. Just remember there are a lot of people watching your every move. Me being one of them. And I'm unimpressed by this. People warned me you would go out of your way to sabotage your own talent. They said, 'He'll be your biggest disappointment. Never live up to his potential.' Shit like this makes me believe they're right."

The muscles in my jaw tense as I shoot to my feet.

"Whoa, whoa," TJ rushes out, adding, "Nate, run block."

Nate grabs a pillow shoving it in front of me to cover my dick because I'm suddenly too mad to fucking remember or care that I'm nude.

"I missed one session," I grind out, gripping the fuck out of that pillow as my blood pressure rises. "You go ahead and tell the fucking coaches whatever you want. I'll still send you a bottle every time I win, sweetheart. I haven't sabotaged shit, but it's good to know you've been listening to the bullshit they leak to the press."

I chuck the pillow across the room as I walk into the bathroom, rubbing a hand over my abs and hearing TJ apologize to Claire.

But from over my shoulder, I toss out, "She's not offended by my dick. She wouldn't be trying to compare hers to mine right now if she was."

Claire doesn't even pause before coming back at me just as hard.

"Matthews, we both know if I had a dick, mine would definitely be bigger."

She walks out of the door, slamming it behind her. But I don't give a shit. There's only a beat of silence before the guys start laughing.

"Jesus, Crew. You really had to go there. That feisty little thing's gonna make you pay for that shit this afternoon. Everything you ate over the past week is coming up," TJ calls out from the room while I pee.

I shake my dick, flushing the toilet, before I turn toward the sink and see a pair of black basketball shorts on the counter. So, I put them on before I wash my hands.

"Hey," I yell. "Someone bring me my phone and order some coffee."

Nate opens the door, tossing my phone to me.

"We're just gonna go grab some grub. We'll bring back coffee too—"

I jerk my head toward my closet, not looking up from the screen as I text my lawyer, saying, "Tell Elvis to grab some clothes if he wants."

"I'm good," TJ shouts, and I chuckle.

I hear my bedroom door close as my fingers fly over the keys.

> Me: Good morning. I hope you're ready to earn your fee today.

> Josh: I was just starting to get bored. You boys have been quiet. What am I dealing with?

> Me: Got drunk married last night. No prenup. I need it taken care of quickly and quietly. I don't want shit interfering with the trade.

> Josh: Jesus, you really did mean I'd have to earn my fee. Girl on board?

Me: Yeah

Josh: Any viral presence we need to worry about?

Fuck. I'm not worried about myself. All my shit is run by other people, but I don't know about her.

Me: Not sure. But her name is Eleanor Thomas…if memory serves. I'll send where she's staying and her number.

Josh: Keep it. I'll be in touch by this afternoon. You realize it's Saturday so we're going to do someone a favor. The courts aren't exactly open.

Me: Whatever it takes to make it happen.

Josh: …Does Barrett know?

The thought immediately gives me indigestion.

Me: She's my next call.

Josh: Good luck, buddy.

I blow out a whoosh of breath because I'll need all the luck I can get. Barrett is a fucking shark and one of the only people who doesn't believe I'm a forgone fuckup conclusion. And I'd like to keep it that way.

What the fuck was I thinking last night?

My mind drifts, thinking over the night, remembering the guys texting me, the fucking drinks…the way she looked in that dress. Damn, I was done the minute she looked up at me when I caught her. A total slave to my dick.

Damn, did we bring out the devil in each other. That wild card was the most seductive experience of my life. I was lured directly down a tequila path and right into her pussy.

Shit, I would've died a happy man had I drowned in it.

A smirk grows on my face, even though Barrett's number is ringing, because my eyes have dropped to my dick.

"This is your fault, buddy," I whisper just as my agent answers.

"Josh texted. What the fuck did you do? Start from the top."

Fuck. My. Life. Here we go.

four

· · ·

"You think they got an Elvis suit I could wear?"

crew, yesterday

> TJ: Hey, dick, get your ass down here. We're at XS. It's time to celebrate.

> Nate: We got booze, girls, and more girls. Especially this one chick. She's wild.

> TJ: Yeah, fireworks are going off in more ways than one tonight.

I groan, staring at the group chat filled with endless badgering by these assholes as I talk to my agent.

"So, the trade's looking good?"

"Yes," Barrett answers enthusiastically. "The Niners are thrilled to steal you away. And I've been reassured they understand where you're coming from and are happy to give you a reset. But that means you have to stay away from anyone and anything that could get you into trouble before contracts are drawn up and signed. Right now, we only have a verbal agreement."

I'm nodding but still smirking.

35

"Does that mean no clubs tonight? Because the boys are blowing me up."

She laughs.

"Club life is fine. How about avoiding public statements telling the team owner to suck your dick?"

"Fair." I chuckle.

Another message pops up as if those two know I've gotten the okay.

> Nate: You can't skip out on Fourth of July. It's time to eat BBQ and pussy. Who are you? GET HERE!
>
> TJ: Come on, dickhead. What are you gonna do...wash your hair? Say affirmations in the fucking mirror? Get your fucking ass down here.
>
> Nate: I'm enough. I love me.
>
> TJ: Five inches is average.
>
> Nate: Nobody chokes, but they like it.
>
> TJ: They aren't faking. Women are just silent when they come.
>
> Nate: We'll do this all night.
>
> TJ: Don't make us use our powers for evil.
>
> Nate: Get. Down. Here.

I can't help but fucking laugh. Barrett chimes in.

"I'm going to assume you're laughing at messages from Tweedle-Dumbass and Tweedle-Dipshit. You know they owe you for what you're doing."

I shake my head.

"They don't owe me anything. If one of us succeeds, we all do. Plus, there's no better defensive end or wide receiver in this league."

"Yeah, but they aren't *you*, Crew. And you know that."

I shrug off her compliment.

"Let me know when the contracts are ready. And maybe try to have some fun this weekend?"

"Contracts and money are my good time, silly. You have fun...just not too much."

I laugh as I hang up before finally answering TJ and Nate.

> Me: Be there in fifteen. And that wild girl you're talking about...I call dibs.

I don't even have to look to know they're texting back an array of *fuck you*'s and *eat a dick*'s.

There's nothing better than a little competition to make shit interesting.

❦

EVEN IN THE DIM LIGHTING, I CAN SEE THEM—MY FRIENDS AND THE horde of women surrounding the table. Jesus.

Fuck it.

We're young and about to seal the biggest trade deal in the league. The three of us are on our way to winning a Super Bowl. Life doesn't get any better.

"Crew" is bellowed above the music as TJ waves me over, smacking Nate's shoulder, who looks over and points at me with a grin.

As expected, they're both already plastered.

I smile as I walk past bouncers who nod their heads and even more people who stare and pretend not to notice me. Until some girl pushes through the crowd and grabs my arm. She's giggling and drunk, staring at me like I'm about to change her life.

Hard pass, sweetheart.

"Oh my god. You're Crew Matthews," is slurred in my direction. "I told my friends if I saw you here, I would totally leave with you tonight."

She's biting her lip, trying for sexy. But I'm not interested. I gently peel her hand off my forearm and flex my jaw before I speak.

"Thanks for the offer, but I just got here. Another time."

She licks her lips and winks, but thankfully, security steps in, ushering her away. My head turns back to Nate and TJ, who are cheering and holding up liquor bottles, making me laugh again.

Jackasses.

The minute I reach the red velvet ropes quartering off the table, a drink is shoved into my hand.

"Took you long enough," TJ yells.

Music thumps, making us have to lean in to speak. But Nate slaps my shoulder, pointing toward the half wall lined against the back of the booth.

"Bro…"

As I look, some girl with a smile that could stop traffic is lifted by security over the back, her feet landing on the shiny black seat of the booth.

Her eyes are bright and her hair a little wild. She looks like she's been dancing all night. She's got a bottle in her hand with a sparkler stuffed inside, spraying bright crackling streams of light into the air, creating a spotlight on her.

"Happy Fourth of July, bitches!" she screams, making everyone around her go wild.

Nate beelines for her as TJ hollers, and the DJ starts spinning more bass, calling everyone's eyes to the sky.

TJ leans in, saying something I don't hear, but I nod anyway because I can't take my eyes off *her*. She's winding her hips, her head thrashing back and forth as sparks shoot up into the sky behind her, exploding in the air.

Fuck.

"Who is that?" I thunder to TJ.

Bright pink rains down, crackling as it decorates the sky, but this chick doesn't even look up. Why would she? She's the main attraction. But whoever she is, she's singing at the top of her lungs while holding the bottle in the air as more people cheer in celebration.

She's in her own world. But I'm mesmerized.

I'm going to eat her the fuck up.

TJ taps my arm, and I make a considerate effort to look away. But she's fucking something. When I finally do look, it's directly into TJ's smirking face.

"That's your dibs... Her name is—"

"Mine." I grin. "Her name is mine."

TJ laughs, then nods. "It's also Eleanor."

I watch Eleanor climb onto Nate's shoulders, high above the crowd. Rightfully so, because this girl is fucking hot.

She's holding Nate's hand, her other in the air holding the sparkler bottle toward the sky as more fireworks explode and the crowd cheers. TJ whistles toward the sky just as the beat drops, and everyone starts jumping, like a massive wave dipping in slow motion.

My brows pull together, not liking what I'm seeing because even though Nate grips her thigh as he joins the motion, bouncing with her on his shoulders, she lets go of his hand.

Nope. She's going to fall.

I shove my drink into TJ's hand as I barrel past him, cutting around the inside of the table. Eleanor holds the bottle higher, dancing with her arms, just as Nate falters and lets go of her leg.

That's when it happens. In a split second.

She falls backward, losing her grip on the bottle, dropping it as she tumbles, headed for the floor. People around lunge, but instinct takes over all three of us.

Nate stops some guy from trying to push me out of the way, TJ's hands reach for the catch, and I make the play.

The entire sky is lit, fireworks detonating one right after another as Eleanor stares up at me, held like a bride in my arms. Caught.

"I got the bottle." TJ smirks as all the sparks begin dying out.

"And I got the girl."

Eleanor's head falls back, her laugh filling my ears before she slips her hand down my chest, pats it, and shrugs.

"This is a helluva way to ask for my number. But okay."

I look down as she bites her bottom lip, so I wink, shifting her around so her legs wrap around my waist, palms laid gently on my shoulders.

"Crew," I offer, our eyes locked.

"Eleanor."

My head tilts.

"Drink? Then your number?"

Her brows raise.

"Shots... then, maybe."

The highlight of my Friday night slides down my body before looking up between the three of us, setting her eyes on me, then Nate, before landing on TJ as she grins.

"Come on, fellas. Let's have some fun."

🧦

"Shots. Shots. Shots."

Eleanor and I reach out, grab our respective tequilas, and gulp them back before snatching up lime wedges and sucking the juice.

She licks her lips, staring back at me.

"You're more fun than I gave your assumed six-pack credit. I thought football players were all healthy and shit."

"Limes are a fruit."

My tongue darts out, feeling a piece of lime left behind before I draw it into my mouth and smirk. Because she's staring at my lips again.

Damn, she's as bad as a dude.

We've been doing this all night—flirting, bantering, and

flirting some more. *Down to fuck* has been volleying between us like we're playing for the championship at Wimbledon. Except on my side of the court, there are three of us playing to win. Not that we're gaining any points. This fucking girl's been running game since she showed up, and my balls are firmly in her hand.

"Where the fuck did you come from?" tumbles out of my mouth as I stare down at her.

"Does it matter?" she teases, blinking up at me as she licks the salt rim of her glass. "Cuz I bet you already know where I'd like to end up."

Her eyes tick between me and then over to the guys before she grins.

A long, drawn-out "Fuck" rumbles in my chest as I tip my head back to the ceiling, simultaneously reaching for her waist.

Our eyes meet again as I pull her flush to me.

"You're a fucking wild card, you know that?"

Nate comes around behind her, twisting his hand around her hair before gently tugging her head back as he lifts a bottle with a pour spout attached.

"Shot, hot stuff?" he offers, his eyes connecting with mine for a moment before he smiles down at her.

Eleanor licks her lips before she leans further back and opens her mouth.

My fingers dig into her hips, keeping her pressed against me as my bottom lip draws between my teeth, then slides out slowly, my eyes never leaving her. Nate lifts the bottle and pours the liquid directly down her throat.

Goddamn, the dirty shit I'm going to do to you tonight.

The minute he's done, she says, "Lime," before swiping her fingers under her bottom lip. TJ holds it up, wiggling it between his fingers.

"Come and get it, sweet thang," he drawls from beside her, but something about how she's corralled us in around her makes me impatient.

Fuck flirting. I want her. Now.

The last thing I hear is *"Oh damn"* before I steal the lime, suck the juice, and seal my lips right over hers.

Nothing about Eleanor backs down or even fucking hesitates.

Her tongue dives inside my mouth as my palms cup her face. I'm hovering over her, the tips of my fingers touched by the dampness just underneath her hair from the balmy night.

Music bounds around us, and I can feel her chest rising and falling quickly because neither of us can get enough. We stumble as her fingers crawl up my back, the taste of tequila and lime bleeding between us, maybe making us drunker, but it really only serves to make me want to taste every fucking inch of her.

I suck her bottom lip between mine, letting it glide out before I dive back in, dipping my tongue inside her warm mouth again.

She moans. And my fucking dick twitches.

Goddamn, that was hot. More.

The last bit of sober me says to stop. To pull away and not fuck this chick in public. But drunk me is more fun and more convincing. So, I drop my arms, disconnecting hers from me before I wrap around her waist and lift her off the ground.

Her legs don't wrap, but our mouths pick up the pace, and the gasp she lets out is eaten by our tongues swirling. Eleanor's hands ghost over the back of my neck before she's wrapped around it, hugging me close as we get sloppier and more desperate.

Fuck, she's a good kisser.

I growl, rumbling my chest, my breath heaving as she pulls away, just as breathless. Her eyes are locked on mine, and she has a smile on her face.

But we're silent, staring at each other as the thump of the bass rattles our bones. She parts her lips to speak but doesn't need to say shit. Because from the way she kissed me back, I know whatever happens tonight will be the time of my fucking life.

"It's about time, QB," she pants. "I thought I was going to have to pull an audible."

My lips part to say, *Come home with me. Right fucking now*, but her friend Millie pops up, a hand on each of our shoulders breaking our drunk bubble. Our heads shift simultaneously as Millie smiles big and bright back at us.

"We've got a party bus, hoes. Let's go. We're blowing this joint."

⚓

I CAN'T HELP THE GRIN ON MY FACE AS I TAKE ANOTHER SWIG OF drink number *too fucking many*. But who cares. Everyone's wasted, and the night hasn't stopped looking promising.

Mostly because Eleanor's ass is directly in front of my face as she stands between my legs throwing dollar bills at TJ, who's swinging around on the gold stripper pole in the middle of the bus like the jackass he is. My eyes tick up to Nate, who's sitting across from me, relaxed, his eyes firmly planted between my Wild Card and her friend Millie.

I know exactly what he's thinking—the guy loves a good threesome where he's the star of the show, but nobody's fucking Eleanor without me in the goddamn picture. He looks up, chuckling as he meets my gaze, and I mouth, *Dibs, bitch.* Not that he gives a shit. So to further my claim, I put a hand on her hip and jerk her backward onto my lap, giving him a fuck-you look before I laugh. She squeals, but it morphs into a laugh too.

I tuck her against me, my lips finding her ear, the liquor I just drank still fresh on my lips as I keep what I say hushed.

"How long do you plan on making me watch the dudes on this party bus eye fuck you before you let me do it for real?"

She turns her head, giving me her profile and a shit-eating grin.

"Your eye's gonna fuck me? That'd be a first for me."

I grumble, biting at her cheek, but she likes it. I know it because she smacks my bicep before turning all the way around to straddle me. My hips thrust upward, bouncing her on my lap as I grab the sides of her dress to make sure it doesn't hike up over her ass. Even still, she keeps talking shit.

"Is that a preview of what I should expect?" She steals my drink, blowing an errant hair from her face and taking a sip before adding, "Because pass. So disappointing. I had such high hopes for you at the club."

Her leg lifts like she's going to crawl off me, but I hold her in place, anchoring her pussy to me.

"Where the fuck do you think you're going? We're not done."

She bites her lip before taking another sip of my drink. It's sexy. But that's not what's got my attention. It's how her hips rock forward, ever so slightly, inconspicuously, as we stare at each other.

"Feel good?" I whisper, but she just grins.

I bet if we sat here like this long enough, she'd slowly get herself off, rubbing that desperate little clit over my cock while a whole bus full of people partied around us, and nobody'd be the wiser.

That thought has my dick growing. Her smile gives away that she can feel it too.

I lick my lips, jerking my chin for her to give me a kiss, but she shakes her head. *Such a little tease.* My hand is already in her hair, gripping it at the nape of her neck.

"I'm not asking. Gimme that mouth," I say with all the gravel in my voice.

I pull, but she pushes back against my hand, resisting, her grin never leaving.

My jaw tenses because not fucking her is becoming painful. I've never wanted a woman more.

I smirk. "You're gonna fucking kill me. You know that? Put me out of my misery and tell me you're coming home with me tonight."

She shrugs, but the glint in her eyes is teasing. "Maybe," she whispers before her voice goes back to normal. "Or maybe I'll go home with someone else. I haven't decided yet."

Oh, she thinks she's funny. *All right. Let's play.*

I steal my drink back, finishing it before setting the empty cup on the seat.

"Someone else, huh?" I repeat, my head turning side to side as I chuckle before I bring my face closer to hers. "Your pussy might as well have *Property of the Raiders* stamped on it. Who's getting through me?"

Her lips slowly form a pout before she presses forward, lingering only briefly until she barely pecks my lips. As she pulls away, she throws out her challenge. "I guess we'll just have to see."

There's a shit ton of conversation happening around us. Even that dumbass DJ Millie is with set up his turntables inside the bus.

But Eleanor and I...we're in a bubble.

This fucking chick. She knows exactly what she's doing. And it's working.

This time, I let her crawl off me, but my eyes are still locked on hers. And as she stands, I do too. *Whoa. I'm fucked-up.*

My hand darts out, grabbing the stripper pole to keep me from swaying too far forward because I almost engulf her beneath my stature.

"What's it gonna take for you to say yes to me?"

She smirks, giving a little shrug.

"Probably more than you got, QB. But go ahead. Give it your best shot—"

The music dies down, and I can feel people staring at us, but I couldn't care less. I don't even care if they hear us or if I look like a beggar.

She issued a challenge. And I'm going to take it.

The three milliseconds my drunk mind takes to formulate what I'm about to say is just enough for me to think I'm a fucking genius. So with all the goddamned audacity I have, I open my lips to speak with far too much confidence.

But I'm cut off, interrupted as she grabs that fucking stripper pole with one hand and the other uses TJ's shoulder to help her stand on the bench seat.

The bus slows, stopping as cheers erupt, and she laughs, pointing at me as she announces shit to the whole bus.

"Crew here wants in my perfectly lovely panties. I think he should try harder to convince me he's the man for the job."

"Miss, I can't go if you're up there," the driver calls out, but nobody's listening. They're too invested in this fucking silly spectacle. A whoosh of breath leaves me as I smile, my hand gripping the back of my neck.

"But," she continues, "if I'm gonna fuck someone in Vegas... in Sin motherfucking City...it should be epic. Right?" More cheers. "So tell the room, QB—how is big dick energy slathered in red flags epic? That just sounds like a Wednesday night."

The whole bus erupts in hollers and oooo's.

"Enjoying yourself?" I chuckle.

She nods, but I shake my head before I turn to my friends. Big mistake.

TJ's clapping and laughing as Nate nods, his eyebrows raised, waiting for my answers. They're enjoying this way too much.

"Well? Answer her," is said from the back somewhere. I reach for her, ready to throw her over my shoulder and walk her back to my fucking penthouse, but she steps back, her ass hitting the window.

"You're gonna get it," I grind out, rubbing the stubble on my jaw because she's cupping her hand around her ear like she can't hear me. So I add, "You want epic? Fine, I'll give you epic—"

But before I can finish, TJ steps up next to her, puts his hands on her waist, and looks up at her with puppy dog eyes as he says, "I'd give you a boombox in the window if you came home with me. We can bring back 1989, sweet thang. Fuck him. I make all the touchdowns anyway."

Her mouth falls open like she's shocked as she runs her fingers through his hair before looking back at me.

That motherfucker.

"I don't know, Crew…TJ's giving me movie reenactments. That's a pretty amazing offer. How do I turn that down?"

I shove his shoulder, pushing him away from her, making them chuckle as I growl.

"Get the fuck off her. You can't make a touchdown with a broken arm."

But it doesn't matter what I say to TJ because I've got two cockblockers. As I turn back to her, Nate's already got her halfway down on his lap, saying he'd tattoo her name on his ass.

"Nope," I grind out, wrapping an arm around her waist and hauling her away before I set her to her feet.

She plops down onto the seat across from them, so I trap her, my palms pressed against the seat on either side of her shoulders.

The smile she's wearing is so big that it's infectious, but I keep my face serious, leaning close enough so my tequila-laced words are only for her. But as I do, out of the corner of my eye, I see it—an epic once-in-a-lifetime motherfucking gauntlet to throw down.

Say no to this, Wild Card.

It could be the booze or the fact that she's made me feral, but what comes out of my mouth surprises me as much as it does her.

"You want epic?" I pinch her chin between my fingers, guiding her face over her shoulder, making her twist to look out the window as I let my lips brush her ear and say two little words that detonate like a bomb.

"Marry me."

Her head snaps back, almost smacking me in the nose, but I

jerk up to standing, falling backward. Luckily, Nate's hand steadies my back.

"What the hell. Are you crazy?" she rushes out.

TJ high-fives me, saying, "Badass," before he looks out the window. "You think they got an Elvis suit I could wear?"

Nate laughs. "I wanna be the best man."

But TJ points at him, saying, "Co...best man," as Nate bends forward with his forearms on his knees, looking between Eleanor and me, completely entertained and invested.

She's shaking her head, so I raise my brows in challenge. More seconds tick by without an answer, and now the bus is starting to throw out *come on*'s and *do it*.

Even her best friend, Millie, chimes in, "Married today, divorced tomorrow...that's a conversation starter for sure, bitch."

I bite my lip, squinting one eye, trying to focus my thoughts —*What am I doing?* That's sober me. *Who cares.* Welcome back, drunk me.

"You wanted epic, right?" I press. "Here it is. Marry me. Then you're mine. Win-win."

She's actually speechless. Just like the whole crew on the fucking bus. Everyone's just staring at us, waiting for her answer. But she wanted to play this game, and I don't lose. Even if I'm plastered. I look around the bus, smirking, my arms spread wide.

"Anyone want to try to beat that?" I shrug, boasting my win, "No? Cool."

An incredulous huff that sounds a bit like a laugh leaves her body before she stands, stepping sideways just a little before she grabs my waist and stares up at me.

"Or are you full of shit?" I press. "Maybe you're just one of those girls who's all bark and no bite? Likes the chase but doesn't wanna get caught."

Her brows raise as she takes a step forward like a little badass, making the backs of my knees hit the seat so we're forced to switch positions—now *I'm* sitting, and *she's* trapping me in.

She licks her lips, and I don't even pretend not to stare at her mouth.

"You think I won't do it? Or that I'll just cave and go home with you because you tried some wack-ass reverse psychology?" She laughs arrogantly, like she's about to mic drop. "No. *You're* full of shit. I'm a helluva poker player, Crew. And I'm calling your bluff. You want me, then dun-dun-duh-dunnn, playa."

We're staring at each other for what feels like forever. Yes, I threw down the gauntlet. But she's also right. A part of me didn't think she'd actually call my bluff. She winks, and that's when the most dumbass decision I've ever made solidifies.

The bus kicks into action, rumbling back to start, so I turn my head, bellowing my words.

"Stop the bus. We're getting married."

five

• • •

"I'm pretty sure there's still cum on my back
from last night."

eleanor

"**H**ome sweet hepatitis," I whisper to myself, walking the three steps from the curb to my motel door, avoiding the décor of cans and discarded strip club flyers in front of the building.

My hair's hanging in my face, so I brush it away before digging into my purse for my key card. All the funny disposition I had before now vanished. Because the moment I hung up with my sister, the adrenaline from my walk of shame plummeted, and all I was left with was a hangover and the mystery filth coating my back.

A tired breath whooshes out as I shove the key card in, but it just beeps, and the little light goes from green to red. So, I jiggle the handle before trying again. But the same thing happens—green to red.

What the hell?

"Dude, I'm too tired for this shit," I grumble, tilting my head back to the sky before I look back at the lock and try again...only to fucking fail.

"Fuck my life."

On the upside, I'm staying in the shittiest motel in Vegas. This means I don't have to walk down luxurious hallways or take gold elevators to the front desk. I can walk about twenty or so feet to the small coffin-sized lobby—that smells like hot dog water—where you can rent a room by the hour, day, or week.

A little bell dings as I open the lobby door, and I'm greeted by a middle-aged guy in a black soccer jersey sitting behind a counter.

He's licking his fingers clean of whatever sauce is on his chicken wings. *Eww, who eats wings at the crack of dawn?* Eh, somehow, that seems on-brand for him.

Regardless, the smell makes my stomach gurgle.

He uses his shirt to wipe his licked hands as he lifts his chin to speak.

"Right. Room 17. I've been waiting for you."

He's got one of those Irish accents that's hard to understand, like Brad Pitt in *Snatched*. Except he doesn't look like Brad, and my attitude is the only snatch I'm introducing to him. I half roll my eyes, not at him, just over the moment as I answer.

"Yeah, my key card doesn't work. Which you clearly already know. Are you guys having a problem or something?"

I gently toss it on the countertop, trying not to react as he clears his throat, hacking up too many sounds. *Ewww.*

"Allergies," he offers, skating my key card across the cheap fake-wood laminate counter toward him.

All I can do is smile tightly because, for fuck's sake, just get me the hell out of here and into my less gross room. The fact that I can think that should be considered a health violation.

"Here's the thing, love," he levels. "I can't make you another key. It's impossible."

"Are you kidding me? How long will it take to get a new one?" I shoot out quickly, but he shakes his head as his words sink in.

What. The. Fuck.

"Your credit card declined. You birds chose to pay by the day. No cash, no room."

Fuck. Fuckkkkk. We only did that in case we could get a better room.

I open my purse, running my hand through my hair. But all that's in there is some Mentos, my ID, and a slot machine cash-out slip for $0.32. I left my debit card in my room and took cash with me last night.

Shit.

My chest begins rising and falling faster because what am I supposed to do? Call Millie? Call my sister? The bank? *Oh fuck, the bank...they think this is fraud.*

"Listen," I rush out, hoping to negotiate. "All my stuff's in the room. Just let me in, and I can change out the card. It probably declined because the bank thinks the charge is fraudulent—"

His face says no before he does.

"No. Can. Do. Call your bank. Clear it up. The room's yours again."

My shoulders sag as I let out a harsh breath, narrowing my eyes at him. I'm going to punch this dude in the fucking face.

I reach inside my purse so I can call said bank, but as I pull it from my bag, staring back at me is a black screen...the kind that only a dead fucking phone produces.

"Come on," I growl-scream. "Are you fucking kidding me?"

All my patience gives. It straight-up leaves my mother-fucking body, and I punch the air like I'm fighting with a fucking ghost. I'm huffing, a little breathless but not embarrassed, as I blow my hair from my face and look back at D-rate Brad, who shrugs, picking up another wing, talking as he chews.

My palms lie gently on the counter as I say my words with forced calm.

"It seems as though my phone is dead. So can I use your landline, please?"

He shakes his dumb fucking head again.

"Nah, can't do it. Guests only."

The rest of my words come out as sarcastically as I mean them.

"That how you got your five-star rating? By being a dick?"

"No, it's because of the blow jobs the cleaning crew gives," he counters, tossing the slurped-over bones back into the Styrofoam carton.

I groan, looking down at my phone before I hold it up to drive home my desperation.

"Look, just let me charge my phone for five minutes. Then I'll call my bank. And I'll get you the money."

Our eyes meet again, and without missing a beat, he says, "Chargers cost five bucks."

I almost scream, *Motherfucker.*

The grip on my phone is deadly. I feel like I could bend the metal. My molars clamp down so hard they might break as I stare back at him. But if they do, I'll look like a fucking crackhead.

I blow out a harsh breath, gripping the edge of the counter as I lean closer to him, my voice perilously close to murder.

"Listen to me. I just did an epic fucking walk of shame through a Vegas casino, wearing this peekaboo tummy dress and dried sweat. I'm wearing whore clothes in the daytime. Whore clothes are meant for the night...for when people are whoring." I hear the bell jingle on the door behind me as my hand slaps the counter. But I'm officially at rock bottom, so I don't care who hears me. "I'm pretty sure there's still cum on my back from last night. Actual fucking dried-up jizz. Check-in Charlie...I just need a Big Mac. Fries. A Coke...*with light ice.* And a goddamn shower. In that order. So, what do I have to do to make that happen? And don't say *you* because I'll vomit all over your shitty lobby."

A laugh from behind me immediately draws my attention.

"Thank god," I breathe out, throwing my arms in the air in celebration, locking eyes with Millie over my shoulder. "My fucking bank card declined. I was dangerously close to giving five-dollar blow jobs for a charger."

Check-in Charlie chuckles and wags his brows, so I flip him off as Millie sashays over, pulling her credit card from her wallet.

"We wouldn't want that... P.S. You look like sex. Like straight-up *fucking*, Eleanor. Exactly what happened last night with the football team after we parted ways?"

Her card hits the counter as she turns toward me with a smirk, waiting for my answer. I smile, biting my bottom lip, and shrug.

"Let's just say I put a quarter into the slot machine of life and got a full house."

six

. . .

"I'd rather have third-degree burns than that
dirty dick in my mouth."

crew

I push my burger away, not hungry, because Claire really did try to kill me during my workout today. My stomach is still fucking queasy, even though I puked my guts up twice on that damn field.

TJ looks up over his food, furrowing his brow.

"You good man, or did itty bitty do you in?"

I rub a hand over my bare stomach, my skin still clammy from the sweat. The good news is if there was any booze still left in my system, it's gone now.

Nate laughs, chugging his water.

"Better you than me. I woulda dug a fucking hole and buried myself if she'd made me run one lap. I've never been so hungover than I was this morning."

I nod, yawning, contemplating the idea of taking a nap since it's almost noon, just as my phone vibrates in my pocket. I lean sideways on the couch, reaching into my shorts before my eyes narrow in on the text from Josh.

> Josh: The judge wants us in chambers to sign papers in one hour. One hour. Grab your Cinderella, and let's get this done.

> Me: Got it. One hour. Cinderella in tow.

"What's going on?" TJ asks, still stuffing his face.

I push off the couch, stand, and grab my T-shirt off the back, answering him as I slide it over my head.

"Nothing. I got a date at the courthouse." My head pops through the hole, and I smile at the guys. "Time to get me divorced. But if I'm lucky, I might score with my ex-wife."

They laugh, but I'm half serious. Eleanor was definitely a fucking memory I'm tucking away for a rainy day.

I snag my phone off the couch, shooting off a text to her.

> Me: Hey, you want the D? Yeah, you do. I'll swing by and pick you up in forty-five minutes for the courthouse.

🧦

eleanor

"Fuck," I grumble, standing next to my bed, messing with the cord attached to my phone.

"What's wrong?" Mills chimes in as I pretend misery.

"This stupid charger wasn't working. My phone's still dead. Where's that other charger you used yesterday?"

She looks thoughtful for a minute as she stretches. We slept most of the morning and into the afternoon, but it was the only real way to survive our hangovers.

"Car," she says, marbled in her yawn.

I give her a wink as I swipe the car keys off the nightstand, shoving my feet into my slides before I head to the door.

"Are you going to put pants on?" She laughs while saying it.

I shake my head, looking down at the long T-shirt that says *I'd hit that*. There was no way I was leaving it behind. It's the perfect memento from my night of debauchery.

"Nah, I'm good. I'll be right back."

The heat hits hard the moment I step outside, making goose bumps bloom over my arms. I'm already fanning myself as I walk over the loose gravel toward the shit brown Toyota Camry we rented. But you can't beat nineteen dollars a day.

My only current regret is that we parked in the far corner of the lot, almost hidden by the dumpsters. Because this place really should be a filming location for *Unsolved Mysteries*.

"Hey, girl."

My Nike slides crunch on the ground as my breath catches, and I look over my shoulder.

Some dude that looks like a Vanilla Ice dupe smiles from where he's leaning against the wall.

"Oh, hell no," I whisper, turning back and picking up my pace, trying not to sway my ass.

I start walking like I've shit my pants, kind of wide-legged and stiff.

Why did I think wearing a fucking nightgown shirt was a good idea? Fuck. What if this is like that documentary I saw once. What did they say again? Oh yeah—if you look a pimp in the eye, you become his girl.

Do not look over your shoulder. Do not look over your shoulder.

I'll kill Millie if I get fucking trafficked in Vegas by Ice Ice Baby.

My breath finally leaves my body as I reach for my car door, clicking it unlocked. *Oo shit, it's hot.* But I tug it open anyway.

I'd rather have third-degree burns than that dirty dick in my mouth.

God. Damn.

The amount of hot air that just bursts from inside my car feels like I'm being hotboxed by nature. What the fuck.

I can't even fucking swallow as I slide inside, closing the door. Jesus Christ. I read once that the murder rate increases when the temperature hits above ninety-eight degrees. I believe that because I want to shank someone right now.

How do people who live here survive? This weather is like a live reenactment of *The Purge*.

I pull the visor down to look behind me to see if Pimp Daddy Lame is still there. But I don't see him anymore. *Thank god.*

So, I shove the keys into the car to start it so I can turn on the air-conditioning because I feel like I'm being subjected to cruel and unusual punishment. My head falls back as I groan because more hot air bursts from the vents before turning cold.

I'm too delicate for this. I live in California. Anything above seventy-five degrees is torture.

Las Vegas is basically waterboarding me. *Jail for you, Sin City.*

My eyes drop to the console as I rummage around for the charger, but I don't see it, so I look in the back seat, twisting my body to try to look at the floorboard. The tip of the cord is peeking out from under the passenger seat, so I lean over awkwardly, trying to reach it.

As I do, tires ripping over gravel fills my ears, but I don't look up, still struggling, scooting myself a little further over to try to get my fingers on the cord.

Did that car peel in?

My gut starts to turn over as the thought lingers.

Oh my god. What if that sketchy dude left and came back with more dudes? No. *Maybe...*

It's one of those thoughts that make you ask yourself, *Am I crazy, or is this intuition?*

I'm either about to save my own life or humiliate myself, like when I was sixteen and I called the cops on our neighbor because I thought he was part of a satanic cult killing people in his basement. Turns out he and his friends were just playing D&D and liked to dress up.

Regardless, I swallow hard and start walking my hands back

to sit right in the seat. But as I sit up, my hair still in my face, the passenger-side door opens.

I scream. Close my eyes. And fucking swing.

I'm not even sure I connect with anything, but I keep doing it. And for whatever reason, like a lunatic, I start reciting all the information from the self-defense class my whole sixth-grade class was forced to take.

"Feet first. Feet first," I bellow.

I try to spin myself around to kick whoever's in my passenger seat, still yelling my thoughts.

"I won't go quietly. But I haven't seen you. I can't be a witness."

My fist connects with something hard, as I hear a deep voice say, "Ow. Fuck."

That's right, bitch. Catch these hands.

I'm wild, feral, throwing all manner of my *one* hand. Because I'm so deep in panic, it hasn't occurred to me that I could let go of the steering wheel and use my other one too.

"Stop hitting me," my attacker growls, swatting me away.

But I yell back, still trying to lift my leg to get into a position like I'm in the UFC as I yell back.

"I'm not even in the age demographic to be trafficked. Google it. Fuck you."

A very strong hand grips my thigh, holding it in place as he yells back, "Would you quit fucking hitting me? Eleanor. Open your goddamn eyes."

Eleanor? They've done their research.

I swing harder, shouting, "How the fuck do you know my name?" I connect again with my open palm, sending shock waves up my arm. "I know someone who knows Liam Neeson's trainer. This bitch is not about to be taken."

My wrist is grabbed, so I blurt self-defense lessons again. "Make my body limp."

As if I'm trying to actively get kidnapped, I go limp, jerking my wrist from his hand as I fall over the console. My head and arms sprawled into his lap.

Why am I getting closer to his dick?

"What the fuck is wrong with you?" The deep voice thunders, "Get off me."

He grabs my rib cage, trying to lift me, but I'm not cooperating, even though he raises me anyway as more insanity tumbles out of my mouth.

"I have gonorrhea. Nobody will pay good money for me. I'm bargain basement. Spoiled meat. Throw me back."

"Is this a joke?" My jaw is gripped, forcing me to turn my face toward his voice. "I'm not trying to traffic you, weirdo. Open your fucking eyes. Jesus Christ. It's Crew."

I'm panting, completely breathless, as I blink, then open my eyes slowly.

Eyes the color of water from somewhere tropical stare back, set against tousled brown hair and lips with just the right hint of fullness.

My chest's still rising and falling too fast as a grin grows on my face. Because Crew's just as hot as I remember...*and* as the fucking gravel in his voice.

"Hey, wifey. Remember me?"

I bite my lip, trying not to laugh as I nod and attempt to fix my hair, swiping it out of my face.

But he winks and rubs his jaw, tapping a finger to it as he adds, "Good. Now, give daddy a kiss and make it better."

seven

. . .

"No commitment, all the fun, and none of the feelings."

eleanor

"Yeah, right. You're insane. What are you doing here?" Embarrassed, I scrunch my face as I add, "Other than getting beat up."

If I had to describe the look on Crew's face, it would be wildly entertained. His eyes drop to my lap before he slides his hand over the console. My eyes follow his line of sight just as he gently plucks my cell phone from between my thighs.

The motion is all too slow and drenched with sex appeal. *Drenched like my pussy.* His fingers graze my skin as he holds up my cell.

"You never answered my text."

"Dead," I answer at the same time he taps the screen.

Crew bites his bottom lip before his eyes lift, locking on mine again as he hands back my phone. God. I feel like I'm in high school. We're just sitting in my car, smiling at each other like the way you do when you have a crush on someone and you're finally talking for the first time.

Except I've already married him and done some dirty deeds.

I think that's what's making me smile so much—all those delicious memories.

Damn. I really got drunk and married this dude, then let the starting lineup for the Raiders rail me every which way. I've never wanted to be a role model, but god has his favorites, so it would be selfish of me not to accept this privilege.

I laugh to myself over my thoughts, still staring at him and those dreamy fucking blue eyes. I should really buy a notebook and write the whole night out while it's still fresh. That way, when I get old, the people at the nursing home can read me my *ho tales*, so I'll die happy.

Crew leans in, resting his forearms on the middle console as he speaks unhurriedly with all that fucking gravel.

"You're cute." His eyes drop to my lips before lifting again. "You should've stayed this morning. I would've given you a personal wake-up call."

I mean, it's only fair since he basically put my kitty in a coma the night before.

My bottom lip drags from between my teeth before I say, "You still haven't said why you're here."

"We have a date."

"A date?"

He nods, then frowns as he rubs his jaw, adding with a wink, "Yeah, with a judge. I'm thinking I should claim spousal abuse and take you for all you've got. You're so mean to me."

I laugh, playfully shoving his shoulder. He doesn't budge like he's extremely comfortable invading my space, so I lean against the door as I speak, glancing at the way his arms fill out his white T-shirt.

"Well, currently, 'all I got' would be this T-shirt. A pack of Mentos. And that jackpot for $0.32 we hit last night."

His brows raise like he's pretending to be impressed, so I sarcastically throw out, "I know. I know. Try not to be overwhelmed. I really didn't fuck you last night for you to become a gold digger today. I'd appreciate it if you could maintain some dignity."

He laughs. And I do, too, before he moves away, grabbing the door handle and saying, "Come on, you pretty little thing. Go put some pants on so we can go do this divorce. No wife of mine will show her ass in public." He narrows his eyes, still teasing. "But if you're a good girl, I'll take you to lunch after. Anyplace you wanna go. I'll be sixteen cents richer, after all." He shrugs. "I mean...I'm definitely taking you for half."

I smile as we both get out of the car, and I look over the roof. Fuck, he's so tall. I raise my chin higher to make eye contact as I speak.

"I knew this would happen. You're a monster. Fine. But I'm going big with that kind of fortune—McDonald's. And I'm warning you...I'm ordering a Big Mac *and* a Coke."

He whistles, lifting his hands like what I'm saying is really taxing, making me laugh again before he adds, "And I bet you'll get that drink with light ice too, just like last night. You're a real ball breaker."

Hold on a minute. Did he just remember my order...from when we were plastered?

He glances at me as we walk side by side, and suddenly, I can't stop grinning again. This guy is too much. Between those fucking muscles and that chiseled jaw, along with the memory of the deep-cut v that runs along his stomach all the way down to paradise—I'm completely hot.

But the fact that he casually threw out the one thing no man has ever known has me rethinking this divorce.

I mean...not really, but like, do I have a crush on my future ex-husband?

Yeah, I think I do, with my whole french-fry-loving heart.

Eww. Why is my pussy being problematic? Vegas is for catching cock, not crushes.

crew

"We're definitely hooking up again."

The words pop right out of my mouth without permission or apology. But I can't be blamed for my frankness. Kissing her is all I've thought about for the last ten minutes of this damn drive. Well, maybe not *just* kissing her.

Her head snaps to mine as her mouth falls open.

"Wow. You're something else," she breathes, ending with a grin. "So sure of yourself. I have bad news for you though. I make it a rule never to double dip, my *fun dick*."

What the fuck? Did she just call me…

I stop at the red light, turning my body to look at her. I hear my phone buzz, but I ignore it. I know it's Josh. He's been blowing me up the whole time we've been driving because we're late.

And we're about to be even later because what she just said is my only focus. I pipe up, almost laughing, "Did you just call me *fun dick*?"

She nods with a deadpan expression as she answers, "Yeah."

When I don't say anything, she smirks, explaining, "You remember when we were kids and there was that candy that like came with the little sugar stick, and you would dip it into the powder and lick it?"

"Yeah…"

I raise my brows, wondering where the hell she's going with this because suddenly, all I can see is *her* last night, dragging her silky tongue up the shaft of my cock before deep-throating.

She smirks like she can see my thoughts before continuing. Shit, she probably can. It's not like I'm trying to hide what I'm thinking.

"I loved that candy," she continues, rubbing her hands over her exposed thighs, making me do a double take.

Tiny little goose bumps bloom over her skin as her hands drag up and down. I blink, lost in my thoughts. I want to push her legs apart and drag my warm lips up her inner thigh just to see how far I could make those bloom. Maybe *all the way* until I reached her pussy... *Fuck.*

I clear my throat and look back up.

"You loved that candy? Sorry, you were saying?"

She nods, amused as she continues. "Yeah...but I could only ever sample one flavor before I'd eat the fuck out of that little stick, and I'd get a stomachache."

Little? I mouth, knowing she'll get the joke, as I reach up to lower the air-conditioning.

She does get it because her eyes roll before she adds, "The point is...your cock, Crew, is my *Fun Dip*. Deliciously flavored but only good for one round, or you'll end up making me sick."

I laugh because I literally don't even know what to say. I have never met a girl like this in all my life. I'm shaking my head, my eyes locked on hers as she smiles back, completely unapologetic.

Jesus, there are so many thoughts traveling through my brain, most of them about how I want to fuck her even more now. *How does she do that?* Make me want her more while holding me under a fucking sea of rejection.

"Light's green," she whispers, her eyes staying connected to mine as she motions to the signal.

I huff a laugh, still partially in shock as the GPS tells me to make a left. The steering wheel is midturn as I glance over at her again.

"Let me get this straight. Now that you've tried me, you'll move on to another *flavor*?"

"Yep."

Damn. And people say men are terrible.

"You're such a player," I goad, pulling into the parking lot. "A love 'em and leave 'em type." She rolls her eyes again, not missing the teasing in my voice, especially as I add, "But don't worry about me. I won't bother you with my tears—"

She interrupts with a shit-eating grin.

"Let me guess, you'll wait until you're in the shower, listening to early 2000 Ashlee Simpson songs before really falling apart."

"'Pieces of Me' got me through some hard times, Eleanor. Have some respect."

"Oh. My. God," she scoffs incredulously. "Give me a break. I'm the player? How many real relationships have you had in the last five months…let alone the last five years?"

I'm parking as she lifts a hand, stopping me from answering.

"Hold on. Let's make it even easier to answer. Name three girls whose last names you know." Before I can pop off my retort, she crosses her arms and says, "Women you aren't related to, Crew."

My head swings back so that I'm staring past the hood of the car with a smirk on my face, shoulders shaking in acquiescence as she says, "Mm-hmm, exactly. So, shut up. You just don't like to lose."

She's right. I don't. Who the fuck does, other than losers? I reach down and lace my fingers through hers, lifting her hand to my lips and kissing the top gently.

I'm trying for charming, even though she looks unconvinced. *Amused* but unconvinced.

"You realize if I win, we both win," I tease. "And technically, ex-husband should count as a different flavor." With my lips against her skin, I lift my eyes. "If you let me dip my stick in, I'll let you lick it off."

She scream-laughs, tugging her hand away before she takes a deep breath and shakes her head.

"You're such a guy…you should've offered to just lick it, and I would've said yes. Now you're screwed, buddy."

Buddy? She's the cruelest little vixen.

She turns away, still smiling as she gets out of the car. But I groan as I exit, tossing my words at her.

"You should work for the military because you definitely specialize in torture."

She laughs, and I follow suit until my eyes land on Josh. He's pacing at the top of the empty front steps of the courthouse.

"Your lawyer?" she breathes out as we meet at the front of the car. "He must stay busy with a guy like you as a client."

I chuckle, but without skipping a beat, I put her in a loose headlock, smiling as she laughs before pulling her toward me so we're flush.

"Wild Card, listen to me...you can't blame a guy for trying. For the record, you're the coolest chick I've ever known. Not just anyone can handle Tweedle-Dumbass and Tweedle-Dipshit so well."

She knows exactly what I'm talking about. Nate and TJ might've been guest stars, but the way she worked the three of us over made her spotlight very well deserved. She's filthy, and we loved...*I* loved every minute.

Those big eyes of hers stare up, her palms pressed against my chest as my lips barely part. But it's Eleanor who speaks first.

"You'll have to tell the Tweedles I said goodbye."

"Deal," I whisper, wetting my lips, making no secret about what I want. "But since we're here...together. Maybe one for the road?" I lift my chin, beckoning her mouth. "You can't divorce me without a proper goodbye, right?"

She shrugs, a gleam in her eyes, whispering, "I mean, it *is* a traditional goodbye in many countries...sooo—"

Her fingers curl into my shirt, gathering bits of it as they crawl up my chest, pulling me down toward her as my words hurry out.

"So does that mean yes?"

"Just kiss me goodbye already, QB."

The smile on my face vanishes because I do just that. My mouth seals over hers, hands cradling her face.

Fuck. She tastes exactly how I remember. Like mint and lavender. Her tongue's like a fucking dessert, and I can't get enough. A low rumble shakes my chest as she nips my bottom lip before sucking it, her hands sliding around my body, hugging me.

There's not a hint of space between us. Not between our mouths or my hardening cock and her stomach. Our heads tilt, lips gliding between each other's, tongues dancing faster and faster. She's stealing my breath, and I'm stealing hers because neither of us seems capable of stopping.

We're fucking. I mean, we're not, but this kiss feels like we're fucking.

I'm hovering over her, my fingers tightening in her hair as we stumble backward before hitting the hood of the car. She moans, and I almost lose it.

Her leg lifts, drawing up the side of mine before lowering, and all I want to do is wrap them around my waist and bury my dick inside her like last night. God, the thought of her tight cunt makes me kiss her harder.

She's clawing into my back as another moan escapes, set free into my mouth. Instinctually, my hands drop to her waist to lift her onto my hood, but Eleanor pushes my chest, humming, "Mm-hmm."

I immediately break away, creating space between us, and stare down at her, totally breathless, before I chuckle.

"My bad."

She smiles as my hands still linger by her body, but I'm on a lag, still sucked in by the moment, adrenaline pounding through me, making my heart beat a mile a minute.

Fuck. Holy fuck.

"Damn," she pants, staring back at me, looking as wild as I feel. "Nobody'll give us a divorce if they saw that. I'm not sure it looked like the goodbye kiss we were planning."

I smirk, lifting my fingers to her mouth, wiping away the

shine around her lips as I try to control my breathing. Eleanor's eyes tick down, so I follow, hearing her chuckle.

Shit. Yeah, there's no missing the outline of my dick in my basketball shorts.

I shrug, looking back at her.

"What can I say? Your mouth puts me in a sexual chokehold—"

Whatever I'm about to say next is lost because Josh shouts my name, making me look over my shoulder. He's tapping his watch too aggressively, so I look back at Eleanor and smile, whispering, "You think instead of I do, they'll make us say I don't?"

She gives me a little push. But as I'm turning, I feel her hand slip into mine, drawing my eyes down to see them joined, making me smile.

Is there such a thing as a non-monogamous girlfriend…who doesn't love you but always treats you like her favorite? Because I want Eleanor to be that.

No commitment, all the fun, and none of the feelings.

eight

· · ·

"Now I know why the lord gave me one heart
and three holes."

eleanor

Oof, I shouldn't be holding his hand. I just told him I
never double dip, but here I am, prepping to do just
that. He's just so fucking dreamy, and that kiss... *If
my pussy was previously in a coma, it's now revived and doing lunges,
getting ready for round two.*

I mean, what's the worst that could happen if we hook up
again? It's not like either of us is trying to be in a relationship
anytime soon, that's for sure. And Crew isn't a *fall-for-the-girl*
type. Soo, maybe we could...

No, nope, negatory. What am I thinking?

The last time I thought a guy and I could swing casual sex
ended with him showing up at the salon. Without an appoint-
ment. While I was waxing some dude's ass.

The poor client was literally head down, ass up, and that
psychopath busted in to show me a portrait of my fucking face
that he got tattooed on his chest.

Guys get addicted when the girl is down to keep things
simple. You suddenly start becoming *the one*. And no matter how

easy breezy Crew comes off, I do not need another portrait of me out in the fucking wild.

I look up at Crew as we take the steps, but my eyes narrow because I just thought to myself—*maybe he's different*. Gross.

Talk about famous last words. Why can't there be a test? A way to know he won't turn into a walking museum of me.

Ooo, hold up. Have I just solved my own problem with a genius thought?

Yes—if I take my hand away and he tightens trying to keep it, I stick to my guns. But if he lets it go easily, then it's cock-a-doodle-me time. I feel like this could work...

The real question is: Have I lost my mind to horniness? Maybe... do I care? Not really.

But before I can test my theory, Crew's lawyer interrupts my plan.

"It's about time you got here. Fuck, Crew. It's not a good look to make a judge wait." Law and Order looks at me, adding, "Excuse my French. Hi, I'm Joshua Maroney, your lawyer for the day."

I grin. "I don't speak French, Stabler, so you're good. Just make sure your fee is covered by the other guy."

I think I'm funny, and apparently, he does too because the Gabriel Macht look-alike huffs a laugh as he starts up the stairs, glancing over his shoulder to throw out, "Technically, Elliot Stabler's a detective. I'm a lawyer. But don't worry, I do pro bono work." He holds the door open for us to walk inside the building, offering his words to Crew this time. "You sure you don't want to stay hitched? She's funny."

No, thanks blasts from our mouths simultaneously before we look at each other and smile.

"Come on, then, lovebirds. Let's hope we didn't piss off the judge."

crew

I like the way her hand fits in mine.

And I'm tempted to keep holding it, but I can't because that's the kind of shit that makes the day go from legendary to restraining order. Thank fuck Josh interrupted because my dick was robbing me of blood flow to my fucking brain.

I was dangerously close to doing something stupid because I know how girls are.

Even with as cool as Eleanor is and as much as she talks a good game about hooking up, even she has a *thing*...something that'll make her think we're a possibility. That there's untapped potential here, and eventually, four little irrational words will make all the sense in the world to her: *I can change him.*

It won't matter that I've been completely straightforward with my intentions. I'll be a guy who broke her heart. No way am I setting myself up for that shit.

I need to let her hand go before I look like boyfriend material. As I'm thinking it, Eleanor slips her hand from mine, so I let it go without hesitation because I'd be a fool to pass up divine intervention.

Still, the irony isn't lost on me. I chuckle to myself, realizing how crazy it is that I'm worried my wife might fall for me.

As if I beckoned her with my thoughts, she looks up, our smiles meeting.

Begrudgingly, I look away because Josh has stopped in front of a door with a gold nameplate affixed to the front before turning to address us in the vacant hallway.

"Listen up, kids. Although it's uncommon for the judge to ask us to chambers, I figure he understands the need for privacy because of who Crew is. Honestly, I've never had a client stupid enough to do something like this, so I'm not sure what to expect." Josh smiles apologetically at Eleanor. "Sorry, no offense."

The way she shrugs makes me grin because Eleanor defines nonchalant.

"None taken. It *was* super dumb...honestly, it makes me regret saying yes. I'd always hoped my first husband would be smarter."

Josh laughs as I nudge her. But his eyes linger. *The fuck?* It's enough to make me clear my throat and make him grin, and he looks at me, saying, "Sorry," before he switches back to professional mode.

"Listen, when we walk in there, just smile and nod. And whatever you do, lie about remembering last night... You two were blackout drunk. Understand? I figured an annulment was best, and that defense is our only hope. God willing, in the next ten minutes, it'll be like last night never happened."

Eleanor tilts her head toward me, so I lean down for her to whisper in my ear as Josh knocks on the door.

"Nice lawyer. Do you have to pay extra when he encourages you to lie?"

There she goes, pulling another smile out of me. I capture my bottom lip between my teeth and let it drag out slowly before I launch more playful sarcasm in her direction. I can't help it. This girl brings out the devil in me.

"You're right. We should tell the truth. Do you want to tell the judge about when your mouth was around my cock while your pussy was getting double-fed? Or should I?"

I don't miss how her eyes turn into saucers as she chuckles quietly, breathing, "I hate you."

I wink. "So we are lying, then?"

My hand drops to the small of her back, ushering her through the door and feeling her pinch my side before she follows Josh, and I hold back a laugh.

A portly, half-balding, older man in a black robe sits behind a massive oak desk, smiling tightly as we walk in, and Josh greets him.

"Judge Reynolds. Thank you so much for doing this on such

short notice. We understand how important your time is. We'll be as quick as possible so we're out of your hair."

Josh motions to two chairs in front of the desk for Eleanor and me as he continues, placing a thick packet of paperwork on the judge's desk.

"I've prepared the paperwork. It's very straightforward. Both parties agree to no exchange of any personal assets, and there is no community property. They're also requesting an annulment. Neither party was capable of agreeing to the marriage due to the level of alcohol in their respective systems. To be frank, Judge, my clients got blackout drunk and then married. Both parties would appreciate a swift no-fault wrap-up."

Jesus, way to cut to the fucking chase. I look at Josh, shaking my head, but he shrugs.

The judge nods as I stand beside Eleanor's chair until she sits before taking my own.

Everyone is silent. The only sound is the crinkling of the paperwork as the judge flips through it.

Josh has stepped behind us, standing between our chairs, but I don't get the sense he's nervous about anything. I figure it's a good idea to treat this like the rules on a plane.

If the flight attendant panics, then we're going down.

I'm midway through my thought when the cell in my hand vibrates, catching my attention. A smile burgeons on my face. *Sneaky, sneaky.*

> That girl I married: I just want you to know that you're my soulmate. They can take away my last name, but they can never take away our love—also, refresh my memory? What's your last name?

I look up, trying and failing to hide the smile on my face. She's ridiculous. My eyes tick over to her, but she's staring straight ahead at the judge, who's still looking at the paperwork.

We're like two kids in middle school passing notes when we're not supposed to.

And I like it.

I'm already texting back, ignoring Josh as he taps my shoulder.

> Me: LISTEN. I'll call this thing off right now. Don't tempt me with a lifetime of YOU. But how do I know you're not just leading me on? You're an admitted heartbreaker.

> That girl I married: No, YOU listen... There's nothing sweeter than meeting your soulmate and finding out he likes it when his friends fuck you too. Now I know why the lord gave me one heart and three holes.

I cough. It's all I can do to hide the laugh that refuses to stay in. It's not fair that she's this funny.

Fuck, now everyone's looking at me. Even the judge.

"Are you okay, son?"

I tap my chest with my fist a couple of times, pretending to clear whatever's there before he adds, "Crew. Matthews. This is quite the surprise seeing you here."

I smile and nod, just like I was told, not even tempting fate with a glance in her direction. We're not allowed to sit together anymore. No more divorces for us.

The judge's voice commands the room as if he's comfortable pontificating.

"I would have thought in the weeks leading up to training camp, you would only have football on your mind." He glances at Eleanor and then back to me. "But I guess there are distractions everywhere, even for the best of the best."

What the fuck?

All the humor I felt is immediately gone as my brows pull together while he looks down at the paperwork.

I don't like his tone or his implication. But mostly, the way it involves Eleanor. I start to lean forward to say some shit, but Josh's hand lands solidly on my shoulder, a whispered "smile and nod" added. So, I let out a silent breath and relax back into the chair.

Judge Reynolds lifts the paper before addressing us again.

"You understand that your attorney stated you didn't know what you were doing. Because in order for me to agree to an annulment, that would mean you were too incapacitated to understand what you were entering into." He looks up, adding, "I believe the term was blackout drunk…"

I can feel Eleanor looking at me, so I meet her eyes and smile, reassuring her before we both look back and nod. *There's no turning back now.*

But Judge Reynolds is staring us down, his eyes volleying between us before zeroing in on me again.

"Lying to a judge, even in chambers, can be considered perjury. I offer this because *blackout* would indicate—say, if I had video of the two of you—that you would be so drunk you couldn't stand or speak, let alone say *I do.*"

He pauses like he's waiting for one of us to come clean. I glance over at Eleanor, and she's sitting there like a gangster, riding and probably dying on the inside but still holding strong with an incredibly unnerved demeanor.

If I ever hit hard times and rob a casino, I'm doing it with her. She's my Ocean's Eleven…TJ would've already caved.

I cross my arms just as Josh begins to speak. Except the judge holds up a hand, halting him, as he keeps my gaze.

"Or maybe Crew here has become too comfortable telling lies."

"Say what?" Eleanor mutters under her breath, her eyebrows hitting the ceiling.

No shit. My face swings over my shoulder as Josh steps forward.

"I apologize, Judge Reynolds, but is there an issue? I don't understand why my client is being impugned—"

"Well, Mr. Maroney, you have two problems. Let's start with the first one. After reviewing these files—" Reynolds breathes out, tapping the paperwork. "—and after doing a bit of research..." He reaches for his cell phone and swipes it open before turning it around, showing a video cued.

"What the—" falls from my lips before Eleanor cuts me off.

"Oh my god. Is that my fucking Instagram?"

Josh coughs, so she looks at him and shrugs, answering the *shut the fuck up* on his face.

"What? Excuse *my* French now. But that's my private Instagram." She turns back to Judge Reynolds. "It shouldn't count."

Whoa, whoa, whoa, whoa. What the fuck shouldn't count? Oh shit, this is what he meant by video.

"It's not private if it's public, young lady," the judge snarks before touching the Play button.

I whip my face to hers as Josh speaks under his breath, but drunk cheers from the phone fill the room.

"What shouldn't count? What's on there?"

I glare at him. "You didn't fucking look for anything?"

"You said there wasn't anything to see."

"I said I wasn't sure."

Eleanor doesn't add anything because she's already leaning forward, slightly cringing, taking in the screen. So I do the same.

Why does this feel like the beginning of the end?

Jesus, we sound as smashed as we look. Which is bad for present-day us because we only look a smashed *five* on a scale of *one through ten*. We're in front of the chapel, TJ in that fucking Elvis jumpsuit and Millie holding up what looks like plastic bouquets. Everyone is howling and shouting because Eleanor's legs are wrapped around my waist as we kiss like we need each other for actual fucking air.

"Pay attention. This is the good part," the judge adds with a smile, making our heads lift before we're sucked back in.

Oh fuck. I let out a heavy breath, watching drunk Eleanor lift one arm and look directly into the camera, shouting, *"I just married Crew Matthews. He's my husband, bitches."*

My own drunk-as-hell voice is right behind her. *"Gimme a kiss, baby. You're Mrs. Matthews now. Fuck Thomas."*

Jesus. Damn. Christ. We are so done. Those aren't people that need to be propped up or even helped to their beds with a bucket by the side. Those are just two horny fucking morons doing some dumb shit.

"Looks like you have been caught red-handed in a lie, Mr. Matthews..." The judge looks at Eleanor, adding, "And Mrs. Matthews."

"What's the punishment for perjury?" I say well under my breath to Josh, who shakes his head just as Eleanor's saucer-sized eyes catch mine.

Judge Reynolds cuts the video right in the middle of our sloppy make-out and begins shuffling the paperwork. But Eleanor's eyes are still popping out of her head as she looks back at Josh and then at me, hissing under her breath.

"I knew this was a bad idea. P.S. No thanks for making my last name the only one you remember in life. You're an idiot. It's probably all the balls to the head."

"This is my fault?" I shoot back. "Who has a public-private Instagram for people to find damning evidence? What are you, eighty? Learn how to work technology."

She rolls her eyes, but I stare at her profile for a hard second before returning to the judge, who looks up and smiles.

"Annulment denied. So now you're going to ask me for a civil divorce...that's problem number two. For both parties to obtain a divorce in the state of Nevada, one of them must be a resident. Otherwise, you'll have to file in your home state. Which, if the records are correct, is California. And that'll take six months."

Eleanor sucks in a gasp, adding, "Oh god... wait, he lives here..."

"Yeah, I'm a resident," I say too quickly, feeling her hand grip my forearm because we're each hoping the universe is throwing us a life vest, but the judge cuts me off.

"You live in a hotel, Mr. Matthews. That's not a permanent residence. Unless you have a PO Box or utility bill, I can't help you."

"Judge," Josh presses, "I know you're aware that Crew plays for the Raiders, so—you have the power to declare him a good-faith citizen."

The judge fucking chuckles like Josh is missing the point. It's enough that Josh stops talking as Eleanor and I look at each other.

What the fuck is happening?

My head whips over my shoulder to Josh, the look on my face loosely translating into *Are we going down?* Because if he's my fucking flight attendant into the maiden voyage of my divorce, I kind of need to know where we're at.

And telling by how hard he just swallowed, the answer is we lost an engine and are careening toward the fucking ground.

"Thank god," Eleanor gasps, smacking my arm to get my attention before I follow to where she's pointing as she adds, relieved, "He's a fan."

Holy shit.

Josh taps her shoulder as all the color in my face drains, trying to get her to shut up, but she doesn't. Because we see something she doesn't.

Judge Reynolds is wearing a Raiders jersey. But not just any jersey. It's a special edition that only the owner gave out to his close friends. I know because I had to sign twenty of them right before the Super Bowl.

The Super Bowl I lost before going on a tirade and telling the owner to suck my dick on ESPN. Now it all makes sense.

Fuck. My. Life.

This is payback for the trade. For fucking the Raiders the way I felt like they'd fucked me.

Eleanor's voice has my hand lifting to her face to cover the whole thing as I feel myself sweating like I've run five miles. I'm having a heart attack. Maybe it's for the best, just bury me in my failed hopes and goddamn dreams.

"Do you want him to sign something?" she rushes out, swatting my hand away, sounding confused as she adds, "What are you doing?" before she motions for me to stand up. "Get up and let him see you do something footbally."

"Stop talking," I breathe out, turning to look at her. "He knows the owner, Eleanor. Reynolds isn't our judge by accident. Do you remember what I told you last night?"

She swallows, and I know she's remembering me telling her the whole story. All about how I went off on the owner, how I not only agreed to a trade but was stealing away Nate and TJ too. It takes seconds that feel like minutes before she grips the arms of the chair and slinks down with a guttural "Noooo, this isn't happening. Tell me this isn't happening."

Judge Reynolds props his hands behind his head with a grin on his face like he's enjoying every moment of our spiral before he speaks.

"To declare Mr. Matthews a citizen of Las Vegas would be a lie, Mr. Maroney. Because in order to do so, there would need to be evidence that he's planning an indefinite stay." His eyes are locked on mine. "And from what I hear, that simply isn't the case, unless the Niners are coming to Vegas. So it's my order that Mr. and Mrs. Matthews will remain married for no shorter than thirty days. Residing *in* the city of Las Vegas…without stepping one foot outside its city limits. Giving their commitment due diligence and so therefore obtaining residency before they may come before me again."

"Fuck," Josh breathes out as I think it.

That's when pandemonium ensues.

I'm on my feet, voice thundering, and Eleanor is lobbing insults like hammers as Josh unsuccessfully tries to shut us the fuck up.

"Fuck you, Judge Judy." … "Thirty days means I miss

training camp with the Niners." ... "You can't just force me to stay here for a month? I have a whole life outside of this fucking city." ... "Thirty days means my fucking deal could go south." ... "This isn't fair. I have work, friends, and work." ... "You tell that son of a bitch nice try. I'll make his life hell." ... "How am I supposed to explain this to my family?" ... "You can make us stay married for forever. It won't fucking change—"

Before I can finish my threat, a body climbs me like a fucking tree, legs wrapped around my waist, mouth suddenly sealing over mine.

Eleanor's kissing me. She's got herself wrapped around me so one of my arms is trapped between her crotch and my body as she clings to me for dear life, mumbling, "Shut your dumb mouth," in between shoving her tongue inside.

"I'm filing a motion—" Josh rushes out, but I don't hear the rest of what he says.

Because I'm trying to break free from her, but the intrusion of her fucking tongue in my mouth and the way she keeps lifting her body to stay up...rubbing her pussy on my arm, makes me grab her ass and kiss her back.

Hard.

She pulls back after a minute and looks me dead in the eyes. "I really don't want to get fucked by him for longer than thirty days. You feel me? Shut your mouth."

My chest is heaving. I'm not sure if it's because I'm mad or turned on. Either way, I nod until the sound of the judge's robe zipping up draws both our eyes.

Reynolds smirks.

"Looks like you lovebirds have some things to work out. If you'll excuse me, I have to get back to my day, but I expect I'll see you back here in thirty days with a new level of respect for my friends and for Raider Nation. Good day, Mr. and Mrs. Matthews. And remember, what happens in Vegas is now ordered to stay in Vegas."

He walks past us as we watch quietly, my hand on her ass,

holding her up. Neither of us moves until well after we hear the door shut.

But as soon as it does, Eleanor lets out a heavy breath before smacking my chest with both hands.

"Raider Nation?" She huffs an empty laugh. "I hate football. Put me down."

My jaw tenses before I drop her, making her squeak before her ass hits the chair. We glare at each other, neither of us giving in first. Because the only thing I truly know is that right now, Eleanor wishes she'd never met me.

And I feel the exact same.

"So, hubby, where do we live?"

"In hell, wifey. In. Fucking. Hell."

nine

. . .

"You can't exist in hyperbole when you probably
can't even spell it."

eleanor

> Samantha: Quit playing. This better be a joke.

No matter how many ways I've explained to Millie and my sister
what just happened, they seem incapable of believing me.

> Me: 30FUCKINGDAYSSAMANTHA!!!!!!!!!

> Mills: Oh shit. Swear you aren't fucking
> with us?

> Me: NOOOOOOO. I'M LOSING MY SHIT
> HERE.

> Mills: Okay. First—calm down before you get
> arrested. Second—answer your FaceTime.

I hit the button on my screen, immediately dropping my
head back, my eyes hitting the ceiling as my sister and Millie
speak simultaneously.

But I can't even focus on what they're saying because my

head's about to explode. I'm so pissed. This wasn't supposed to happen. We were supposed to get married, then divorced. The latter being the most important part of that sentence. But now I'm fucking collateral damage because of some dumbass football vendetta.

Fuck.

Alcohol is bad. So. So. Bad.

"Shit, what are you going to tell Mom and Dad?" Samantha mutters from the little box her face is in.

"Who cares! That's the least of my worries right now, Sami. What am I going to do about all my clients at the salon? I'm going to lose them when I tell them I won't be back for a month. I can't leave the fucking city limits. And that's not exactly ideal when you're about to start your own fucking salon."

Millie's shaking her head as she cuts in.

"I won't let that happen. I'll explain or make shit up to keep them. Listen, if you have to come back and live out your days with everyone thinking you single-handedly saved the world on the president's command after you met a secret service detail in Vegas, bitch, so be it. You won't get fired, and our salon will not fail. I have zero problems lying for a good reason. And what's better than for a best friend?"

My shoulders start their descent down from my ears, a tiny bit relieved. I trust that Millie will hold it down for me. Plus, I'd kept my July light client-wise so I could focus on starting our own thing. But this is still the most fucked situation.

I'm still frowning as I glance at Crew. He's been talking a mile a minute about ten feet away on his phone, arms flying in every direction. Clearly, he's just as mad as I am. *Which is rich since this is all his fault.*

As if on cue, I hear him say, "This is a fucking disaster. I'm stuck with a girl I picked up at a goddamn nightclub because the good ole boys club is real. The owner can kiss my ass, and so can that judge. They're literally trying to ruin my life using last night's pussy."

My eyes narrow. *Using my pussy?* Is he serious? Dick. How about using your stupid fucking temper tantrum because you lost a dumbass game nobody but a bunch of old dudes cares about. In fact, this unholy matrimony consequence is everyone's fault but mine *and* my pussy's.

All I did was marry some dude who grown-ass men would let spit on them, just so they can tell their friends about it. The penalty for that is a next-day divorce and some ribbing from your friends—not sanctioned corrupt-ass revenge.

Again, I say…I hate football. I'm banning it from my vocabulary. I won't even read about it anymore. From now on, I'm only reading hockey romance.

I'll take those toothless, ice-skating yahoos over lame-ass quarterbacks any day. Or those linebacker guys with the thighs that could crush steel. I mean, nobody loves those football pics where they're always wearing half shirts showing off their sweaty abs, holding balls and putting those veiny arms on display. The ones that could probably never tire of holding me up against the wall while I was basically getting fucked through it—*goddammit.*

I give my head a tiny shake, trying to ward off my traitorous thoughts. But my pussy is literally an enemy of the state. The state being my anger.

He was just blaming you, you dumb bitch.

My sister saves me from my thoughts as she chimes in.

"Okay. We're not freaking out. We're here now. And there's nothing you can do about this. Everything will be okay. We'll work it out. Okay?" I'm staring into the phone, nodding, knowing she can see my worry, but she does the one thing only a big sister can do—states the obvious, then pivots. "I second what Millie said, Elliebelly. We got your back…but only because you're a dumbass and couldn't help but lie on it." A grin grows on her face. "If you think I'm ever letting you live this down…wrong. Dead wrong. This will be like when you found out that I inadvertently named the hamster in my eighth-grade science class Queef because I didn't know what it meant."

Millie's mouth drops open as she laughs, and Sami smiles. I know what she's doing...trying to pull me into the bright side. But I'm not going, half shrugging and digging in my heels as she continues.

"Remember that? You took out a whole page dedicated to Queef in the back of my senior yearbook with the title 'Never forget how far you've come.'"

I chuckle. I can't help it—that was my best troll work to date. But I don't want to laugh. I want to be angry. Very angry. Living in the feeling until I morph into my villain era. An airy breath drags from my lungs just as my eyes tick back to Crew.

"What are you looking at?"

I whisper my answers back to my sister, half under my breath.

"Him. He's mad."

I flip the camera, letting them see him pacing as he runs his hand through his hair, half facing us as he talks on the phone. His head falls back for a brief second as he lets out an irritated groan before he grips the back of his neck. If I didn't currently dislike him so much, I would think it was sexy.

I bring the screen back to me, rolling my eyes. "He has some fucking nerve acting like he's a victim. This could've all been avoided if he wasn't a dick to the owner and did a whole under-handed trade thing...I don't know. All I do know is that if I ever hear a man make fun of a woman for loving Harry Styles or anything, for that matter...I am going to out them for the fangirls they are. My life is being ruined because this judge is the equivalent of a Swiftie. The Raiders are basically his Taylor, and I'm paying the price for Crew's betrayal."

"Yeah, that judge is a real antihero..." Mills throws out, making my sister smile before she answers in the exact way I knew one of them would the moment I made a fucking Taylor Swift comparison.

Here we go. They're always like this together. I'm already shaking my head, but there's no hope that they'll listen.

"You'd think he'd be more understanding of their *love story*."

Millie laughs harder as she piggybacks off my sister.

"Right, but he was basically *'You're on your own, kid.'"*

Samantha's almost wheezing as she answers.

"Exactly, it's not like she was the *mastermind* either."

Millie's picture is shaking, probably because she's smacking the bed she's lying in as she laughs harder.

"He knew *all too well* she wasn't. But ruining Crew's *reputation* was *better than revenge*."

Samantha can't even speak—neither of them can as they say three words, then stop in a fit of laughter before a few more words come out.

"I bet our girl... I bet our girl was wishing...wishing she was... in a *lavender haze*." They're laughing so hard you can't hear them making any sound anymore.

I hate them. I roll my eyes, trying not to smile. Trying really hard. *Whatever.* I drop my phone down by my side, letting out a harsh breath and shaking my head before I lift it and hiss at them.

"Assholes."

They scream. It takes everything in me not to join in the laughter because they're too much. But I'm staying mad. I don't care how hard they try to pull me out.

"I'm dying a slow death, and you're doing Tay Tay puns. Really? You guys are the worst."

They still don't care, more laughter spilling out. Dammit. It's happening...I'm buying in. *I swear to god.* It's impossible to be angry when I'm surrounded by clowns.

"Fine, consider this my Dear John letter. Where my love for you once existed, there's now only a *blank space*."

Clapping. They're fucking clapping.

My sister raises her eyebrows, doing a little shimmy as she veers in a totally different direction.

"Can we also acknowledge the elephant in the room?"

"Yeah," Millie cuts in. "When am I getting picked up because I'm not staying at the house of horrors without you."

"I'll let *you know* as soon as *I know* where I live."

My sister shakes her head.

"No, I meant that the guy is fucking hot."

I scowl, kind of nodding but still rolling my eyes as Millie chuckles.

"Yeah, he totally is. And his personality is Eleanor's kryptonite. Super cocky, flirts by giving her shit, and can't keep his hands off her. At least last night, he couldn't."

I huff a tiny growl.

"Would you two read the room? Look where that got me. I'm living the dream, hitched to a guy who regrets me about as much as I regret him right now. My life is ruined. Focus."

My sister and Millie laugh. *Again.* I might as well be a damn HBO comedy special with how much these two are belly-laughing it up. *I'll be here all night, folks, and twice on Sunday.*

"Okay. Settle down," my sister teases. "Inconvenienced, yes. Ruined? Take it *down*, Meryl. You can't exist in hyperbole when you probably can't even spell it."

"Y-o-u-a-r-e-a-t-w-a-t. Am I close?"

"Shut up. You've basically been ordered to an extended vacay…with a *hottie* who's paying. So, while I want to be sad for you…"

Is my sister right? A little. While the situation is very much fucked, I'm aware it's not apocalyptic. But I am not at all ready to bright side or listen to reason.

Absolutely. Fucking. Not.

"Excuse me," I snarl sarcastically. "Roll it back, Samantha. This is not the time for reason. We need revenge plans and shit talk. Get on board. Mills…you need to handle your bestie."

Millie points to herself, chuckling.

"Oh, she's mine now?"

"Yes, when she's dumb, she belongs to you. That's how it works when you're raising children together."

Samantha smiles back at me as I contemplate throwing my phone in the trash so I don't have to witness this traitorous conversation anymore. Obviously, she knows I'm not really mad at her, but I am mad at Crew.

And I'm holding on to it. Letting it fester. Because grudges are like comfort blankets for haters. And I'm definitely his hater today.

"Listen to me," I protest. "The next thirty days will be all-out war because he's left me no choice other than to make him as miserable as I am right now. That's the only silver lining I will acknowledge."

As if beckoned, Crew starts walking toward me, his jaw tense as he pockets his phone. Shit. Did he hear me? Millie calls my name, but I don't answer.

Crew's eyes are locked on mine as he starts speaking.

"There's paparazzi in the front. That asshole judge must've tipped them off. We're being picked up in the back. Get off your call."

"Um, noo. You can wait," I spit back, staring up at him.

God, he's too close, hovering, and for the life of me and despite how angry I am for being in this position...other parts of me, however, are getting *too* excited at being in this exact position. I'm the definition of *I hate his face, but I'd still sit on it.*

I take a step back, feeling heat rise up my neck.

"Just get off the fucking call."

"When you get off your high horse."

I look back at the screen at Sami and Millie and their eyebrows, slow matching smirks blooming on their faces.

Crew lets out a heavy breath before tossing his words back.

"That mouth is only cute when I want to shut it up with my—"

"Call us back!" they yell in unison, cutting him off, but I shake my head.

"Absolutely not." My eyes lift back to his, and I dig my heels in. "Absolutely. Not."

Crew grabs my wrist, extending my arm out so they can see him too.

"Ladies, I need to speak to Eleanor for a hot minute. Privately. I'm stealing her, but I'm more than happy to give her the fuck back when I'm done."

A laughed *Oh shit* pops from Millie's mouth before he ends the call.

I swear I see red as his palm presses to my stomach and I'm walked backward until I'm against the wall. His face comes too close, his body touching mine.

"We need to call a truce. Right now. Before your little war starts."

So I was heard. Good, because I'm ready to press nukes.

I huff a laugh, crossing my arms, feeling too enveloped by his scent, by him, but ignoring it anyway.

"No."

His hand presses to the wall next to me, cornering me in even more.

"Eleanor. I'm not fucking kidding."

"Neither am I. I did you a favor in the chambers place when I climbed up and kissed you to shut you the fuck up so we didn't get buried further down in your bullshit. You got a favor out of me…so now there are no more fucks left for me to give you."

We're deadlocked, eyes laser focused on each other. Crew pushes off the wall and turns around, walking a few steps away and wiping a hand down his jaw before he spins back around.

"If this gets out…that we got drunk-married like two idiots, my entire life goes up in flames. The deal I have in place with the Niners will go south because it makes me look too impulsive and untrustworthy…"

"That's a you problem, QB. I'm over here fighting for my life, trying to figure out how to keep my job and not get fired. And news flash, I don't have millions to land on when I fall."

His eyes search mine as his brows pull together.

"I'll give you money. Whatever you'd make for the month."

I instantly recoil.

"Eww. No, that is not what I meant...I don't want your money."

"Then what? I get that this fucks with your life. And I don't want to be stuck with you any more than you want to be stuck with me. But the consequence of what we did is about to hurt two people I care about. So, you need to help me make that not happen."

He means TJ and Nate. I forgot about them. He said they were a part of his deal. I was so focused on my own shit that I never even considered them.

I might be good at being a twat, and he may be just as good at it too. But I'm not a monster. My eyes close as I nod my head, saying my words on a hard exhale.

"Fine. What do I have to do? But to be clear, this is for TJ and Nate because they're cool as hell. Even if they have shit taste in friends."

He lets out a quiet, relieved breath, ignoring my dig.

"Barrett, my agent, is spinning this as two people in love. A real love-at-first-sight kind of thing."

I huff. He shrugs.

"Yeah, I think it's dumb too. But the organization won't. You just have to pretend to like me in public for a few weeks. And keep the truth between us...and the two on the phone. That's it. Once everything is signed, you can go back to regretting me all over again."

My teeth find my lip, scraping over it as I consider what he's saying. It's not a terrible idea. I could use it to look like less of an asshole to my clients and even my parents.

What's the harm in a little white lie?

"Fine," I rush out. "But no kissing or anything like that. Our couple vibe is *'are they siblings, or are they dating.'* You get me? Close enough but not too close. Because our physical proximity is what got us into this shit in the first place. So, keep your hands to yourself, QB. I'm not even risking falling into hate sex at this point."

"Done. Trust me, Wild Card. The last thing on my mind is your pussy."

ten

· · ·

"Is she or isn't she a brotherfucker."

eleanor

We've been in the back of the car for what feels like an hour because Crew and I are entrenched in silence as we drive to his penthouse. Apparently, the hotel room I thought was a five-star honeymoon suite was his actual house.

It seems wrong to go back to the scene of the crime, but alas, here I am.

My phone is still vibrating, more messages flooding in. I know my sister and Millie are having a field day. He was such a dick. And they ate it up. Because if the charming, cocky guy is my kryptonite, the asshole dickhead is my 3:00 a.m. "you up" destiny. So says my sketchy hookup record.

I sneak my cell from my purse, looking up discreetly to make sure he's not looking at me before I open the message thread.

> Samantha: Hundred bucks says she folds in the first week and does the dirty with him.
>
> Mills: Oh, that's a guarantee. There's no bet there.

Samantha: A week is generous now that I think about it...

Mills: I give her two days, tops. If there's anything we know about Elsinore it's that there's no if you're a bird, I'm a bird shit—she's an if you're a turd, I'm a pooper scooper kind of girl. And Crew Matthews is definitely a little shit.

My fingers type so fast I have to correct three typos before I hit Send.

Me: The ways in which you are both DEAD wrong. Neither of us is remotely interested in even sitting next to each other at this point. He's not even that hot in person. Forget about the fact that his personality cancels out any interest I had from before.

Samantha: Mmmkay...

Samantha: *GIF of an old lady on a stripper pole

Mills: ha ha that's going to be your pussy in a week feeling dusty and thirsty ya' whore. No way you share a space with that piece of meat and not cave. I have no faith in your willpower.

Samantha: Zero.

My mouth falls open as I laugh, drawing Crew's attention next to me. So, I give him a mildly dirty look, making him look away as I go back to my conversation.

Me: I have self-control.

Samantha: Funny. Earlier it was—He's not even that hot in person. His personality sucks. Now it's—I have self-control...which is it, Elle?

Mills: Ha ha ha. Caught.

Me: Shut up. I'll bet both of you I can last the whole month without even touching him. Whoever wins gets a thousand bucks.

Samantha: Done. But you might get fired. So you're not good for the money.

Oh nice. Jerk.

Mills: I want your new sparkly boots WHEN I WIN.

I gasp. The gravity of this bet deserved the gasp. Again, Crew's eyes meet mine as I glance up before huffing a "What?" at him so as to not even remotely let on that we're talking about him.

I splurged on those boots. After she and I had watched *Urban Cowboy* for the millionth time and then happened upon them at an upscale thrift store in San Francisco. I negotiated for over an hour and threatened to cut the leash of some woman's dog and set it free in the Bay because she tried to butt in and offer more.

Those Betsey Johnson rhinestone cowgirl boots are my fucking precious, and I'm their Gollum.

Me: Now you know you're going to lose, Mills. I would go to jail for those boots. I almost did. That Pomeranian was about to be a free doggie.

Samantha: Perfect, then wagering…I don't know…admitting to Mom, to her face, that you accused her fucking the whole cul-de-sac, shouldn't be a problem.

My eyes almost pop out of my head.

> Me: You terrible whore of a sister. Karma's giving you a yeast infection for that treachery. You know I would rather chew glass than let our saint of a mother know what a menace she raised.

> Me: You know what? You're both on. If Crew Matthews touches me...

My forehead wrinkles as I specify, unfortunately thinking of all the parts on him he could touch me with.

> Me: ...If his giant cock touches my holy grail then I will become the worst shoeless daughter in history.

Samantha: Fingers count too.

Mills: And his mouth.

"Oh my god." I inhale sharply before waving off his curious face.

> Me: If any part of his body sexually touches my body, I lose.

Samantha: Mills...friends too?

Mills: Yep...his friends count.

> Me: Not the Tweedles. How could you? You fucking hate me.

> Me: Then you know what...I hate you dirty cockblockers too and I hope you both get syphilis.

I can hear their scream-laughs in my mind. Because that's exactly what they did the minute they read that. And it's making me smile until I look up directly into Crew's face, who narrows his eyes.

"What's so funny?"

Nothing you ever get to know. My head draws back, my eyes looking him up and down, searching for my words carefully.

"None of your business."

It's not inventive, but it gets to the point.

"You were talking about me, weren't you?"

He looks amused as he reaches for my phone. But I snatch it away.

"Are you crazy? Don't try to take my phone. Also, no. You weren't even mentioned."

Crew bites his lip, tilting his head as he stares at me. So, I shrug, really trying to sell my bullshit, but I can feel it the minute he decides to call my bluff.

I squeal, jumping in my seat as my phone is snatched from my hands.

"Give it back," I yell, but Crew laughs, nabbing my chin and holding my face in place.

"Dickkkk move," I grind out, making a hundred weird crazy expressions, trying to fuck up the facial recognition.

But it works faster than legs spread for tattooed guys.

"You're so rude," I rush out, trying to unlock my seat belt. But I can't see what I'm doing because he's holding me away with his palm outstretched on my face.

"Who's Patty with the Fatty?" he levels. "And New Year's Chris… Thick Fingers Steve… Why do you have so many guys in your phone?"

I smack his arm with one hand, trying to undo the belt with my other as I yell.

"You really are a walking red flag. This is an invasion of my privacy, you asshat."

"Whatever," he snaps back, keeping my face covered with his big-ass mitt of a hand as he adds, "Wives shouldn't keep secrets from their husbands."

"I'll make sure to tell the next guy everything."

The chuckle he lets out makes me ravenous for murder,

coupled with the horror that he's going to see the damn bet. I'll die. I'll fucking jump straight out of this car onto the freeway, tuck-and-roll style, and wish for the best.

He cannot see that I was talking about his "giant cock" and that "I had self-control." He doesn't get to know I think he's hot still. *Shit.*

"Crew," I growl, wrestling with his arm. "If you don't give my phone back right now, I will hold a pillow over your head tonight. You'll sleep with the damn angels."

He whistles, finally letting me go and tossing my phone back onto my lap.

"You're so violent. You should work on that."

In answer, I smack his arm once more for good measure, but it only serves to make him laugh louder.

Damn that laugh. It's disarming and sexy as hell. It's like hot fudge on vanilla ice cream. All melty and decadent, and it makes me want to lick him. But I won't because he's an asshole, and those aren't keto-friendly... Also, I love my mom and my boots.

God, why did Millie have to be right. I have the worst taste in men. Because I can't deny that there's a tiny piece of me that is turned on right now.

I string my words together, brushing my hair out of my face.

"I'm convinced that whatever I saw in you last night only exists with tequila goggles."

His face slowly lowers to mine as he leans over, suddenly invading my space. I hold my breath, swallowing as his minty warmth brushes over my skin.

"Maybe you just need a reminder. Dirty things happen in the light of day too...but that means we'd have to break your little 'is she or isn't she a brotherfucker' rule."

Nooo... I can feel myself turning into weak Superman. It's the mix of sexy and shitty. It's doing me under.

"Shut up," I whisper, pressing my hand directly over his mouth, and quote my favorite movie. "You shut your mouth when you're talking to me."

But Crew presses his face closer into my hand, turning his head and growling like an animal as he takes a bite of the side of my palm.

The way in which my thighs squeeze together gives away just how much that turned me on. And if it didn't, I fucking shiver.

"Ow."

"Liar," he mumbles before pressing a lingering kiss to the spot. "You know what I love about Vegas, Wild Card?"

That's the third time he's called me that. But that's not the only thing throwing me off. I can't foresee where he's going with what he just asked, not that I actually care because Crew's mouth on me has me all hot and flustered.

God, give me strength, or just let me break my legs so I'm not running straight for his dick.

Crew smirks, moving back into his seat as I shake my head and answer his question.

"No, what do you love about Vegas?"

"Betting on the house...because it never loses."

What? Betting on the... oh my god. My brows draw together as my hands scramble for my phone, swiping it open.

Holy. Shit.

Are you kidding me? He made a new group message.

One that includes him.

Son of a bitch.

> QB with the giant cock: Fuck around and find out, ladies. Old bets are dead. Here's the new bet. A thousand bucks says I have her screaming my name by midnight tonight. If I don't, each day I fail you earn another thousand. If I win, Eleanor deletes her roster in her phone.
>
> Mills: That's 30k... You're fucking on, buddy. For the sisterhood Elle—DO NOT CAVE!!!

Samantha: Now we're talking. Eleanor…you better not fail this mission! Be like Tom Cruise. Millie, we're splitting it… I could do a lot of damage with fifteen thousand.

Eleanor has left the chat.

eleven

. . .

"Shirtless, gray sweatpants, and quad rolls."

crew

Having her here, in my fucking space, is exactly as hard as I thought it would be.

That's part of the reason why I made the bet...I'm never going to be able to *not* shoot my shot with her. And it's clear the same shit is on her mind too.

Because she stared at the seat cushion of my couch for ten fucking minutes with a grin on her face and her legs squeezed together. The same couch her knees sunk down into when I bent her over it last night.

I'll never make it thirty days before I turn into one of those little Chihuahua dogs that see a leg and start humping the air.

Because everything she does and every room she's in makes me think about sex. There's no safe space...my house is unsafe for me.

When she walked by the kitchen island earlier, I thought I was going to pass out because all I saw was her parked on top, legs spread as TJ ate her out.

I'm losing brain cells by the second here.

There's no blood circulating anywhere in my body other than

in my dick. Because I've had a half chub for way too long to be medically healthy.

My hand runs over the marble countertop as I chug back a water, before heading to the couch, trying not to think about the fact that I never got to sample her last night after TJ was done.

The regret is real.

Ironically, just as real as my regret that I even met her. I chuckle to myself because this is why women think men are stupid and led by our dicks.

I've got agents and public relations people working overtime to clean up my mess, but I would one hundred percent sell Nate to the highest bidder to be in Eleanor's pussy right now. I swear I can't stop thinking about her body and doing dirty shit to it.

If I don't win this bet, I might actually combust. Problem is, I would never pressure her—that's nasty and fucking illegal. I'm not *that* guy. But I am the guy with a plan: I have to be so irresistible that she jumps me.

She'll come to me.

It's weak, but it's all I got. I have to be *irresistible* to a girl who basically despises me. Therein lies the problem. If it works, I'm a gambling genius. But I have a sneaking suspicion I'm more of a world-class fucking moron, who's about to be out thirty thousand dollars to boot.

Especially since I was dickish to her earlier...but, I mean. I was having feelings. Really pissed-off ones.

I was going to apologize, but that group text had me in a hard Ross PIV-AUGHT...her bullshit felt like a challenge. And history's already proven that if she issues one, I'll accept.

However, this challenge is proving more difficult than I thought. Considering I've already lost day one's bet since the moment after she left the chat and the ice in her demeanor got even chillier, and when we got home, after staring at the couch, the only thing she said to me was "Go get my friend. She's staying here until her flight leaves tomorrow."

Then she walked right into my room and closed the door. A few minutes later, a pillow and blanket were launched out.

Eleanor: 1

Me: 0

So now here I am, staring up at the ceiling from the couch, surrounded by my bedding, not even trying to hide my grin. Because while she's been in the shower, I've been strategizing. And I'm going to turn the next thirty days into relentless temptation. I'll make it impossible for her to stand by what she said.

Is it immature? Yes.

Am I too old to act like this at twenty-eight? Yep.

Do I care?

Nope.

There's something about the fact that I've never had to work this hard in my life. Usually, I just have to show up and girls are down. But now, I have to reignite the flame. How the fuck do I do that?

It's like we're real married people. I should have a dad bod and a penchant for fixing shit that doesn't need fixing. Still, I'm in it to win it. Her pussy is my Super Bowl, and I want that ring. So fucking bad.

I just have to figure out how to drive her crazy. I can't call the guys…they don't know how to woo women any more than I do. But then a thought strikes, making me sit up and grab my phone to text the only person I know who will be brutally honest and answer me without asking for context. Because she won't care.

> Me: You're single, right?

Claire: Not interested.

> Me: Same…I need someone on the dating ground floor.

Claire: Are you drunk again?

Me: Claire. I need help. I'm trying to get this girl.

Claire: Agreed. You do need help. But don't the girls you like usually tell you how much up front?

Me: Come on. I need to know what girls like. What do they find irresistible? Help me. You're the only girl I know who owns stock in Bumble.

Claire: I hate you.

Me: I won't complain all week. Not a peep. Especially when I wear the weighted vest during the sprints.

Claire: Two weeks.

Me: Done.

Claire: I'd say be yourself...but the objective is for her to like you, right?

Me: Forget I asked.

Claire: Omg. Stop being such a baby. Truth? We like guys who listen to us. Guys who are funny. Kindness. You know, the basics.

Me: I want her to like me enough to want to sleep with me, Claire. Not want to marry me.

Because we already did that.

Claire: Oh. Then—stay shirtless, add gray sweats. And stretch in front of her...specifically, the quad roll-out. We love that.

Me: Seriously?

Claire: Seriously. Godspeed, Matthews.

I toss my phone on the table and look at my bedroom door. Shirtless, gray sweatpants, and quad rolls. Check.

Damn. Women are no better than men.

But if objectifying me gets me in her pants, then I'll let her slap my ass and call me pretty all day long. A win's a win.

Get ready, Wild Card. I'm about to make you feral.

twelve

• • •

"I don't know if there's such a thing as being dickmotized, but I think I'm that."

eleanor

Jesus, what is wrong with me.

How am I the main character in my own life and simultaneously completely unreliable? I can't be trusted with my thoughts. Case in point: I already had to take a cold shower. Because all I could think about in the car was Crew's cock. The whole time.

And there wasn't even a fucking detachable showerhead.

This place is amateur hour. Two stars. Also, how am I surviving this bet? I will though…for the sisterhood.

But I swear I feel like it's been imprinted on me.

Like I'm Jacob and his cock is my Renesmee.

I have to stop watching Twilight *before I go to bed.*

Why can't I want a guy who's into charity and like helps old people across the street? Not one who fucked me with his friends and only speaks caveman. All I know is Millie better hurry up and get here with my shit because I am not walking out in this towel or my failed divorce clothes.

My fingers brush back and forth on the soft comforter on the bed. A soft exhale leaves my chest as I stare up at the ceiling from where I've been lying. It feels like a week has passed, but it hasn't even been twenty-four hours since we met. Jesus.

I close my eyes, trying to relax, until a ruckus clammers on the other side of the door.

"Crew" is bellowed before another equally deep voice says, "Where's our girl?"

Oh fuck. I snap to sitting, clutching the towel, eyes growing wider by the minute.

Our girl? Oh my god.

"The Tweedles," I whisper to myself conspiratorially.

My head swings side to side, looking for my clothes, because I'm suddenly filled with the urge to put them back on just so I can run out of this room and see these two.

It's not every day a girl gets to re-meet two one-night-simultaneous stands.

Laughter bleeds through the walls, and I hold my own in because Crew's voice rumbles with irritation.

"Shut the fuck up, Nate."

My fingers find my lips, amused. *What is he mad about?* I don't have to wonder long because he adds, "TJ, you open that door and I'll break your fucking arm."

Wait. Door! Fuck.

I scramble off the bed, turning in circles, looking for anything to cover me. For fuck's sake, I look like a drowned rat with unbrushed hair. Can someone, for the love of god, just re-meet me when I'm hot?

Now that we have a new bet, the Tweedles are fair game. And if I have to be here for a month, I'd really like them to play with me.

The handle turns, and I hit full panic, grabbing the comforter and yanking it hard. But it's not tucked in like on a normal hotel bed. It's loose. And now, so am I from where I was just standing.

My feet kick up into the air as I squeal, making me drop my towel as I fall, spinning and wrapping myself up in the blanket.

The thud my ass makes is followed by a *"Fuck"* from my mouth as laughter rings out.

"She's covered," I hear yelled out, followed by a different voice saying, "And on her ass."

I laugh. I can't help it.

I'm sitting on the damn floor, butt-ass naked, covered in a blanket.

Like a dog rubbing on a rug, I scooch around underneath my fluffy little tent, gathering the material around me before I carve out a little opening for my face to peek out.

A piece of my hair flies off my forehead, landing back in the same spot as I blow it before unsuccessfully hiding my smile.

"Hi."

Two incredibly handsome behemoths stare back, and I instantly like them…again.

What's not to like?

Nate is built like a brick shithouse with black hair, brown eyes, and a decent amount of stubble on his face. He's wearing shorts that must be custom-made because his tattooed thighs are thicker than sexy intended. Yum.

And TJ is an extra-dirty, auburn-bearded god. He's a little shorter and leaner than Nate but just as sexy because his hazel eyes make you want to melt in them. The showstopper is his insanely well-defined forearms. The veins alone could make a nun sweat.

Suddenly, the memory of TJ pulling the front of the Elvis jumpsuit open and pretending to lick his nipple during our complimentary wedding photos blesses my mind.

"Hey, Elvis."

TJ chuckles and walks over to me, staring down before he squats.

"Girl, you look like a real cute version of ET." He winks and points to himself. "Not Elvis, TJ." He then hooks a thumb over his shoulder to the brick shithouse. "Nate."

Oh, I'm a little swoony because I'd forgotten about TJ's

twinge of a Southern drawl. It's enough to make my panties wet...if I had any on.

"I know...I remember you. I wasn't that drunk. But it's nice to meet you again."

In fact, I remember everything way too acutely right now.

TJ smirks, staring into my eyes.

"It was more than nice the first time, sweetheart."

I press my lips together as he winks and reaches out, gripping where my shoulders are hidden under the fluffy comforter, and lifts. I squeal but hold the blanket tight as he sets me to my feet.

"Atta girl. Let's get ya off your ass."

"Thank you," I say sweetly, eyes shifting to Nate as he holds up a bag of McDonald's. "Yes!" I draw out, shuffling toward it like a clumsy penguin.

I rock my head back and forth because my hair is stuck inside the blanket before stopping in front of Nate.

"You are a lifesaver. Seriously. I'm starving. I was promised lunch, but seems my ball and chain's already set on disappointing me."

I jerk my head toward the bed, where TJ is now sitting, and Nate's eyes follow.

"You should let us make it up to you. We never disappoint."

Oh, hello.

Nate grins and winks at me, whispering, "It's true," before slipping his hand around the back of my neck, adding, "Let me," as he pulls my hair free.

Oh, man. As if one of these charmers wasn't enough. The way these two fuckers seem to tag team everything makes my skin heat. I let out a quiet half laugh before I bite my lip.

I'm about to say something when Crew clears his throat from behind Nate. And it's not the kind people do because they have something clogging it. No, it's the *excuse me, I'm here* kind.

My teeth immediately find the inside of my cheek to stop myself from smiling. Mainly because Nate doesn't move as he stares down at me with mischief in his eyes. *I like him.* But before I can tell him that, Nate gives and takes a step away, clearing the doorway.

I shift my head, and all I see is Crew.

Fuck. Me.

The not-love of my life is seated on the arm of the couch... shirtless...and in gray sweats. When did he get those? He must've snuck into the room while I was in the shower.

Good *god*. And I mean that.

Because there has to be one. I believe now.

Only someone who created miracles could think I was making it out of this moment without breaking all ten of the *'ments.*

My eyes peruse his body. Shamelessly.

If I could stop them, I would. But...*for fuck's sake*...he has that v thing that disappears into his sweats like it's pointing to buried treasure. I remembered it, but in person, the drunk memory didn't do it justice. And he has a six-pack when he's sitting. Nobody has a six-pack when they're sitting.

He's perfect... I hate him. I hope he gets the stomach flu. *After we fuck.*

No. Goddammit. Keep your legs closed for the sisterhood, ho.

Crew brings a hand to his chest, rubbing it, and I feel my mouth water like my body's actually embarrassed that I'm this thirsty.

I wonder if all girls are this horny? There's got to be medication for this. Like the anti-Viagra or whatever the equivalent is for women. I roll my eyes at myself, going for snarky as I look at him, trying to hide the *bang me* leaking from my pores.

"Gray sweatpants...really?"

Crew smirks as I continue. "You're a filthy whore. Put some clothes on."

I did not hide anything.

A voice from behind him makes my eyes pop open wide.

"I told you she wouldn't fall for it. Nice try though. But my bestie isn't caving."

"Millie," I shriek, jumping up and down and almost dropping my bag of Mickey D's as she laughs.

Crew's eyes stay on me. And for the first time in the last hour, I smile at him before tugging my blanket tighter.

I can't help it. He lost, and I won this round. *Cha-ching.*

He bends down to grab my bag, the one I didn't even notice, before he stands and walks toward us, but Nate blocks the doorway, crossing his arms as he leans against the frame.

"Do I have you to thank for bringing my friend?" I all but purr.

He nods slowly, eyes on mine. TJ comes up behind me and whispers in my ear.

"You can thank Nate first...or both of us at the same time if you'd like."

I don't know if there's such a thing as being dickmotized, but I think I'm that. These two don't give a girl time to think straight. I'm already being tag teamed while our clothes are on...or theirs are, at least. My teeth find my lip before Crew jerks Nate backward, making me laugh.

"Go get dressed," he grinds out, setting my duffel at my feet as Nate chuckles, holding up his hands before turning and walking toward the couches.

But Crew doesn't move, eyes only ticking to TJ before my Southern Tweedle says, "Fun's over."

TJ touches my blanket-covered waist to gently push me aside before joining Nate.

But Crew hovers over me, a smile peeking out. We're just standing there staring at each other, and it feels a little like déjà vu. I'm already instantly flustered when he's this close, but now with him shirtless...it's having an effect...everywhere.

He takes a deep breath, and the dirtiest thought soaks my mind. The idea that he could smell me, like know how turned on I am right now, exactly the way the guys in all the romance books I read do. Because this pussy is wet and throbbing just enough to remind me that not fucking him is a hardship.

Crew lifts his hand, dipping his fingers inside the collar of my blanket, and my breath catches. He grins, pausing only for a moment before he slowly pulls it open...just enough so he can peer down.

My entire goddamn body is burnt to a crisp. I've already gone up in flames. Now I'm cooked. It's the way he's smirking, daring me to stop him...it's the way I don't, in fact, stop him as we sexually double-dog dare each other.

"Are you trying to torture yourself?" I whisper, hidden in our bubble. "Because do not forget that everything underneath this blanket is for looking and not touching."

He licks his bottom lip before pressing his fingers under my chin, forcing it up, our eyes locked.

"Wild Card, no more flirting with the bench. I'm the starting fucking lineup."

thirteen

• • •

"That's a good fucking girl. Now, let me clean
you up."

eleanor

The coffee cup warms my hand as I hold it and stare out
the penthouse windows. It's so wild that Crew lives in
a hotel. The perk, though, is that late last night, after
much drama, Millie and I had an array of desserts delivered to
top off our sleepover.

I lift my coffee, blowing on it before I take a sip, letting the
caffeine seep into my system and bring me back to life. Truth is, I
was up really late, not just because Millie and I were reliving our
middle school sleepover days by bouncing on beds and having
dance parties...yes, we did that. But only after I texted my boss,
just barely keeping my job. And also called my parents.

That call sucked. Which is why dessert was ordered.

Nothing kills the pang of knowing you disappointed the
people you love like chocolate tiramisu. Thankfully, my sister
swooped in with a follow-up call to them and saved the day.

It's all fun and games, kids, until you drunk-marry a
stranger.

Speaking of said stranger, Crew left about an hour ago.
Apparently, he works out every day, sometimes twice a day. The

idea not only sounds terrible, but I'm convinced that it is actually terrible. And I'd said as much when I found him this morning engaged in a live-action thirst trap.

He was using one of those roller things on the ground, gliding back and forth over his thigh. I literally almost dissolved into a puddle.

I was unprepared. My whole body just got all wobbly, knees trying to buckle as I watched him—palms pressed into the ground, his left foot digging into the ground as he rocked forward and back, forward and back…in and out… I shiver, almost spilling my coffee as I relive it again, making me chuckle.

"Jesus."

But it was the hottest thing I've ever seen in my life. It far surpassed any video I've ever seen of any guy doing that on TikTok. However, I knew what he was doing, even if it took me a minute to compose myself. And I wasn't falling for that shit.

Even if I had.

So, when he looked up with that sexy smirk, I wrinkled my forehead and said, "Why are you humping the floor, weirdo?" Then I stepped over him and headed straight for the kitchen.

I'm still smiling at my second victory in two days as Millie's sleepy voice catches my attention.

"Hey."

She pads through the room, joining me in the kitchen and taking my coffee from me to sip. Her nose scrunches up.

"This doesn't have Baileys in it. I thought we were partying today. Where's Crew?"

I laugh before I walk over to the fridge and open it, pulling out her iced coffee mixed with Baileys and handing it to her.

"He's at his workout training stuff. And yes, we're partying, but unless you're going to cancel your flight today and stay with me, ensuring your thirty-thousand-dollar win, then this girl is partying with mimosas minus the champs."

She laughs and nods.

"Fair. One-K down, twenty-nine more to go."

She takes a sip of her coff-tail as her phone buzzes, drawing her eyes down and mine to what she's doing.

Her head pops up, excitement written on her face.

"Guess what?"

"What?" I answer playfully.

"Turntable Tony is doing his thing down at that club here. The one we were at the other night. I didn't even know there was a pool outside. But there is, and they do a pool party day club kind of thing. He has bracelets for us." Her eyes lift to mine. "How do you feel about ending our weekend off with a bang, baby?"

My choices are to stay cooped up in this room, waiting for the husband I never wanted, or to party with my friend for the end of our weekend. Duh.

"I feel like we need to get our bikinis on because it's party time, bitch."

AN HOUR LATER, MILLIE AND I ARE IN A CABANA...*CHARGED TO THE room.* Stacked with food, water, and bottles...*charged to the room.* Wearing the cutest red, white, and blue ass-out bikinis we could find...*charged to the motherfucking room.*

I'll pay him back, but not before I poke the bear.

Millie lifts her phone, catching me off guard and making me laugh as she takes another picture of us.

"Tag me in that." I smile, grabbing my drink—cranberry juice with a splash of Sprite and a lime twist—before holding it in the air and yelling, "Happy Fourth of July weekend."

People around us cheer, and even Millie's DJ points at us. *Actually, to her. Hmmm.*

"I know you had the worst weekend." She smiles, gulping back some water. "But I kind of had the best weekend ever."

I laugh because had I not been sanctioned to matrimony hell,

I would've said the same thing. We cheers anyway before I smirk at her.

"What's Turntable Tony's real name? Because it feels like casual isn't so casual anymore. When we FaceTimed yesterday, you weren't at our motel... That means you left after I did when I went to the courthouse."

Millie flings her arm over my shoulder, completely ignoring me, refusing to answer in a way that makes me one thousand times more curious. All she told me last night was that they had indeed slept together, but my drama took up most of our night, so she was able to stay under the radar.

"I will beat it out of you, Mill Valley. I want all the torrid details."

She lifts her arms, grinning ear to ear and jumping in place as the beat drops, and everyone in the pool starts creating waves as they jump too.

This sneaky little link.

I'm smiling, laughing, and thoroughly enjoying this moment until my head turns like an obedient dog, as if my name's been called. Not that I could hear anything over the bone-deep bass taking over my ears. Except maybe I did because my entire body stills.

Oh shit.

Barreling my way is a six-foot-five, shirtless, sweaty, dirt-smeared, angry-as-fuck-looking quarterback flanked by his two sexy besties.

I guess he got the room charges.

The chuckle that escapes is accompanied by gentle taps to any part of Millie I can hit without looking at her, desperately trying to get her attention.

"Ummm, that's my boob," she yells humorously.

But I don't say anything. I just point, then look at her, my eyebrows hitting the top of my forehead. She slaps a hand over her mouth before saying, "Oh shit, the jig is up. Wait, what is he doing?"

I look back to see Crew hasn't bothered to walk around the pool like a normal human. He's opted to walk straight through the foot-and-a-half shallow ledge where people are sunning, splitting the crowd as he tromps, shoes and all.

My stomach flips, but I don't look away as he closes the distance between us, his words as unfriendly as the expression on his face.

"What the fuck do you think you're doing?"

Oh hell no. People in proximity stare at us as they begin to whisper. My hands hit my waist as Millie gives TJ and Nate a small wave, and I narrow my eyes on Crew as I make myself clear.

"Excuse me? You better rephrase, buddy."

"I'm not your fucking buddy," he throws back.

So, I snap back as quick. "And you're not my daddy either, so watch your mouth."

You'd have to cut the tension with a chainsaw. But I won't be intimidated...because I'm intimidating. There isn't a person in the world that needs more than an hour with me to know I'm not available to babysit anyone's audacity. You have to take that shit home with you.

Crew takes a deep breath, his eyes closing before they're on me again, but this time, so are his hands as he gently touches my waist, guiding me backward further into the cabana.

Although we're unseen to the world around us now, he still keeps his voice quiet.

"I have too many messages on my phone from people trying to convince the world that we're in love, saying you're making it hard for them to do that. Barrett even sent a fucking messenger to the goddamn field to interrupt my workout."

What? Wait...what? So this isn't about the room charges.

I shake my head, trying not to stare at the dirt mark on his jawline. Because then I'll get lost in how strong and fucking defined it is.

"How am I doing anything to make their job hard?" I push back.

He looks me up and down, his tongue darting over his lips before he says, "Wild Card, you look real single right now."

Are you fucking kidding?

I spin around, putting my ass on full display, and look over my shoulder, hearing him growl as I restate the ridiculousness of what he just said.

"Single because I'm ass out for the world to see?" I turn back, staring at him expressionless. "I have a feeling you show your ass on a daily basis. So, I'll take *literally* over *figuratively* any day of the week."

The smirk on his face isn't friendly; it's more of a *motherfucker* kind of look. Still, I don't stop because nobody gets to tell me what to wear or what I choose to wear means.

"What is this? The 1950s? Does football culture expect me to be a good little wifey? Let's get one thing straight, Crew Matthews—"

I'm cut off, rant left on pause as his mouth crashes down over mine. *Oh fuck.* His lips are warm and his tongue intrusive. He's taking this kiss, not asking for it.

I wish I could say I push him away, especially since I was knee-deep in my feminist manifesto. But I don't. My palms are already on his chest, pretending like they're about to push him away, like liars, because all I'm really doing is feeling the speed of his heart under my flesh.

Because Crew's kissing me like he couldn't stop himself from doing it. And that feeling is way too goddamn familiar. Our lips glide between each other's, tongues playing, licking, teasing as our heads tilt faster and faster.

Crew's rough fingers wind their way through my hair, and I lift to my tiptoes, wanting more, as he cradles my face, stealing more of my breath.

He's hungry and aggressive, kissing me like he wants me to

collapse into a heap, pussy wet, begging for more. *And damn, am I close.*

But as fast as it started, it ends. He pulls back, fucking breathless, his chest heaving as he stares down at me with those stormy blue eyes. My breath matches his as I blink, lost in a haze as my hands begin to drift from his chest.

Crew licks his already wet lips as he nabs my left wrist, holding it to his chest before he reaches into his pocket. My brows pull together, trying to make sense of what he's doing before he lifts my wedding ring, the cheap dice one we got married with.

Oh shit, I'd taken it off last night and forgotten it by the sink.

His voice is chock-full of the gravel that makes me feel weak.

"You can wear whatever the fuck you want. But don't ever fucking forget this again."

He slides my wedding ring back on my finger and drops my hand.

That's what he meant by I looked single—no ring.

I blink a few times, still trying to get my bearings, before I chuckle. Because *my bad.*

"Sorry?" I say insincerely, slightly entertained over how wrong I just got that moment.

Crew shakes his head, letting his eyes peruse my body, even tilting his head to do so.

"That's not an apology," he offers, skimming his finger just under the stringed knot on my hip.

I'm dizzy, head swimming.

First off, he's touching me. And I can't think straight when that happens.

Second, he's touching me...and all I've thought about since yesterday has been about *not* letting him touch me. Which, in a way, is still about him fucking touching me.

Crew's lips part as I stare at them. And without a doubt, I know that any apology he'd accept would only be in the form of my pussy. *Never happening.*

"What *is* an apology, then?"

He huffs a laugh as he raises his hand and skims his thumb over my bottom lip while he speaks.

"You don't think before you speak like you're allergic to tact. Has anyone ever told you that?"

I nip at his finger, watching him almost smile before pulling back his hand.

"Are you going to answer my question or stand here and insult me?"

Crew growls before bending down and lifting me at the waist so that I'm standing on the couch in the cabana, bringing us almost eye to eye.

"That's better. If you're gonna act tall, you might as well be it too."

I chuckle, a grin peeking out and not going away as he continues.

"And for the record, an apology comes without a question mark...but I'm not looking for one. I like that you speak your mind without apology. I like it so much that it makes my dick hard as fuck."

My eyes nearly pop out of my head. My face shoots down, eyes locking on the impression of his cock through his shorts.

Oh.

I want to reach out and rub my hand over it. Feel it jerk, wanting me to relieve it. I'm thinking about it so much so that my fingers twitch.

Crew lifts my eyes back to his.

"Now that we're on the same page, let me be frank. I'd planned to make you wild. To make you come to me. But I'm just gonna put it out on the table for you."

His fingers curl around the nape of my neck, anchoring me to him.

"I want you upstairs, on the island, legs spread with my tongue fucking that tight pussy. I want you to come until you're squirting and sliding all over the goddamn marble like the dirty little slut you are. And when you're done, I want you sitting on my face so we can do it all over again."

Holy. Fuck.

My heart has stopped beating...but I can still feel my pulse. It's just a little further south.

I swallow, trying to remember why I'm supposed to say no. There was a reason...what was the reason? Money...that was it.

But you know what? People are too greedy nowadays...they invest in too much materialism. Money shouldn't be a factor in people's lives, especially and specifically, say, like, thirty thousand dollars. That's a dumb amount. Nobody cares about that much.

"Tell me you want that."

Five little words and I can't speak. I'm too stunned, but I can feel my head nod.

Crew keeps his eyes on me as he yells over his shoulder to the boys.

"Fellas, make sure Millie makes it to the airport. Her shit's already at the valet."

My mouth pops open as I rush my words out.

"I'm not leaving—"

But without skipping a beat, Crew bends down and tosses me right over his shoulder.

"You sure as hell the fuck are," he growls.

I squeal his name, slapping his perfectly hard ass as he spins around and looks at Millie.

"Say goodbye to your friend."

She's laughing, the smile on her face way too big as she points at me.

"Bye, friend, and goodbye, thirty thousand."

Oh my god. Crew barely waits as I yell back, telling her I love her and to call me when she lands. The moment we hit sunlight, the hordes of people begin to cheer, and some asshole yells out, "Nice ass."

Crew pauses, and I can feel him looking around before I

scream again as he leans sideways, grabbing a pillow off a lounge chair and slapping it over my bare ass.

"Oh my god," I yell as he traipses back through the water the way he came past people clapping and cheering. "This is so embarrassing."

I bury my face in his back because I could die. But he doesn't care. Crew carries me out of the day club, through the fucking hotel, and into the private elevators, making enough of a scene that my other cheeks are bright red.

But the minute the elevator doors close, Crew runs his nose up the side of my leg, inhaling the scent of coconut tanning oil and my sweat before he drops the pillow and bites my ass.

I can't help it. I suck in a gasp, gushing wetness between my squeezed-together thighs. And as the ding sounds for our floor, Crew pushes his fingers between my legs, tucking just inside the lining of my bikini bottoms and dragging over my arousal before he brings those fingers to his lips and sucks them loudly.

"Fuck yeah. That's a good fucking girl. Now, let me clean you up."

fourteen

· · ·

"Open wide for Daddy."

crew

I carried her all the way to this fucking counter, kissing and nipping at the side of her leg as my hand closed in tighter around her body. Just the smallest sample of her pussy's turned me into a fucking animal.

It took everything I had not to sink right in when I placed her down, bare-assed, on the cold fucking marble and heard her suck in a hard breath. Instead, I growled my words like a goddamn caveman thinking about fucking her raw.

"Open your legs."

My chest is heaving, my jaw slack, as I stand an arm's length away, rubbing my cock from the outside of my shorts. Her eyes are locked on mine as her chest rises and falls in a matching rhythm. I'm so fucking hot for this girl that it makes me feel as if my senses are heightened.

Eleanor slowly glides her tongue over her top lip. Oh, she's going to fucking get it.

I half blink, following every fucking glistening movement, feeling drunk, before I shorten the first three words I said to one.

"Open."

Her hands move slowly, positioning between her legs, and her slim fingers curl around the edge of the marble, blocking my view as she parts her legs.

"You dirty little fucking tease."

Her lips tip up, but her eyes stay locked on mine before she bites her lip.

"That grin on your face is gonna be why I turn your ass red."

She smiles wider, not moving her hands.

"Push back until you're on your back, baby."

This is one of the reasons I liked her so much the other night. A smaller but packs a punch other reason is that she's clean and on the pill.

"Hands behind you."

Her eyes never leave mine as she lifts one hand at a time and presses her palms behind her, making her tits jut forward, leaving her bikini-covered pussy on display.

My eyes drop, looking at her thighs spread on the counter, legs gently dangling, kicking back and forth slowly. Her waist rocks right as she stares me down.

I take a step forward, nestling myself between her legs as I skate my fingertips up her shins and over her knees slowly. Watching goose bumps bloom over her thighs as I spread my fingers over her soft skin, I let my palms ghost her flesh until I stop at her hips.

"Are you fucking taunting me?"

She shrugs, feigning innocence because there isn't an innocent bone in her body. Thank fucking god because I'd be overly disappointed if this girl wasn't exactly as slutty as I'd hoped her to be.

"I'm gonna bite this." My hand trails over to the inside of her thigh. "I'm gonna sink my teeth hard enough to leave a fucking mark before I tell your pussy exactly what I'm gonna do to it… spelling every goddamn word with my tongue."

Her head falls back, soft exhales cascading from her lips as I tug at the strings on her bottoms, letting them fall open before I sweep my hand inside the front. Inhaling deeply as I touch the soft hair on her cunt, I bunch the fabric and jerk it from underneath her.

She lets out a little squeal, laughing and catching herself, then smacking her hands down on the counter again.

I chuckle, smirking as my hand glides over her stomach, up through the middle of her breasts.

"You're fucking gorgeous, you know that?"

My bottom lip draws between my teeth, then drags out slowly as I apply the gentlest amount of pressure, forcing her to crawl backward until she's lying down, arched off the marble with her tits pushed forward.

On display like... The rest of my thought tumbles from my lips. "My perfect little whore."

"Okay," she purrs in acceptance.

Fuck. I feel wild, as if I'm being led by instinct only. I want to touch every inch of her fucking body. I want to taste, lick, bite, and mark...but mostly, I just want to own her cunt.

To use it for however long I want until I'm fucking done.

I grip her thighs, spreading her so I can get the perfect look at her sweet pussy.

"Jesus," I groan. "Your cunt is beautiful."

My fingers dive between her soft, curly hairs, parting her lips, opening her, and watching as she contracts, spilling wetness over her rim.

"Fuck yes," comes out hoarse and strained just as I dive down between her legs, flattening my tongue and drawing it all the way up, devouring her arousal.

"Oh shit," she hisses, sucking in a breath and slapping the counter.

But I want to taste all her fucking pleasure. Take her into me. Drink her cum. The tip of my tongue flicks her clit before I suck it between my lips and let it go with a pop.

"Goddamn, you taste so fucking good."

I spit on her clit before diving down and sucking it again.

"Fuck," she gasps, already writhing underneath me, but I pull back again, trying to shove her legs wider.

"I would've never stopped eating you out had I known you tasted this good."

My mouth covers her swollen clit again as I growl and hum, gliding my tongue between the fold of her lips and back over her clit again.

I promised to clean her up, lick her fucking clean, and I'm going to do just that.

Eleanor lifts her head, already breathless, as her fingers weave through my hair before she tugs, forcing me to begrudgingly leave heaven.

"What do I taste like?" she pants.

I like you filthy.

With my eyes locked on hers, I let go of her leg and rise up, bringing my hand between her legs. We never break eye contact as I circle the rim of her cunt before pressing inside with two fingers, making her gasp and arch her back again.

"You taste like pussy..."

I can feel the arrogant smirk on my face as I stroke the inside of her warm cunt, feeling it contract around my knuckles. I press in and out slowly, curling them to hit that spot that's making her eyes roll back.

All the while licking my lips because my mouth's jealous of my fingers.

She exhales small, begging mewls. So, I draw my fingers out slowly, reaching out with my free hand to grab the string of her bikini between her tits and pull, forcing her forward as I bring my lust-coated fingers to her lips.

"And pussy tastes good. Open wide for daddy."

She grabs my wrist, sucking my fingers between her lips before circling her tongue over the rough skin.

"You're a dirty little bitch, aren't you. You keep being a good girl, and I'll let you do a little comparison between your pussy and my cum."

Her eyes meet mine as a string of her spit lingers between the tip of my fingers and her lips as she draws back before it's broken with one word.

"Heard."

I shove my fingers back inside her mouth as I dip back down, thrusting my tongue between her hairs to get an even better taste of everything I missed. Eleanor licks and sucks my fingers like she wishes it was my cock, but it doesn't distract me from what I'm doing.

Nothing could. Her pussy is my newest obsession. I could die here and be happy.

Her head bobs as I press her back down to the counter, my fingers staying in her mouth as I grab one of her legs and hook it over my shoulders, sealing my mouth over her throbbing clit again.

"Oh fuck. Yes. Just like that," she moans, pulling my hand from her mouth to palm her tit.

Her hips rock and circle as I lick and suck, tracing figure eights around her clit. I'm eating her harder and faster like I'm fucking starved for her as my other hand dips underneath the fabric of her top, pinching her beaded nipple.

"Oh my god, don't stop. You're so good at this."

My fingers dig mercilessly into her thigh, my other hand trying to spread wider because I feel feral. My feet are digging into the ground, my face buried in her pussy.

I can feel her pulse, the quickening throbbing beat on my tongue as her clit engorges. It's fucking incredible. The hand I have on her opened thigh runs closer to her cunt until my thumb dips inside, crassly fucking her pussy.

"Yessss," draws out husky and full-bodied before she props up on her elbows, tangling her hands in my hair and grinding into my face. "Eat it like that. Oh, fuck. Lick me clean."

I wasn't lying when I said she fucking tasted good. Her cunt is addictive. It's the embodiment of eroticism. And the way she circles her hips faster and faster, gripping my hair, urging me to devour her, is shameless and unapologetic.

The girl is brazen, and it makes me want more.

I want her to come. All over my face. Screaming my name.

She's panting and moaning, begging and fucking my face.

"Please. Please. Please. Please. I want to come. Please."

I chuck her other leg over my shoulder, gripping her ass with ferocity as I eat her like it's the last thing I'll ever do. She's pulling my hair, desperate for my mouth to fuse to her pussy as I rake her flesh with my fingers, growling, wanting her fucking release.

I'm a slave to my basest instincts, jerking her body closer to my mouth, sliding her halfway off the counter with ease. Because every bit of her fucking desire has spread between her thighs and in between her ass cheeks.

And all over my face.

It's fucking heaven.

"Oh my god," she gasps, a hand grabbing my shoulder.

I chuckle deep and menacing because her panting sounds like a desperate whine. And it's music to my ears. She's coming.

Her gorgeous chants fill the space mixing with the slaps of her hand on the counter as my tongue moves faster and faster. I suck on the swollen flesh until I can feel her thighs begin to quiver. Her hand on my head viciously pulls at my hair until she's screaming.

"Yes. Yes. *Yes. Yesss.*"

A violent gush coats my lips as she squirts into my mouth, her cum slathering my chin as I tilt my head, rubbing my cheek over her wet cunt, wanting her on me before I lick from her ass to her pussy.

Her hand falls from my head as she whispers to herself, but I don't stop licking her clean. I want more of her taste and her scent. I slide her back onto the counter before I drag my face away from her cunt with a deep inhale and wipe my face with the back of my hand.

On shaky, unsteady hands, she crawls back to sitting, staring at me as I tug my shorts down with one hand and toe off my still-wet shoes.

My cock springs forward, bobbing heavily against my stomach.

"C'mere."

Her panting is the only sound in the room before I reach for her legs again, slapping my hands down on her thighs. Eleanor doesn't hesitate, wrapping her legs around my waist, her arms doing the same around my neck as I lift and carry her toward the bedroom. But we only make it as far as the couch because her pussy's a magnet for my dick.

It's already trying to find its way inside.

I set her to her feet, spinning her around and smiling as she squeals before I bend that sweet ass over the back of the couch.

"Oh my god," she rushes out, laughing and looking back over her shoulder as I stare down, grabbing both her ass cheeks and pulling them apart to expose her tight, puckered hole.

"I'm gonna fuck this too."

She locks eyes with me just as I kick her legs open, forcing them wider as I line my cock up with her pussy.

I tease the tip, my tongue gliding over my bottom lip as she lifts to her tiptoes. The head of my cock is engorged, topping the veiny shaft as I drag my hand down, letting my precum mix with her glisten before dipping just inside her tight hole.

"Fuck," I heavily exhale, unable to tear my eyes away.

My stomach contracts, eyes closing before I run a rough hand up her spine, gripping her hair and reminding her of my promise.

"You remember when I said I was turning this ass red?"

I tug her hair for an answer, and she gasps before giving a breathy "Yes."

The tip of my cock dips inside her pussy again, cruelly teasing her and me. But I can't wait anymore. I thrust inside, filling her cunt and cutting off her breath, losing mine along with her.

She just took my soul.

I can't breathe…I can't focus.

My head falls back, eyes staring up at the ceiling as I just exist inside her tight pussy.

"Tell me you're my dirty little slut. Tell me you want me to fuck you raw and come on your ass as I turn it red. Tell me I get to use you."

I pull back slowly, threading the rim of her entrance before I push back inside again, pulling a hard whoosh of breath from me. Then I do it again. And again. And again. Until the pace picks up, and she's moaning, her body jostling, tits bouncing as I fuck her, my hand gripping her hair.

Fuck. Me.

No part of me wants to be gentle. I let her hair go and grab two handfuls of her ass, kneading the soft flesh as I bottom out faster and faster.

"This is my ass. Say it."

She's breathless, her words almost swallowed up.

"It's yours. It's your ass."

"That's it. Take it, baby. Take that cock like a good girl. Squeeze me. Make that pussy beg for my cum."

She's moaning loudly, constricting around me, her hands gripping the back of the couch as strings of curses spurt from between her lips.

Goddamn, this feels good. I'm hammering inside her. My fingers are leaving red marks on her ass, but I want my whole fucking handprint.

"Yes," she moans. "Give it to me. Fuck my pussy."

The sound of our skin slapping against each other, the remnants of her cum still coated on the back of her legs smearing between us, sounds like a goddamn sexual symphony.

But it's not enough. I want her soaking my cock.

"Fuck yourself, baby. Put your hand between your legs."

She scrambles, shoving her arm in between her legs, moving her fingers against her clit as I thrust into her faster and faster, harder and harder, listening to her cries. My lips are parted as I stare down at her ass, watching my dick glide in and out of her pussy. The sweet sounds of her building, wanting that release, fill my ears.

And all I fucking want is to tip her over.

My teeth grit together as I rub her ass before lifting my hand and slapping it. Hard.

With my other hand, I reach out and wrap it around her throat, squeezing just enough to anchor her in place.

Her panting sounds like stuttering cries as her arm moves faster and faster, meeting the pace I'm fucking her at.

"More."

She exhales as I tighten my hand and slap her ass again, feeling her pussy tighten. My cock feels impossibly hard as I smack another blow, rubbing the reddening skin before doing it again.

I can barely hold on anymore.

Eleanor's soft warmth contracts, locking around my cock as a guttural moan rises from her lungs. I break, growling, hunching over her like a goddamn animal, relentlessly fucking her desperate cunt as my whole body engulfs hers.

She doesn't even need her hand anymore because I'm grinding her wet pussy all over the fabric.

"You better soak my fucking dick. Come on, baby."

The thought of her leaving a mark on the couch, as evidence for anyone to see I fucked her here, almost pushes me over the edge. But I can feel her building again, and I want it. She's whispering, almost in hysteria.

"I'm coming. I'm coming. I'm coming. I'm...I'm—"

Her whole body contracts, stiffening from head to toe as she screams. My arms immediately wrap around her body, hugging her as I fuck every ounce of breath out of her.

But the minute her body softens, I stumble back, jerking my dick out of her swollen cunt. Heaving breaths as I listen to her trying to catch her breath, I don't really give her any time as I demand more.

"Knees."

Eleanor flips over lazily and slides down the back of the couch directly onto the floor, looking up at me before she licks her lips and opens her mouth wide.

My chest expands as I grab the back of her head, guiding her forward and tilting her head, dragging her mouth up my shaft before pushing my dick as far as it'll go down her throat.

"You taste good on me, don't you."

My jaw tenses as she gags before I pull back and push in again.

"I told you I'd let you compare."

Her hands grip my skin, tugging me forward for more as she hollows her cheeks, eating both of us.

"Oh, fuck. That's right. Suck that dick. Your mouth is so good, baby."

I take two steps forward, forcing her to lean back as I grip her hair.

"I'm gonna come down your throat. You gonna be a good little whore and swallow what I give you?"

She hums, sucking hard as I take over and start fucking her face. Between her moans and the silkiness of her mouth, there's no fucking way I'm going to last more than a few seconds.

Her head bobs, guided by my hand as I thrust inside her mouth over and over, faster and faster, all the breath in my body ripping out like a bull.

My head drops back as I feel her throat contract before she swallows, massaging the head of my cock.

"Oh, fuck. Again."

My hand tightens in her hair as I pull out and thrust back in, cutting off her wind.

"Swallow, baby. Fucking swallow me back."

Her throat closes around me, tears pricking her eyes as her lips stretch around my hard cock, only finding relief when I draw back quickly to let her take a breath.

But Eleanor's already wanting more, her hands gripping my ass, urging me forward.

So, I give us what we both want.

I fuck her mouth without any regard for her. I hammer inside over and over, ignited by the sloppy sounds of spit gathering around her lips and her gagging each time I hit the back of her goddamn throat.

"Take it. Be a good whore. Take it all the way back."

I can feel my balls draw up and my stomach tighten until it feels like I can't breathe. Until mercifully, I explode, coming inside her mouth and down her throat, cradling her face as I stare down and watch as she swallows.

I can't move. I'm standing, suspended in the moment, looking down into her upturned face as I pet and caress her head.

"Your mouth is heaven, Wild Card. Your mouth...is fuck-ing...heaven."

Eleanor takes every drop, gently and slowly running her tongue up my softening shaft, making my body quiver before she lets go and sits back on her heels, letting out a deep-seated exhale.

"That was..." She smirks, her voice raising in weak celebra-tion. "Touchdown."

I chuckle, and with the rest of the strength left in my body, I bend down, hooking my arms under hers, and help her to her feet.

Our lips meet, and we kiss in slow, languid motions like two people who have nothing left to give but can't seem to get enough.

My arm circles her body, pulling her flush to me as my face nuzzles her neck. A smile breaks out across my face as I let my next words drift across her skin, kissing it gently.

"I'm glad you enjoyed yourself. I figured if you were throwing away thirty thousand dollars, I'd better make it worth it."

She hums a laugh and reaches for my face, forcing me to look at her.

"I didn't lose."

My head draws back as I stand to my full height.

"Yeah, you did."

I jerk my chin toward the bedroom, and she nods, slipping her hand in mine as we start to walk together on weak-ass legs. But Eleanor smirks, looking up at me the minute we hit the door, swinging around and blocking me with her hand on the jamb.

"You said that you'd have me screaming your name."

My brows raise as I nod. But before I can say anything, she adds, "And last I heard from my own lips, I never once said your name."

Motherfucker. That sneaky little cheat.

I tip my head back and laugh.

"Are you fucking kidding me?"

She grins back.

"Absolutely not. Those were your terms, and I'm sticking to them."

Eleanor gives me a wink before sashaying that fine ass directly into the bathroom, tossing her words over her shoulder.

"Don't worry, buddy. You can always try again."

All I heard in my head was challenge issued, challenge accepted. It looks like for the next four weeks, my dick's going to be happily working overtime.

*

Me: Bets off.

That girl I married: You're a sore loser. Ps. making a new chat when I left the old one...dumb.

DJ Mills: Oh, this is interesting. Do share with the class. I'm bored in between clients.

Wild Card's sister: You can't call it off because you're losing. Someone has to cheat or something.

Me: Wild Card IS cheating.

DJ Mills: Andddd we have nicknames.... This is an unexpected new development.

Wild Card's sister: Oooo...wild card. That's kind of perfect for her. Not gonna lie.

That girl I married: Don't encourage him! He's like a puppy. He'll start pissing all over the rug if you give him attention.

Me: Would you rather me hump your leg?

DJ Mills: Hahahahaha

Wild Card's sister: *GIF of dog humping air.

That girl I married: The bet is not off. Stop texting my people. Go get your own people.

DJ Mills: Technically we are his people by marriage now too.

That girl I married: You are pick-a-side friends. Get it together! We're a sham.

Me: Thanks Millie, that means a lot. Maybe you can talk to my wife about being nicer to me.

Wild Card's sister: Aww, come on Elle, he's adorable...be nice to your poor husband.

THAT GIRL I MARRIED HAS LEFT THE CHAT.

Me: Something we said?

Wild Card's sister: *laugh emoji

DJ Mills: This just keeps getting better and better.

fifteen

. . .

"Like you want to get tacos and then let me eat
your taco."

eleanor

I flip through the channels for the millionth time, but there's
always the same shit on. My phone buzzes from where I
have it lying on my stomach, so with the laziest effort, I tilt
it up to read my text.

> Mills: Um, random thought in between clients.
> Can I call myself your pimp since your pussy is
> really putting in the work for me?

> > Me: Inside voice, Mills...let's not share all our
> > thoughts.

I laugh, propping my feet on the back of the couch as I grab a
handful of grapes.

> Mills: All I'm saying is that I truly appreciate
> updates saying I'm $4000 richer. Your loophole
> is clutch.

Wait a minute.

> Me: Are you seriously still in a group chat?
> Fucking traitors.

> Mills: Duh, how else would I know how much
> I'm earning? He's so funny too.

My eyes roll of their own volition. What is wrong with him? I can't help but grin because, of course, he's still in a group chat… with *my* people. There's no point in making a bet unless you have someone to brag to about winning. And he really does think he'll wear me down and get me screaming his name.

I'm enjoying the effort.

I wipe the dew from my freshly washed grapes on my shorts before texting her back.

> Me: You better be more concerned with being
> nice to me. Or I'm going to throw this bet. Truth
> —my roster can be replenished. *salute emoji

> Mills: Speaking of throwing it back, I feel like I'd
> be a bad friend if I didn't state the obvious…

I laugh. That's not even a good segue.

> Me: And that is?

> Mills: That having sex with someone in the form
> of a one-night stand is one thing, but living
> together…sleeping together… Do you see
> where I'm going with this?

I see and hear what she's saying. And truth be told, I already gave myself the same gut check. Because the last few days have been weird. Almost kind of awkward. We basically fuck, he trains, we fuck again, and then stumble around conversations. It's like we're back at the beginning, sitting in my car, smiling at each other.

Which I guess is better than plotting murder scenarios, but still, it gave me pause.

But once I thought about it, Sunday was kind of a reset. As if everything we were pissed about got settled after he carried me upstairs and fucked my brains out. And now the dust has settled, and we're just back to being two people who are attracted to each other while sentenced to marriage and allowed to do dirty shit to each other.

I chuckle as I type out my exact thought.

> Me: Mills. I can like someone, even fuck them, and not fall in love. It's called friends with bennies. C'mon. You know me. I tap out at the idea of catching feelings and he's allergic to relationships. We're good. Plus, I'm totally planning on fucking the friends again. Ha ha.

> Mills: Rub it in, bitch. RUB IT IN.

Oh, I'm going to be rubbing something all right.

> Mills: Oh…P.S. —4, 7, 22, 30

I frown, confused, holding my phone above my face as I whisper to myself, "What the fuck?"

> Mills: Your horoscope says those are your lucky numbers. And that big life changes will alter the road to your happiness. Bet on red!

The sound of a duffel bag hitting the floor grabs my attention, making me drop my phone on my nose but immediately shoot to my knees on the couch, almost choking on a grape.

"Hey."

Crew stretches his muscular arms, sweat still soaking his shirt.

"Fake honey, I'm home."

I rub my nose as I smile back at him.

"We gotta go to the craps tables."

He runs his hand through his hair, grinning before he chuckles. "What?" His expression drops as I raise my brows, so he adds, "Am I getting a choice?"

I shake my head, pushing off the couch.

"Duh...happy wife, happy life." My shoulders pop in a quick shrug as I smile big, and my voice raises in celebratory cuteness. "Let's go!"

🦋

"THIS IS THE WORST GAME," I GROAN, POUTING AND NOT EVEN embarrassed about it.

"That's because you lost all your money."

He gently flicks my bottom lip as I swerve my head, scowling.

"Exactly."

Crew laughs, shoving his hand into his pockets, and smiles down at me as I keep grumbling. It only took fifteen minutes for me to lose the hundred dollars I had.

I turn to him, ignoring the fact that people keep staring at us...really at him, only occasionally looking at me. Which is weird in itself because I know they know about my life, seeing as quite a few news stories have reported about our married-in-Vegas cliché.

However, considering how I look right now, it's more likely that people are wondering why he's with some girl who looks homeless. Jesus, if Sam doesn't get my shit here sooner, I'll be stuck rotating the same four outfits for the whole month. I had five, but a dress without buttons will not do.

"We can go," I offer, turning away from the crappy table. "Clearly, Millie doesn't know what she's talking about...lucky numbers, my ass."

My stomach growls, kicking me while I'm down, and he

grins, motioning with his head for me to follow. I don't ask where we're going because I'm too irritated over losing my money until I see the entrance to the Mexican joint I saw on television on the channel that tells you all about what the hotel offers.

Shit's getting dark in the entertain myself portion of life.

"Hungry?" he offers, still smirking.

I nod. "Always."

"Tacos to the room?"

My shoulders do a little dance in answer as I wag my brows, even though I'm about to protest and say let's eat down here since I spend almost all my time in the damn room.

"All my time" dramatically being three days, but still, it's boring.

As I open my mouth, our path is suddenly co-opted and halted by a middle-aged dude in a button-up shirt with flamingos on it. He looks like he sells insurance.

He's holding the hand of a woman with a gold band on her finger who looks mortified to be standing with him. And I'm certain it's because the man is speaking a mile a minute, elated to be two feet away from *"The Crew Matthews."*

Oh wow.

"You're the GOAT." The guy excitedly looks at his wife. "Babe, it's Crew Matthews. He's the fucking GOAT. Holy shit, sorry, I didn't mean to cuss in front of your wife. Congratulations, by the way."

Crew slips his hand in mine, folding my arm behind me as he tucks me into his side. I blink, not stunned by the move but because this energy is a lot. I smile, knowing my eyes are open a bit wider than normal as I try to take it all in.

This is so strange. I mean, I know who Crew is and that he's a big deal. But it's bizarre to see the reality acted out live and in person. Because he's still the same guy who argued the validity of me calling chicken wings "Buffalo wings" if they didn't have sauce on them. Which is ridiculous.

"You can't call them Buffalo wings if they don't have sauce because

that's how they originated...with sauce, in Buffalo, New York. I thought you read books."

I set my plate on the nightstand since we're eating in bed.

"Listen. You better stop treating me like I'm Jessica Simpson and I don't know the difference between tuna and chicken...of the sea... Circa 2003."

Crew's hand grips my thigh as he drags me across the bed toward him, making me laugh.

"Well, if the designer shoe fits, Wild Card. Because the only correct answer is you're eating chicken wings, and I'm gonna eat pussy."

My zone-out is interrupted as the guy hooks a thumb at his girl.

"We got married this weekend too. She finally talked me into it." He laughs like we're all supposed to, except nobody does, and somehow, that doesn't stop this dude from talking. "I bet *your* wife didn't have to talk you into anything though. She's smoking hot."

Dude.

Crew wrinkles his forehead, a grin peeking out as the guy's wife smacks his arm. *I'd smack more than his arm, lady.*

Crew clears his throat, squeezing my hand before he lets go. "How about a picture?" he offers as his face turns away from his biggest fan, his eyes locking with mine.

He mouths, *You good?* before I nod and smile back. The man is almost vibrating from excitement as he steps in next to Crew.

"I can't believe I'm meeting you. You're on my fantasy team."

Crew nods politely. But I chuckle, locking eyes with him, mouthing, *Same.*

Number one fangirl tosses an arm up, trying to get it over Crew's shoulder. But even standing as tall as he can, it's not happening. So ever so discreetly, Crew Matthews leans down.

Aw, he's letting his nice guy show.

The wife steps up and takes a few pictures before nodding, but the guy isn't done. He grabs Crew's hand, shaking it.

"I really appreciate it, man. I'm going to frame this and put it on the wall." He looks back at his wife, who looks at him like he's crazy. "Babe, we could put it next to our wedding portrait."

Oh my god.

Crew steps away, his hand finding the small of my back as he urges me forward before he gives another wave to his biggest fan, saying, "Have a good one, guys," and we walk away.

But I'm still staring up at him because...I don't know, just something.

He looks down at me, eyes narrowing.

"Why are you looking at me like that?"

I scowl before it morphs into a smirk.

"Like what?"

"Like you want to get tacos and then let me eat *your* taco."

A laugh explodes from my chest as I shove his shoulder and shake my head.

"Let's just order the food and go back to the room before we get assaulted by any more people who think you're the equivalent of a farm animal."

sixteen

. . .

"I'm nice to you in public, but I still get to play
with their privates."

crew

"Where are we going?"

I don't answer, glancing over my shoulder and grinning at her as I tug her up another flight of steps, holding the bag of our dinner in my hand.

"Oh my god, will you slow down, please? I might drop the drinks," she huffs, the smile on her face too big for her to really be irritated.

I've been second-guessing myself for the last five minutes because this is uncharted and dangerous territory for me. I don't want to give her the wrong impression, but she was so cool when we were approached by those fans.

And although I know we made a deal, a truce, to be nice to each other for the sake of my deal, she was genuine and gracious under pressure.

So, if anyone deserves what I'm about to share...it's her.

I stop, turning around before turning the corner to take the last flight.

"So, here's the thing. You know how you've been watching that same movie over and over again every night?"

She nods, looking impatient.

"The Hangover?"

I chuckle. "Yeah, that one. And you were rambling on about how it's so unrealistic that they put shit like going on rooftops in movies…"

Her eyes grow wide as her mouth drops open before she stomps her foot.

"Shut up right now. Quit it."

Eleanor lets go of my hand, starting around the corner past me, but I grab the back of her shorts, forcing her to stop and look over her shoulder.

"Settle down." I laugh. "Let me make the grand gesture. You're like a toddler."

Her hip pops as she turns around, smiling at me.

"Look at you, QB…being all nice to me. Careful, I might start to think that you like me just as much as you dig my pussy."

My head draws back before I walk past her, taking the four steps to the door labeled ROOFTOP, and shove the door open, the entire sky coming into view.

"Oh, come on, Wild Card. I could never. Only *one of them* isn't annoying."

She laughs as she walks out onto the roof, shoving the drink holder in my hand before looking up at the sky. I smile as she spreads her arms wide and stares up at the stars.

The door closes behind me, ruining her moment, because in sheer panic, she spins around, her hand covering her mouth.

But I shake my head.

"Calm down. That's the thing movies do get wrong. The door reopens."

I lean back, pressing it open before letting it close again. She smiles before going back to her moment as I walk over to two lawn chairs I snuck up here months ago.

It squeaks as I sit down, setting the drinks on the other chair before I open our dinner bag. Eleanor looks over her shoulder and spins around, walking over to join me.

"This is pretty amazing," she breathes out, taking her tacos. "I bet you bring all the girls you marry and end up having to live with for thirty days here?"

"Obviously," I throw out with a wink. "Why else would I invest in this kind of luxury?" My hand motions to the cheap lawn chairs we're sitting on.

She laughs, and I join before I watch her take a ginormous bite of her taco. She leans over the paper to catch the spillage. Eleanor really is the definition of authentic. The girl doesn't give a shit about being anyone other than who she is. It's refreshing.

I also have no idea what to do with her because people like this make it so whatever guard you have up is hopeless. She makes me want to be myself.

And that's not someone I can really ever be with anyone. A thought strikes.

"I've actually never brought anyone here. Not even TJ or Nate. This is my hideaway. I figured…"

My voice trails off because she mumbles through a mouthful of food, but I still make out that she's saying, *I thought you guys were in love.* My shoulders shake, and I abandon what I was about to say, opting to take a bite of my food as she starts talking.

"I guess I should be honored. But why do I feel this is more about escaping the public eye? Back there in the casino…you were really nice to that guy. You even leaned in for the shot. But that has to get overwhelming. I mean, I was a little tripped out. And there aren't nearly as many eyes on me as there are on you."

I take a swig of my beer, then hold it between my fingers, letting it dangle.

"My first year as a rookie, that was hard. People were really intrusive, and my privacy felt like a sacrifice I had to make in return for the fame. But now, I guess I'm kind of used to it."

I look up at the sky, smirking before adding, "But it is nice to be able to eat without people taking a photo of me and ending up as a meme. You know?"

My face turns to Eleanor's. She's mid-bite, mouth wide open, staring up at me before she lowers her taco.

"No, I have no idea what it's like."

The grin on my face grows. "Lucky...for them and you. Because you eat like an animal."

"I'm hungry," she growls.

"You're feral," I toss back.

She shrugs. "That too."

We laugh before eating in silence for a few minutes, only moaning over how good the food is. I take another swig, relaxing back on the chair before she steals my beer.

"You know, you're not terrible to hang out with," she muses. I raise my brows, smirking, as she grins. "How is it that you haven't had a girlfriend? I mean, I know I was joking the other day, but I get the vibe that you've been single for a hot minute."

I prop a hand behind my head, stealing my beer back with the other.

"Jesus, I haven't had a serious relationship since I started in the league. At first, the worry was *is every girl a gold digger?* Then that morphed into *what are they willing to do to tie it down?* And I know there are plenty of nice people out there too. But mostly, I think I didn't commit because love is a distraction."

"I get that. The whole distraction thing. I feel the same way. I have things I want to accomplish, and if part of who I am is someone's girlfriend, the expectation is set that I'm supposed to consider them above myself."

I'm nodding. She totally gets it.

"Exactly. There's shit I want to accomplish, and it doesn't include learning to compromise to make someone else happy. This is all I've ever wanted to do since I was a little boy." I glance over at her, suddenly talking about shit I never talk about. "I grew up in foster care, but football was my one constant. I was lucky enough to take it from place to place." My forehead wrinkles. "Stop me if you googled this."

She laughs, rolling her eyes and cutting in as she wipes her hands on a napkin.

"Why would I google you? Nobody does that."

"Yeah, they do," I bark playfully. "I did it to you. And after reviewing your Twitter, I could totally understand why you don't have a boyfriend. You're a troll of the finest degree. But who has the balls to take that on?"

She gasps, chucking her napkin at me. I laugh and turn to block it with my shoulder.

"Weak. My Twitter is legendary, you son of a bitch. And if you'd really googled me, you would know that I am the premier esthetician in the Bay Area."

I'm smiling because I'm pretty sure she's not saying that sardonically. She lets out a deep breath before rubbing her tummy and lying back on the chair.

"Gimme," she whispers, wiggling her fingers for my beer.

"Why didn't you get your own when I asked if you wanted one?"

She smirks. "Why are you acting like sharing isn't your favorite thing?"

Damn. Set and match.

I don't say anything. I just give her a fist bump before handing it over and sit in silence, staring up at the stars.

The silence only lasts five minutes, though, before she wiggles around sideways on her chair as if the thought in her head can't stay bottled any longer.

"Okay, here's something Google can't answer. How long have you and the Tweedles been tag teaming women?"

My tongue darts out over my bottom lip before I turn my head and look at her.

"Long enough to be good at it. Why?"

Her voice is quieter, husky, like a phone sex operator, as she gives a very coy and telling shrug.

"Just wondering."

I adjust in the seat so that I'm on my side too, facing her.

"Wondering what exactly...and use all the dirty words, Eleanor. I like when you do that."

She says nothing for the longest handful of seconds as she stares back at me, her eyes locked on mine. I don't know much about her, but I know she's thinking what I'm thinking.

Her lips are slightly parted before her tongue coaxes that plump bottom lip between her teeth. When it drags out, she smirks.

"I'm wondering if they're part of our divorce settlement. Like, I'm nice to you in public, but I still get to play with their privates."

She's got a way with a phrase.

"C'mere."

I grip the metal frame of the lawn chair, scraping it over the concrete, making her gasp, then smile as I bring it closer to mine.

Without any words said, I slip my hand between her legs, dipping my fingers just inside her shorts.

"Let me see how wet you are."

Eleanor rolls onto her back, bending one leg at the knee as her head stays sideways, keeping her eyes on mine.

Fuck, she's not wearing any underwear.

My fingers dip inside her soaked pussy, getting swallowed into her warmth as she contracts around them.

"You wanna get fucked again, Wild Card?"

My lips find her neck as I press in and out, finger fucking her into bliss as I burn dirty promises into her neck.

"We'll fill you up, baby. Make you beg. Take you to heaven... All you gotta do is scream my name."

The smile on my face is remarkably wide as I hear her yell, *"Motherfucker."*

seventeen

. . .

"I want to taste me inside you."

eleanor

rew... I don't know if I said it aloud or in my head, but what I do know is my clit is throbbing, and my hand is between my legs.

I'm rubbing myself.

I dreamed about him the whole night. The way his lips felt on my skin. The way he teased the fuck out of me on the roof only to deny me. I dreamed about his cock in my mouth while TJ fucked me from behind and sitting on Nate's face.

There's nothing my dirty mind didn't cover. And now my entire body is needy, hungry, and desperate to come. A soft moan escapes my lips as my fingers work of their own accord because I'm only half awake.

"Don't stop."

Crew's deep voice tickles the back of my neck. I suck in a deep breath, eyes fluttering open as my hand stops, reality finally fleeting in.

"Eleanor." This time, his voice is menacing, deeper, and fucking sexy as hell. "I said, don't. Fucking. Stop."

My heart beats faster because his voice has that gravel men get in the morning, but it's also laced with his arousal.

The distinct sound of his spit hitting his palm makes goose bumps bloom over my arm as I feel him stroke his cock against my ass.

"Fuck yourself, baby."

My fingers touch my swollen, sensitive flesh again, making my stomach immediately contract, wanting more.

"That's it. Be my good little slut and do as you're told."

I push into the feeling and let my mouth fall open, unabashedly moaning again, feeling every nerve ending in my body standing at full attention.

He groans from behind me, stroking himself faster before he swipes my hair from my neck and bites. His tongue follows, licking over the sting before he does it again.

My breath is stolen, sucked in, and held.

What we're doing, the way we're fucking, feels crude and animalistic. We're just sounds and instinct. Quiet panting with our eyes closed, urging each other closer to release as we tease erotic ideas.

"I want to be inside you when you come," he whispers against my neck. "Tell me when you're close."

The weight of his body presses me forward, rolling me toward my belly as his knee hikes my leg up. I'm rubbing faster and faster, circling my clit, rocking my hips, almost dry humping my hand and the bed as Crew jerks off, letting the head of his cock tease my asshole.

"Say my name," he whispers, rimming my ass just enough that I want more but not enough to hurt.

I suck in a breath, gripping the sheet, fingers curling around the fabric as my body builds.

"Say it." He exhales harshly. "Fuck. You're so fucking sexy, Wild Card. The way you move your body is gonna make me cover your ass in my cum."

He spits in his hand again before the wet sound of him

stroking sets me off. I grind my hips forward, rubbing and fucking my palm as breathy mewls cascade from my lips.

"I'm going to come."

My hand is jerked away just as Crew sinks inside me. His giant body engulfs mine as his strong arm hooks around me. He grabs my face, forcing it sideways and sealing his mouth over mine.

Crew's tongue dips inside my mouth, our lips gliding over each other's before he lets me go and stuffs a pillow down between my legs, never stopping the slow undulating thrust inside my pussy.

"Fuck it. Fuck it like you would TJ's face."

I'm breathless as his fingers intertwine with mine on the bed, his hard cock rocking in and out, moving my body...my center against the fabric of the pillow.

I shiver. My eyes squeezed shut as I picture TJ underneath me, licking and sucking my clit.

"That's it, baby. Let us have that pussy."

Crew rocks me forward against the pillow over and over until my leg hikes up higher, my body pressing into the fabric as I circle my hips and fuck myself. But he fucks me too.

We don't speak, only the sound of our breath serving as evidence of our debauchery. But that doesn't mean nothing's said. Because I'm living in the repetition of five words—*let us have that pussy.*

I bite the pillow, wanting more, rubbing harder, feeling my stomach tightening and my fists insatiably squeezing harder and harder.

Crew follows my lead. As I move faster and faster, so does he. His hard body's pressing against me more and more until I'm flat on my stomach, grinding against the pillow so hard that I'm lost to sensation. I'm in a deep haze, chasing my release and uncaring of what I look like or what's happening.

All I want is to come.

"Take it. There you go...soak my cock."

A deep, guttural scream rises from low within my belly and erupts from my mouth, muffled by my face pressed to the mattress.

Crew's not long after me, jerking my hips up so I'm face-down, ass up as he pounds inside me, grabbing my shoulders to anchor me as he groans, bottomed out inside of me, his cock pulsating as he comes thundering.

"Fuck."

I wipe the hair from my face as I come down from my bliss. But before I can open my mouth to creak out my words, I'm flipped over as Crew growls, "*More.*"

He covers my cunt with his mouth as my hand slaps his back. I gasp, feeling overwhelmed with sensation as he licks over my raw clit before his face tears away, our eyes connecting.

"I want to taste *me* inside you."

His head lowers, slower this time, as he glides his tongue over my clit, making my eyes close as all the air leaves my lungs because he's pressing inside me. Fucking me with his tongue, tasting our cum from the warmth of my pussy before he shines a spotlight on my clit and makes me come for the second time this morning.

...without saying his name.

eighteen

. . .

"I've also been fucking my future ex-wife to death."

crew

The sound of weights clanking around me fills my ears as I swipe my towel from the bench, wiping my sweaty forehead. It's a miracle Claire let me take it easy today and only focus on weight training. She's made it her mission to try to kill me since her failed-ass advice.

Jesus, I still shake my head thinking about Eleanor's face when I was fucking out there in the living room like an asshole doing the quad stretches.

She's not even the type to fall for some bullshit. I know because I've been working overtime to get her to scream my name, and all I have to show for it is a seven-thousand-dollar loss.

TJ's voice bellows from behind, making my head snap over my shoulder to see him and Nate walk in. The grin on his face gives away he's about to say something stupid. *And he does.*

"I'll be goddamned. You're alive. We thought that sweet little thang killed you and buried you in the mattress. Where the fuck you been, man?"

I chuckle as Nate zeros in on me, throwing out his two cents.

"Come on, TJ. We know exactly where he's been."

Here we go.

I chuck my towel at Nate, but TJ catches it with lightning speed.

*Best hands in the business...*so said Eleanor last night, making me want to prove her wrong, leading to a lot of fun. I'd thank him, but that'd just be rubbing it in.

I smirk, aiming to give it back as good as they give it.

"I've been busy, you fucking assholes. I don't know if you heard, but I'm stuck in Vegas, about to miss training camp for the team I traded to because I married a horny little disaster. So, I need to keep myself fresh, or a Super Bowl isn't in *our* future."

Bullshit...that's the definition of their expressions as they stare back. So I shrug and add, "I've also been fucking my future ex-wife to death."

They both laugh, shoving my shoulders before Nate bends down to add more weights, doubling what I was doing for squats.

"I told you he was bogarting her," TJ tosses to Nate, but I laugh.

Of course I am. I fully admit that I'm being selfish. But screw them—I'm the one paying the consequence, so I get all the reward.

"You like her?" Nate groans, always a man of few words, squatting with four hundred pounds across his back as TJ and I spot him.

I nod. "Yeah..." TJ looks up, surprised, but I clarify. "Not like that. *Yes*, I like her. She's fucking likable. The girl is funny and easy to be around. But I'm not developing feelings. Trust me, she and I are completely on the same page. In fact, I've been holding debauchery with you two over her head to try to win a bet."

Nate grunts, "You're a dickhead," through four more reps as we focus on spotting before TJ chimes in.

"What's the bet?"

"She screams my name...I win...she deletes her roster. Or I pay her sister and her bestie a grand a day."

Nate cracks his neck after banking the weights in place, narrowing his eyes on me.

"A fucking grand a day?" He chuckles. "Nah, come on... you're into her, because then why give a fuck about her roster?"

I don't even hesitate with my answer.

"Because it's petty, inconvenient to her, and hilarious. Plus, she started that shit. She made a bet with her friends that she could resist temptation, knowing we'd already made a deal not to fucking touch each other. I just bested her hustle and put *fucking* back on the table."

TJ's still amused as Nate crosses his arms, teetering on skeptical.

"You care if we join the party?" he throws out.

I'm already shaking my head. It was a matter of time before Eleanor got what she wanted. *And I get to watch her get it.* Frankly, I like that she's down for dirty shit because I'm all in, but the way Nate and I are staring at each other makes me say something I've never said before.

"No. Like I said, she's down. But it's a team event. You get me? Dibs still applies, dick."

How old am I? Jesus.

Nate smirks, but TJ taps my arm like he's about to tell me a good joke.

"Look at it this way. Maybe we can help your cause...get her to scream your name, seeing as your dick is unconvincing."

"Shut the fuck up." I laugh. "Anyway, once I'm back at the penthouse, I'll ask her if she wants to hang out...with all of us."

Nate exchanges a look with TJ before he leans his shoulder against the metal weight stand and grins.

"How much longer you still got here?"

I take a drink from my sports bottle before I cock my head.

"Like three more hours...why? You can't keep it in your pants for that long?" I'm joking, but I pause for a second, looking between them. "What kind of dumbass plan are you two Jedi mind sharing?"

Nate produces a chuckle that makes me even more nervous. But it's TJ who props his forearm on my shoulder as he lays it on thick.

"Us? Dumbasses? Never..." Before I get a word of protest out, he adds, "You're nuts, bro." And his fist connects with my junk.

"Fuck," comes out strained and empty as I suck in a vat of air and double over.

I'm going to kill him.

Between their laughter and the fact that I can't even look up, I'm committing this to memory so law enforcement will know their deaths were premeditated.

"Deep breaths, dude."

I can't even tell who's speaking because I feel sick to my stomach.

"Payback's a bitch. You bogarted our girl—"

"And now we're going to show her the time of her life."

Motherfuckers.

I'd laugh if it wasn't me that was in pain. But that's fine because by the time I feel better, I'll have figured out how to drown them both in the goddamn water fountain.

nineteen

. . .

"I am the Daddy."

eleanor

QB with the giant cock: Incuming.

Me: What?

QB with the giant cock: *wink emoji.

"Hey, where'd you go? Are you listening to me?"

"Sami, I have to call you back. Crew sent me the weirdest text…and I think he's stupid and doesn't know how to spell *incoming* because he put a *u*."

A beep, like someone's coming into the penthouse, makes me lift my head as I immediately hang up in the middle of what my sister was saying. Because the smile on my face can probably be seen from space. All caused by my favorite naughty duo, Tweedle-hung and Tweedle-back facial, who are currently standing in the entry.

I push off the couch, walking toward the guys, finally in on the joke from earlier—InCUMing.

"What are you two doing here?"

The sexiest smirk grows on TJ's face, making that beard of his look even more delicious as he holds his hand up like he's telling me a secret.

"We're here to kidnap you."

My eyes pop open, but Nate holds up a bag of doughnuts.

"We even brought snacks to tempt you into letting us."

I groan, my eyes rolling back into my head dramatically.

"Tempt me? You may never get rid of me if you keep giving me doughnuts."

TJ grins, propping himself against the kitchen island with one hand, making the veins in his arm act slutty.

"So whaddya say? You wanna spend the day with us...do something other than Crew?"

I laugh, taking the bag from Nate and inhaling the deliciousness as I open it before looking up at the guys, letting my eyes peruse their massive frames.

God, they're so...*tasty*. The only problem is there's one missing.

"Sweetheart," TJ offers, looking at me the way I'm looking at him. "Say yes and we promise to show you a good time."

There's just something about that drawl of TJ's and the cockiness of his smile that wins me over without him saying a word. Plus, if memory serves—and it does, over and over in all my dreams—TJ's a real, real good time.

My tongue darts out, drawing my lip between my teeth as Nate butts in.

"Or would you rather stay here, alone, watching..."

His eyes flick to the TV, where I've been watching *The Hangover* again for the millionth time on mute. I chuckle and shake my head.

"Nah, I've seen it. My only question is, you said you brought me a snack..." I cock my head. "So, what am I supposed to do with these doughnuts?"

Nate thunders laughter as TJ bends down, rushing me, making me squeal as he lifts me in the air.

"Girl, we're gonna have so much fun today."

I'm all smiles, hands pressed to TJ's shoulders as he slowly lowers me before Nate throws down the gauntlet. He motions to my cell on the table.

"Hey, make sure you let daddy know."

The moment my feet hit the ground, I walk toward the couch, shove my feet into my flip-flops, and grab my purse and cell before I stare them down.

"Come on now, Nate...I *am* the daddy."

❧

"So, what exactly are we supposed to get here?"

Nate's looking around, confused even though I already explained it. TJ takes my hand and lifts it above my head, twirling me around as we walk down the aisle of clothes at the Goodwill. I laugh and turn to Nate.

"I'm going to explain this again, but this time, try to listen instead of looking at my boobs."

Nate shrugs noncommittally. "No promises."

But he still manages to steal another smile from me as I forge ahead.

"Okay, so, what we're doing is this: each of us is going to take turns walking down the aisle. When you hear the word *stop*, whatever your hand is on is what you're going to wear. And we're going to keep doing that until we have a completed outfit."

"And why are we doing this again?" Nate half-heartedly complains, and for the life of me, I can't explain why it's attractive, but it is.

It's like the grumpier he seems, the more I want to fuck him into submission. *Maybe I really am the daddy.*

TJ throws his arms in the air.

"Jesus Christ. You don't listen for shit. I hope you're paying attention to play calls better than this. We can't just be out in the city looking like ourselves if we're playing tourist for the day. We gotta play the part. And baby girl's only got a duffel full of clothes to choose from. Shit's limited."

I motion my hand to TJ, giving an enthusiastic "Exactly" as my voice morphs into a terrible Swedish accent. "I'm Greta, and I'm from Sweden."

TJ picks up a Boston Red Sox hat, but it's kid-sized. That doesn't stop him from trying to cram it on his head as he adds, "And I'm Matty from Boston. Go, Red Sox."

Nate's looking at the two of us like we're aliens, but then his brow relaxes as he grabs a plaid scarf and wraps it around his neck, giving the worst Scottish accent I've ever heard.

"Well, little wee lass, let's get ourselves some outfits."

TJ claps his hands together, dropping character as I do a celebratory dance, prompting Nate to smush my face with his hand.

"Shut up... Okay, who goes first?"

"You," I snark, shoving his hand away.

Nate walks to the end of the aisle and puts his hand over his eyes, waiting as TJ motions to give me a piggyback.

"Ready?" I call out as I jump up, now able to see above the world.

Nate nods, but TJ turns his head my way, and I'm suddenly reminded of the night we met. When his face was so close to mine before he kissed my cheek.

"Déjà vu," he whispers.

I grin and shiver, feeling his whiskers tickle my face.

"Yeah, I was thinking the same thing."

TJ turns away, but his words leave a lasting imprint.

"Maybe we can do that some more because I can think of a few things I'd like to relive."

Dirty, filthy, horny butterflies erupt in my stomach, not the sweet kind most girls get when they vibe with someone. No, the bitches in my tummy have a bottle of Jack in one hand, and the other is holding a stripper pole as they flutter around in a circle. Because any déjà vu coming from that night will require me finding myself in very dirty situations.

"Go," rings out from TJ, and I smile because that felt like the kickoff to a game...one where my kitty gets to be the field.

twenty

· · ·

"I can already feel the vomit giving me a salute like, see ya soon, fucker."

crew

TJ: *video loading

A smile grows on my face because Eleanor's dancing in the fucking Caesar's Palace fountain, wearing a boa, cowboy hat, and a T-shirt that says, "If you like my meatballs, you'll love my sausage." All with the *Friends* theme playing in the background.

What the hell are they doing?

I'm laser focused on the video, listening to them and trying not to laugh.

"Nate...come be Ross!"

She's belting out the song, waving her hands in the air, before TJ shouts, "Oh shit, security."

Water splashes, and the camera jostles before TJ's face comes into frame.

"Damn, she's never boring. Don't worry, we'll keep her out of handcuffs...until later."

Claire's voice interrupts my focus just as the video cuts.

"Why the frown? I thought we agreed no complaining."

I look up and shake my head.

"It's not you I want to murder."

I type out a message, my fingers hitting hard enough to make a thumping sound on the screen.

> Me: She goes to jail? You two get cut from the team.

I LET OUT A BREATH AND PUT THE WEIGHTS BACK ONTO THE RACK AS I relax on the bench. Until I hear my phone ding, so I swipe it off the floor and open the message.

> Nate: *a photo of Eleanor cozied up to TJ on the Ferris wheel.
>
> Nate: I paid the guy to stop at the top and give us an extra fifteen minutes. What do I get if she screams my name?

I might chew a hole through my cheek with the viciousness I'm gnawing on it as I stare at the picture. These motherfuckers. I should've known they'd torture me. My eyes tick up to the top of the screen...fuck, two more hours.

> Me: You get thrown from the fucking bucket.

Claire yells, even though she's next to me. "Crew. What the hell? Are you listening? I said another rep."

I let out a breath, tossing my phone on the ground before I grip the fucking barbell to grind out another ten presses. The bright side is I'm going to need to build more muscle because throwing Nate off anything will take superior upper-body strength. Motherfucker.

THEY TOOK HER TO HOOVER DAM. COME ON.

Eleanor's straddling the Arizona-Nevada border. But not really—her foot is hovering as TJ holds her hand like he's saving her from teetering over. I stare down at the photo, smiling at how wild her hair is. It reminds me of the night we met. When she was lifted over the back of the booth with a sparkler in a fucking bottle, dancing to "Get Low."

Her text comes in as I'm looking.

> That girl I married: Not one foot outside the city limits that judge said...does this count?

I laugh. TJ's right. She's never boring. Damn, but the FOMO is real right now. I'm getting played so hard. And it's working because I want to cut out and have a good time.

They're the worst. Full of bad ideas and trouble... although maybe I *should* cut out early. What's the worst that happens? I can't really throw Nate off a building; I need him sacking quarterbacks. And I really only have another hour left.

An hour isn't making or breaking shit.

My phone is snatched out of my hand, grabbing my immediate attention.

"The fuck? Do you need to make a phone call?"

Claire stares me down, figuratively speaking, seeing as she's looking up at me from her munchkin stature. Her brows raise.

"No. And neither do you. Or have you forgotten that this is my time? You can have it back when it's not interfering with *my time*. And I'm adding another fifteen for all the texting."

I start to laugh, but then I stop. Jesus Christ. Claire could put a fucking drill sergeant into a fetal position, questioning his whole life.

She tosses the weighted vest and points to the treadmill, and

I can already feel the vomit giving me a salute like, *see ya soon, fucker.*

"Fifteen-minute jog. Forty-five sprint," she grinds out.

Fuck. My. Life.

The whirl of the machine hums before my feet hit the belt. Sweat's already dripping down my chest, but all I can think about besides the fact that I might die is what they're doing.

Are they sending the photos in real time or strategically trying to torture me? Because that would mean they're heading back into town. But it's almost feeding time for my wifey, the ogre, so... Ah, I fucking hate them. This is inhabiting my brain.

The smile that's peeking out is completely against my will, but honestly, game well played, assholes.

My eyes are fixed on the wall, arms slicing the air as the pace starts picking up. But I'm still only barely winded, focusing on form until midstride, I hear that ding. Like a fucking siren's call. My face snaps to my cell, taunting me from the counter, and my whole body buckles.

"Fuck," I shout as my feet topple over each other in a tangle, and I grab the treadmill handles, saving my ankle but not my pride. I still manage to pull the emergency cord, stopping the belt before I jump off and stumble toward my phone.

"What the fuck are you doing?" Claire barks, but I'm nodding and waving her off.

"Sorry, I just have an important message..." What I'm saying is cut off because, this time, it's Barrett proving me true.

> Barrett: We have an impromptu phone call with the Niners. Drop what you're doing and get to my office. I don't know what to expect, so just prepare yourself for anything, Crew.

Claire's voice bounces off my back because I don't give an explanation as I stalk toward the locker room to grab my shit and see if my future just went up in flames.

twenty-one

. . .

"You didn't tell us she could suck the meat clear off the bone."

eleanor

"He didn't text back."

My bottom lip protrudes as I pout. It's been hours of us torturing Crew. And every time, he texts back.

Mostly it's threatening to end TJ and Nate in more and more inventive ways. But it's still encouraging because it means we're getting underneath his skin.

And that's the whole point.

We don't have to send pictures to him. He doesn't need to know what the hell I'm doing. I might be his wife, but I sure as hell am not his girlfriend. But when Nate presented this plan to drive him crazy, to get back at him for keeping our love apart…

I wholeheartedly supported it. Am I a menace? Yes.

But I am also the Justin to his Britney—what goes around comes around, motherfucker.

People don't forget, to quote my all-time favorite movie.

Get me to scream your name now, beyutchhh.

TJ looks down at my phone and scowls.

173

"Boo, you whore."

I smile, my mouth falling open for a minute, surprised.

"Wow...TJ...you're a man who, by all arguments, is a prime physical specimen, but you know your *Mean Girl* quotes. It's proof god really is a woman."

He laughs, holding my hand and letting it swing between us as we walk toward our next stop. Today has been an unexpected blast. Well, maybe not totally unexpected. TJ and Nate did promise a good time, and I can say with certainty that they always deliver.

Nate throws his arm over my shoulder. "If god was a woman, then men would be able to find a woman's clit."

The laugh that rips from my chest makes TJ join.

"Now," Nate adds in his Scottish brogue, "don't fret, lass. If we can't lure Crew out with those other videos and pics...this place should do the trick."

My head lifts, taking in the signage.

According to TJ, this place has the best chicken wings in town. Which is awesome because I'm starving. About twenty minutes to hangry. But I have to wonder if chicken wings are code for hot ass since the Spearmint Rhino is a strip club.

crew

I walked into Barrett's office with my stomach in my throat. But thankfully, the call was positive right out of the gate. And now it's been an hour of hype and game planning.

Of all the fucking days for this. The universe really has it out for me today. And to make matters worse, I felt my phone vibrate about ten minutes ago, but I can't look because I have to stare at the three faces on the video call that belong to the Niners owner, my new head coach, and the assistant coach.

My knees bounce a mile a minute as the owner speaks.

"We couldn't be happier, Crew, to welcome you to this team. We really just wanted to have this call to reassure you that TJ and Nate's place here with our organization is solid. Everyone on this side knows what's going on there over at the Raiders. And we see this as a bump in the road."

Barrett reaches out and claws my knee to stop it from moving before withdrawing her hand back to her own lap. I feel like a kid who's getting in trouble with their mom.

God, Barrett, let me live.

I'm smiling at the stupid fucking thoughts in my head as my eyes tick down to my phone as it vibrates again, hearing the coaches drone on.

"We're extending some time before preseason for you to get your feet wet, and the plan is to have you hang back and not play those games. We want to keep you healthy and ready for the regular season."

I smile and nod, looking up again before I feel Barrett tap my leg.

"I appreciate that, sir," I rush out, smiling at the camera. "And I couldn't be happier, really. You guys don't have to worry about me. Claire, my trainer extraordinaire, is keeping me game ready. I'll be ready for the season."

My new coach chuckles.

"I bet, and I'd also bet that being a newlywed has a way of putting a spring in your step. Congratulations from all of us, by the way. I only know what I saw online, but she looks like a sweetheart of a girl."

Oh yeah, a real sweetheart.

The smile on my face is saying too much because like an asshole, I flipped my phone over and saw the group message... the one fucking labeled *Gang Bang Niner Gang.*

I swallow, trying not to give away what I just saw. But damn. It's impossible because a 4K photo of Eleanor with a plate of chicken wings in front of her and *tits* in the background is now permanently imprinted on my brain.

They took her to a fucking strip club.

What is wrong with them? Who the fuck... Actually...the funniest part is I'm not sure whose idea it really was. Each one of them is capable of this ridiculous shit. Equally.

"Crew," Barrett whispers, guiding my eyes back to the screen as the owner speaks.

"We'd love to let the media have a taste of you two during the game opener. Maybe a photo op or some reel of her watching you on the field."

I must frown because he adds, "Unless she isn't planning to come to the games?"

Well, she can come but as my ex-wife.

But I don't say that; instead, I nod and lie. It's really only a partial truth because I have a feeling Wild Card and I might be long-lasting roster buddies.

"Absolutely." I grin. "The little wifey is up for anything."

Like a gang bang.

My phone vibrates again as they start talking about capitalizing on the media attention. But I'm not listening, again, because I'm too busy reading my texts.

> Nate: Hope that workout's working out.
>
> That girl I married: Dolla dolla bills y'all.
>
> TJ: You didn't tell us she could suck the meat clear off the bone.

That's it. I'm done. My face shoots up, the excuse to bail on the tip of my tongue. But I'm circumvented as the screen suddenly shifts to a play board, and the coach throws out his plan.

"If you don't mind, I'd like to take this next hour to go over some plays and get your thoughts on how to best utilize TJ."

Shit.

What I want to say is the best way to utilize TJ is to let him finger fuck Eleanor from behind, keeping her bent over as she sucks me off. But I can't fucking say that, so I opt for, "Absolutely. Let's talk about the man with the hands."

twenty-two

. . .

"What's in your boobs?"

eleanor

"**K**eep your eyes closed," TJ scolds.

I wiggle, standing with my back to his front.

"Even if I open them, I wouldn't be able to see with your big-ass hand in the way."

I hear Nate laugh behind me as I'm shuffled forward a few more steps. We got to the Neon Museum right at sunset, but they didn't want me to see everything until the lights come on.

Nate said all the old casino signs lit up was the closest thing to what the lights in the stadium feel like. And who's turning an experience like that down? Not this girl.

Holding tight to TJ's wrist, I sway back and forth, getting impatient.

"What's that sound?" Nate tosses out. "It's like clinking..."

I laugh because I know exactly what it is—tiny liquor bottles. Like the kind you get on an airplane. A few of the girls at the Rhino hooked me up as we left.

"Okay, are you ready?" TJ whispers.

I nod, bouncing in place.

"I was born ready. Show me already."

The guys count down together as I squeal.

"Three, two, one—"

TJ's hands drop from my eyes as ultra-vibrant, neon light explodes around me.

"Holy shit."

I take a step forward, my gaze drifting from one old, discarded sign to another as my mouth refuses to close.

"This is incredible. You guys did not lie."

I don't know when the objective pivoted, but somewhere back between lap dances and makeup conversations, I was bummed that Crew wasn't here. We've literally had the time of our lives today, and he missed all of it.

And even though I'll never admit this out loud, he's pretty cool to hang out with. I spin around to TJ and Nate, frowning.

"I can't believe he's missing out on this—"

But what I was saying stops short as a smile creeps over my face. Because standing behind the guys is everyone's favorite QB and the object of my torture.

"Hey, Wild Card."

TJ's and Nate's heads snap around, and they immediately become celebratory, slapping hands in greeting and laughing.

Crew walks toward me, staring down before he frowns and leans forward a little more, peering down my shirt.

"What's in your boobs?"

I laugh, reaching down the front of my shirt and pulling out the mini Jack Daniel's bottles.

"Contraband," I answer. "The girls at the club and I exchanged services..."

Crew smirks. "Don't skimp on the details, I beg of you."

TJ and Nate come up on each of my sides, so I hand them the bottles and reach into my back pocket for the other two as I keep explaining.

"I gave them the ingredients of this cream I use that works miracles on razor burn and bumps. I mean, they're in next to nothing, but since their bottoms have to stay on, rashes happen. So, I hooked them up with a fix...and in return, these—"

I clink the two bottles in my hand like I'm cheersing them before handing one to Crew.

TJ looks at Nate and grins. "This was not the story I was hoping for..."

Nate nods, twisting the cap on his booze as he cocks his head.

"Elle, can you retell it, but this time describe how you were all touching each other's boobs."

I laugh, but it's Crew's eyes that catch mine. He opens his bottle, his tongue darting out over his bottom lip before he looks around the group of us and back to me, a question brimming in those eyes...*one I really want him to ask.*

"You know, the last time we did this"—he wiggles his bottle —"the four of us got into some trouble."

The rim of my bottle skims my lips as I look at each of them, their eyes on me, waiting for what I'm about to say. For permission. *I mean...it's called Sin City for a reason, right?*

"We *did* get into trouble...and here's to getting into some more."

I shoot my shot, literally and figuratively. Because if you don't, you never know what the universe could have planned. And right now, I'm hoping that bitch wants me to get plays run on my pussy until I scream, *Touchdown Niners.*

TAKE OFF YOUR CLOTHES.

Those were the only words spoken as we walked into the penthouse.

Nobody even turned on the lights.

But I did as I was told and peeled off every piece of fabric clinging to my body with my back to them, knowing their eyes watched my every movement.

The glow created by the Vegas Strip illuminates the window just enough so that I can see three giant shadows standing behind me. And it's the most erotic fucking thing I've ever seen.

There aren't enough words in the dictionary to describe the feeling of being owned and completely taken by multiple partners, but I plan to pay really close attention tonight so I can come up with some.

The rustling of their clothes has my chest rising and falling faster than normal because each second I don't turn around, my adrenaline goes through the roof. But who can blame me? The memory of last time is front and center in my mind's eye.

"Turn around."

I shiver at Nate's voice.

My tongue glides over my bottom lip, and I draw it between my teeth as I blink, turning slowly, my gaze connecting with each of their moonlit faces.

Jesus. Christ. They're fucking gods.

Each is different than the other, but gods nonetheless.

Nate has his hand on his cock, standing tall and showing off all his well-defined muscles and those tattoos all over his thighs as he looks down at himself, then back at me.

"Come get it wet for me," he grits out.

I saunter over, letting my hips sway. My eyes tick to TJ's, watching him lick his lips and peruse my frame as Crew walks toward the couch. But as I stop in front of Nate, I lift my face to his. He stares down at me with a mix of dominance and unbridled lust.

He wants to fuck me until I'm screaming his name before he flips me over and starts again. And I want that too. But as I begin to lower, his hand grabs my waist, stopping me.

He shakes his head.

"Open."

He means my mouth. I like him like this. I smirk before I do as I'm told.

"Tongue."

Slowly, I slip my tongue from my mouth, pressing it out until it's fully extended. Nate hums, wiping his palm directly over the wetness before wrapping his wet hand around his hard cock.

I suck my tongue back into my mouth, rolling it around and tasting the saltiness from his skin, and stare back at him. My eyes drop to his arms, watching the way his veins protrude as he strokes himself.

God, that's so fucking sexy.

"C'mere," is growled from my left, drawing my attention to Crew, who's sitting on the couch and calling me over with his fingers.

I turn in his direction, but Nate palms my breast, stopping my motion as he drags his hand up and down over his cock, letting the movement brush against my skin. My eyes close as my lips part.

This feels dirty. Mainly because it is.

Nate's letting his precum wet my skin, and it's making it impossible for my feet to move. But TJ comes up behind me, whispering into my ear.

"Come on, Elle. You're being a very bad girl. Crew told you to come to him."

I gasp as Nate pinches my nipple, making me lean into him as I bite my lip, feeling overheated as TJ continues whispering in my ear.

"Do you remember what we do to bad girls?"

I nod, already breathless, because Nate's abandoned my nipple and reached for my fingers, pushing them between the wetness that's grown between my legs as he rubs himself off, circling his hand around his thick shaft.

TJ ghosts his bottom lip over my earlobe before he bites in words and with his teeth. "Get your ass over to Crew and put his fucking dick in your goddamn mouth, or I'm tearing that ass up."

My knees almost buckle because just as TJ gave me his warning, Nate molded his fingers over mine and dipped both of ours inside my pussy.

Nate's voice is gritty and sexy.

"Do you want Crew's cock down your throat? Or do you want a red ass? Which is it...or do you want me to make you come while they watch?"

Yes. Both. All.

Oh my god. They did this the first night. Made me a competition.

And I literally—Ate. It. Up.

Nate's fingers move faster, curving inside with my own as TJ palms my tits, but my shoulders jump as Crew claps his hands together once, immediately drawing my eyes to his.

"Get the fuck over here. Now."

I'm released. Pussy abandoned, chest ignored, left to suck in a breath as TJ leans down again like the devil as Nate brushes my hair over my shoulder.

"Crawl to him, darlin'. But be a good whore, and let us watch."

My legs are already shaky, but Nate extends his hand, giving me support as I drop to my knees before pressing my palms into the ground...and fucking crawl.

I slink over the marble floors, hand then knee against the unforgiving marble, feeling Nate and TJ just behind me, knowing they're watching my ass.

But the minute I get to Crew, he jerks me up so my palms land on his defined thighs.

I gasp as he stares at me, his legs spread like an arrogant prick on a throne. But that's what he is. An arrogant prick with a really big fucking dick.

He's stroking himself off in front of my face in long drags, his skin kissed by the moonlight. My tongue darts out, wetting my lips, craving that gorgeous cock in my mouth. The veins on his shaft make me wish I could run my tongue over them before he pushes his smooth head past my lips and stretches my mouth. I'm salivating at the thought.

It's like he reads my thoughts because he draws his hand all the way up, strangling his tip as he says, "Start there," exposing the underside of his dick.

I lean forward slowly, running my tongue up and over those goddamn veins, just like I wanted, before I take the head into my mouth as he releases his hand.

Crew sucks in a harsh breath, immediately gripping my hair.

"Put your hands on my legs," he grinds out, guiding me down his cock as I hollow my cheeks.

I do as I'm told, but he continues.

"This is for not listening the first fucking time."

I'm lifted to my feet by one of the guys behind me so that I'm bent over, sucking Crew off.

I squeal into Crew's cock, but he lifts his hips as he brings me down, hitting the back of my throat. Oh fuck. I gag, then fucking moan because a hand lands hard against my ass cheek, leaving a sting before it's rubbed out.

Fingers glide around my cunt before TJ's voice rings out.

"Oh fuck, she's so wet. Does our little whore want more?"

I'm nodding, whimpering as Crew takes over fucking my face. Another slap bucks me forward, and I dig my nails into Crew's skin.

Fuck me. That feels so good.

Another slap, then another burns my skin, no doubt making it red as I become feral, sucking Crew off faster and faster, wanting to taste his cum while they punish me.

I'm whimpering and squeezing my eyes shut, begging for more around Crew's cock thundering in and out of my wet mouth.

He's breathing heavily, no tenderness offered as he uses what I'm giving.

I moan again, screaming onto his cock as another slap hits

my pussy. But Crew's deep growl almost makes me come on the spot.

"Shut the fuck up and take this dick like a good girl."

Yes, daddy.

I hear the boys behind me heaving deep breaths, making no mistake about what they want. Crew pulls out, holding me by the throat, and stares into my eyes.

I lick my lips just as he dives in and kisses me. His tongue swirls with mine as our heads tilt before he tears himself away and hooks his hands under my armpits, tossing me directly over his shoulder as he stands, growling.

"Who's got next?"

twenty-three

· · ·

"Throat ... Ass ... Pussy."

eleanor

I'm laughing as I'm carried toward the bedroom when he suddenly stops, and my legs are spread.

"Me," I hear TJ say before he dives in, licking my cunt from behind.

"Oh my god," I gasp.

Crew kneads my ass as TJ's tongue explores, licking and kissing me. He dips his tongue inside my entrance, fucking me for a few languid strokes.

"Yes," I moan, gripping Crew's body with more and more ferocity.

But as fast as it began, it stops, leaving my clit throbbing and begging for more attention. The moment we're through the bedroom door, Crew slides me down his body. His hands are on my waist as he walks me backward into the room.

His eyes stay on mine, never breaking, as his words are said for only me.

"I get your pussy *first* and *last*. You hear me? No exceptions, or I'll let it fucking starve to death."

I nod, biting my lip as he reaches down to my waist and, without warning, tosses me on the bed.

My scream erupts, as does my laughter, before the guys descend.

I'm laughing as Crew spreads my legs and pushes my knees up, putting my pussy on display, their eyes devouring what they see. I can feel myself getting wetter and wetter, wondering if they can see it dripping out of me.

My eyes volley between them, watching how they appreciate the view. It makes me feel wild and sexy. Completely uninhibited.

I want to put on a show. So, I run my hand down my stomach and through my soft curly hair, spreading myself open before my fingers dip inside.

Deep appreciative groans ring out in chorus, making me gasp and arch off the bed as I drag my fingers back over my clit.

"Goddamn, that's pretty," TJ whispers. "Gimme a little."

He crawls closer, intermingling his fingers with mine, rubbing my arousal over his cock before bringing them back and repeating the same thing.

"More," I breathe.

That's all I have to say. It was tantamount to ringing a dinner bell.

Hands begin gliding, dragging over my legs and drifting over my stomach. They take turns palming my breasts and playing with my nipples. Fingers fight with my own, shoving my hand away from my cunt as I'm fingered.

Nate puts his tainted fingers between his lips, saying, "That's a sweet fucking pussy," and sucking me off them before running his hand down the side of my body. My body writhes, my back arching again as my eyes roll back into my head.

"Look at you," TJ whispers. "You were made for filth."

I gasp as he cups my breasts before sucking my nipple between his lips just as a hand cups my cunt, holding still to it and letting me press against it.

My back drops back down to the bed as my eyes connect with Crew's, whose hand it is. He smirks, gently tugging the hairs before thrusting his fingers inside me.

"You're so fucking wet. It makes me think you like to be used. Is that what you want, baby…for us to fuck your body and come all over you?"

TJ's thumb drags over my bottom lip before pressing inside my mouth, drawing my eyes.

"Would you like that, Eleanor? Answer his question, darlin'. Because I'd really love to treat you like a whore."

I bite down teasingly on his thumb, scraping his skin as he slowly draws it from my mouth while I nod. TJ's eyes stay connected to mine before he says, "That's a real…good…girl."

"Oh fuck. Yes, daddy," I gasp, but then my body fucking shudders.

Because Crew slaps my clit.

"Put your fucking eyes on me," he barks. "What the fuck did I tell you about flirting with the bench."

Oh. My. God.

Crew crawls over me, smothering my body and moving everyone else away as he kisses me violently, bruising my lips. My arms wrap around him, as do my legs, as he grinds his cock against my pussy.

"QB gets what he wants," I whisper into his lips. "My bad. Won't happen again."

Crew pushes off me and glances over his shoulder.

"Now, you two can take what you want."

TJ grips my legs, dragging me toward the bottom of the bed and flipping me over, making me yelp before he shoves my hips up and settles his face underneath me.

Instinctually I lift, but he growls.

"Get your fucking pussy on my face."

He grabs my ass cheeks, using them to grind my pussy over his mouth as I gasp, barely able to focus on Nate and Crew, who are on either side of me.

"Oh fuck."

Crew guides me forward by my hair, making my hands walk out toward the top of the bed as TJ hooks his arms around my thighs, spreading my knees wider but keeping me on all fours as he rubs his mouth over my wet cunt.

I feel Nate beside me, rubbing my ass, kissing where handprints probably still exist before he spreads my cheeks and licks. My asshole tightens, but my body quakes.

God, that feels good.

They're just taking from me, like animals.

"Holy fuck," I say, sucking in a breath. "Oh my god."

I rock into TJ's mouth, panting as I feel his tongue circle. His fingers spread my cunt so there's more for him to devour.

"Yes," I draw out long and gutturally.

"C'mere," Crew demands, his cock shining with more cum on the tip. He trails it over my lips slowly. "Look how pretty that mouth is now. You should stay covered in my cum."

I'm dizzy with lust. *Fuck. Me.*

Crew's running his cock over my lips, teasing it in my mouth each time I open, begging to suck him off, while Nate bites my ass before kissing it. I'm panting, already breathless, as TJ's tongue flicks my clit, urging me to come on his face, eating me like he's starving.

"She's beautiful," Nate groans, pushing his finger inside my entrance, so close to TJ's face. "And her pussy is calling my name."

I suck in a breath as his finger glides in and out as TJ sucks on my clit.

Crew lifts my chin, pinching it between his fingers.

"Naw, who gets your pussy, Wild Card? Tell him."

TJ starts eating me faster, making my breath catch as the wet sound of Nate's finger fucking me beats a chorus of lust.

My lips part, but I can't speak, so I swallow, trying to get the words, but Nate gathers my wetness and runs it up toward my ass, rimming the tight hole.

I moan, still panting, beginning to stutter Crew's name.

"That's it. Tell him. Scream my name."

This motherfucker. He's such an asshole. I'd laugh if I wasn't over-fucking-whelmed with the need to come. My mouth falls open as Nate presses against my ass just enough to make my back arch, begging for his finger to sink in.

"You…you…" I say breathlessly, getting fucking worked. "I…hate…"

TJ thrusts two fingers inside my pussy as he fucking eats me, and I almost lose it, moaning loudly.

Crew cocks his head, his smirk ever so arrogant as he slides his dick over my lips. And despite his little game, I open my mouth, darting my tongue out to try to invite him in before he says, "You can't say it with a mouthful. But if you wanna be difficult, Wild Card…then let's play…time-out."

Nate's hand vanishes, and my hips are lifted, stealing me from TJ before they move off the bed, leaving me stomach down on it.

I whine, rolling over to glare at the three smirks looking back at me. I'll kill them.

"Fuck you," I chuckle.

Crew shrugs. "Scream my name and you can have what you want."

I scoot back on the bed, opening my legs, and close my eyes, fingering myself. My voice is raspy but serious as fuck.

"This isn't a game you can win. I have the prize. So you can either fuck me in every goddamn hole, or you can watch me fuck myself. Either way, I'm good to come."

I open my eyes, grinning as the three of them stare back, hands on their cocks as I rub faster and faster, circling my hips, letting my legs fall open with unashamed need.

"Throat." … "Ass." … "Pussy."

That's all I hear before one of them grabs my ankle and drags me down again as I laugh, and my head shifts around, watching them engulf me. TJ's on his knees at the top of my head, a little off to the side, as he tips my chin up, winking.

"You suck me good, baby, you hear me? I wanna fuck that throat."

Before I can say anything, Crew's tongue runs over my neck, then sucks and shifts my body so I'm lying mostly on my side before he runs the head of his cock over my clit.

"Oh fuck," I breathe, but it's cut off as TJ presses his tip just past my lips, teasing himself.

Jesus, I'm already overwhelmed in the most delicious way. My eyes are closed, and my hands are rubbing over Crew's chest, then TJ's thigh, as I feel Nate flush behind me, so I graze his ass.

His deep voice sends shivers through my body.

"We're gonna fuck you so good, baby."

Crew's voice cuts in. "I want this pussy crying all over my cock. You better fucking soak me, Wild Card."

I can barely breathe as TJ's cock thrusts down my throat, but I still do as I'm told because my pussy gushes.

"Oh yeah, that's it. Feel that shit."

Crew thrusts a finger inside me, pulling out before sharing my cunt with Nate's fingers. They're both inside, fingering me as TJ fucks my face, making me gag.

TJ's gripping my hair, slowly pressing inside my mouth before hitting the back of my throat and cutting off my air. Tears well and spill out the sides of my eyes before he draws out completely, and I gasp for air.

"Oh fuck, girl. That's so fucking good."

He does it again as my body begins contracting around Nate and Crew's fingers, lost to the depravity of having my fucking breath stolen by TJ's cock and thick fingers fighting for space inside my wet pussy.

TJ's Southern drawl gets deeper as he caresses my face, stroking himself. "You're doing so good." He looks up at the guys. "She's so fucking filthy. We got ourselves a good one."

"Are you filthy?" Crew groans, rubbing my clit as Nate continues finger fucking my pussy, making me nod vigorously.

Crew slaps my pussy again, biting my nipple just hard enough to make me scream-moan.

"I guess we'll see, won't we..."

I feel Nate withdraw and Crew's cock at my entrance. I'm mewling, rocking my hips toward Crew's cock, desperate for him to slip inside my wet pussy. My mouth falls open as another moan rips from my throat.

"Fuck me. I want your cock inside me. Please. Please."

But Crew keeps teasing my entrance, circling the head of his cock around my wetness and dragging it up over my clit. A warm drip of slippery liquid streams over my ass cheek before Nate's fingers gather it and use it to press inside my tight asshole, making me cry out.

"Oh fuck. Yes."

He spreads more lube over my ass, and my body doesn't know which way to grind. I'm rocking back and forth, my hands all over them, gliding over taut muscles, panting like I'm in heat.

Oh god. I feel like I might come the minute they fill me.

TJ's dick slides back inside my hungry mouth as he grips my hair. "That's it. Be a good whore. Swallow my dick because I'm gonna fill this dirty fucking mouth with cum."

I'm slurping, hollowing my cheeks, ravenous for his cock. Crew's hot breath ignites my body, making goose bumps bloom, starting at my throat, where he's already panting like a fucking bull.

The tip of his cock pushes inside me, and I moan around TJ's shaft, making him groan just as the head of Nate's dick presses against my ass.

Oh fuck. My heart is hammering. I want *this* so bad. I want them inside of me, fucking me until I don't know my own name.

Crew hikes my leg up further over his hip as Nate spreads my cheeks, and they press in together, filling both my holes while TJ owns my mouth.

I feel like my vision goes black. I can't breathe or move. I'm frozen, locked in the most mind-blowing pleasure.

"Fuck," Nate grinds out between gritted teeth as Crew bites at my chest.

They're almost too much to handle at the same time. But I like the twinge of pain that comes from being stretched. Crew's breath is uneven and harsh as he stays still inside me as if he's trying to control himself.

His hand closes around my throat just as TJ's cock touches the back of it, and he says, "Swallow."

I do, hearing him hum and seeing his stomach contract until, mercifully, he draws out, letting me gain air again.

But it's only momentary because it's cut off again as Nate and Crew begin alternating their thrusts. One in, the other out. One in, the other out.

In and out, in and out. Faster and faster until TJ's back in my mouth, and I'm getting fucked by three men as they unload their filthy mouths all over me.

"Your ass is fucking heaven," Nate grits out. "I'm gonna come all over it and rub it in, and you're gonna fucking let me."

My stomach tightens, fingers gripping flesh as I moan.

TJ's voice is strained. "Goddamn, you suck me good." He pushes in deeper, wanting my throat again. "That's it, take it all. Deep-throat that cock with your pretty mouth."

My pussy contracts, feeling the build start. This is too much and still not enough.

Crew's hold tightens around my throat. Between him and TJ, my breath is gone, cut off just enough to make my fucking clit throb.

But that's what Crew wants because he's a dominant son of a bitch in bed, and to prove my point, he growls his words into my skin.

"You don't come until I tell you to. I don't fucking care what your body's feeling. You come with me, slut."

Crew and Nate hammer inside my pussy and ass, and my

body becomes only sensations. It's no longer mine. I'm a slave to the need, the want. The fucking sheer determination that my pussy has to come hard.

Because they're taking what they want.

Nate's fingers dig into my hips as he fucks my ass, grinding inside me and slapping my body with his own. And Crew's got me by the throat, doing the same. Our legs are a tangle as they fuck and fuck and fuck me, making my entire body quiver and shake.

TJ's moving faster, holding my jaw roughly as his other hand lands on my hip to support himself because he's fallen forward, his legs spreading wider, fucking my mouth with ferocity.

Spit runs down my face as he thrusts in over and over, tensing his jaw with each movement.

"I'm gonna come," TJ grinds out. "And you're drinking every last drop, baby girl."

Crew tightens around my throat, fucking me harder as Nate fights for just as much of me from behind, his large hand pawing at me.

Jesus Christ, I'm owned, filled, and fucked. My body's growing warmer and warmer as I clench around all of them, sucking, contracting, and digging my fingers into their flesh.

Nate groans as his forehead presses to my back, and he thunders inside me, chasing his release like an animal.

"Come on. Come on. Give it to me. Give me that ass."

TJ thrusts once more before drawing back, leaving just the tip in as he fills my mouth with warm cum. His body jerks, making his abs contract.

Crew's fingers press harder against my throat as he growls, "Fuck. You're such a good girl. I can feel you swallowing his cum. Take it all, you little whore."

I gasp just as TJ's cock falls from my mouth and lick my lips as Crew grinds my pussy harder. Nate kisses my back, biting and sucking my skin as they take me higher and higher.

I can't focus. I don't know who I am.

All I know is that everything in my body is tensing up, grabbing at me so tightly that I can feel every muscle contracting.

"Not yet. Not fucking yet," Crew growls, but from behind, Nate's cock leaves my ass as cum hits my back.

"Oh fuck," Nate groans, coating me in spurt after spurt.

"Eyes on me," Crew demands.

He doesn't have to ask twice because we're locked on each other, his jaw tense as he fucks my pussy harder than I've ever been fucked. His mouth is on my jaw as he grunts, gripping my leg hard enough to leave a mark. I wrap my arms around him, slapping his back, desperate for the release. And that's when he gives it to me.

"Soak me, baby."

His body rubs my clit, grinding over me harder and harder until I scream, feeling the white-light explosion. My cries are guttural and boundless as my body quakes, completely taken over by the pleasure.

I come and come, squirting my arousal and coating his cock as he grabs my hair, pulling it, and hammers inside me three more times before he bellows, "Fuck."

Crew comes inside of me, lying over me.

I don't know when the guys moved away enough for it to be just me and Crew, but we're lying here, heaving breaths as he keeps rocking inside of me like he can't stop even though he's come.

"Your pussy is fucking heaven," he pants.

His hand releases from my hair before he rolls off enough to let me breathe again, and I laugh, looking around at TJ and Nate before I pat Crew's cheek.

"That's good because you're out another grand."

twenty-four

. . .

"Your dick's been in my ass. You can't be worried about my armpit."

crew

"I wanna wake up like this every fucking morning."

I push inside her, gripping her thigh as the shower beats down my back. Her pussy feels so good, but I haven't stopped thinking about fucking her ass since the other night. Watching Nate fuck her like that while she sucked TJ off was fucking hot. It reminded me of our wedding night and I know just how fucking good Nate's position felt.

"Fuck," she pants as her palm smacks the granite wall.

My hips press forward faster as I tug at her leg.

"Hook your arms around my neck," I grind out.

The moment she does, I wrap an arm around her rib cage and lift her up.

"Your cock feels so good inside me," she whispers into my neck as I hold her flush to my body.

My other hand cradles her ass to ensure she doesn't slip as I pound her fucking pussy, listening to her sweet mewls, knowing she wants to come so badly.

"Goddammit, your pussy's so good." I nuzzle her neck, smiling as I kiss it. "Let me live in it."

She laughs as her fingers weave in my hair, gripping it and tugging my head backward as her mouth assaults mine. Kissing her feels erotic. It never feels sweet; it's always a dirty promise she's making, and I fucking like it a lot.

"Make me come," she rushes out as I thrust inside her deeper.

I spin us so I'm sitting on the granite shower bench, propping her feet on either side of me. Her hands clasp around my neck as she starts to ride me, letting my cock glide in and out of her pussy. I grab her by the nape of her neck and begin rubbing her clit with my other hand. My fingers get straight to work as I watch her mouth fall open.

"Fuck me," I growl. "Take what you want."

She's panting, eyes connected deeply to mine as I keep speaking filth, rubbing her swollen clit.

"You want to come on that cock before I coat your tits? Huh? Tell me. You keep bouncing those tits in my face and I'm gonna put you on your fucking knees."

She moans, rolling her hips, squatting over my dick, bouncing up and down. I can see it happening—her eyelids flutter, and her grip gets stronger. I massage her clit faster as her head falls back, and she screams, spurring on my own need.

Her body's quivering, jerking as she comes, but I barely give her time to come down before I lift her sweet ass to standing and growl.

"Get down."

She drops, her lips parting as I stroke my rock-hard cock, coming all over her tits and her goddamn mouth. I'm panting, completely sated, as I watch my cum drip down her chin. And I don't know what comes over me, but I reach down and swipe it back into her mouth as she smiles and licks her fucking lips.

"You're gonna be the death of me, Wild Card."

She winks.

"I'm gonna be the death of you? I should buy stock in Tylenol because my pussy getting murdered is keeping them in business."

I'm laughing as she stands, washing me away before she grabs my razor.

"Hey. Isn't that my razor?"

She glances over her shoulder and nods before slathering her armpit with some homemade shave cream she concocted and proceeds to go about her business like the audacious little thing she is, throwing her words over her shoulder.

"Oh, come on, QB. Your dick's been in my ass. You can't be worried about my armpit."

⚜

"How much for your car?"

The kid standing at the valet service counter stares at me, confused. But I just saw him coming to work. He drove past me in a beat-up pickup truck, and I wanted it.

I point toward the garage, where I saw him park inside.

"Wasn't that you…who drove by here about two minutes ago in a red Chevy pickup?"

He runs his hands through his hair, looking nervous.

"Oh man, Mr. Matthews, I'm sorry. I'm not allowed to park in that garage. But I was running late for work… there's this girl… anyway. I swear I'll move to employee parking on my lunch break."

I chuckle, putting my hands in my pockets.

"I don't care where you park. How much to let me borrow your car for the night?"

More shock bleeds out over his face.

"Ummmm—" he draws out. "How would I get home when I get off?"

I motion with my chin to the wall of keys behind him.

"Swap our keys out. You can take my Range Rover." I pull out my wallet. "And this too."

I peel a couple of hundreds off and hand it to him, adding, "For your discretion... There's this girl."

His eyes look like they're about to pop out of his head before he chuckles and nods. He digs into his pocket, showing me the keys before walking over and exchanging them with mine, turning to look at me.

"Mr. Matthews, you are now the proud owner of a beat-up red Chevy." He winks. "There are blankets in the bed."

eleanor

"Why are we in a car owned by"—I open the glove compartment and pull out the insurance, reading the owner's name—"Steven Larson."

"Because we need the bed in back," Crew says so matter-of-factly that I almost smack his arm.

Instead, I laugh and look out the window, wondering where he's taking me. All I know is that one minute I was lying on the couch, scrolling through comments on Instagram of this guy who posted that women can't really orgasm, as I laughed my ass off—because sometimes the internet really just wins—and then I was told I needed to put my shoes on and *come with* him.

Now, here I am, in a truck that might be stolen, in my pajamas at 10:30 at night.

"Crew," I muse. "This feels almost romantic. Are you taking me on a date?"

His answer begins on the tail end of my question.

"I'm not allowed to take my wife on a date?"

I laugh, giving one shoulder a pop.

"I mean, whatever keeps the magic alive for what...like...

half? Oh man, we're almost at the halfway mark in this marriage of convenience."

He nods, chuckling.

"This marriage is anything but convenient."

"Truth."

We're kidding-not kidding, but saying that out loud really makes me think. It's been two weeks-ish since we got stuck in this arrangement. And it's been strangely easy, which is unexpected.

I've spent my days getting to know everyone at the casino, eating at every single restaurant the Encore offers, and even hanging with TJ and Nate for what we now call Adventure Tuesdays. But when I say easy, I'm talking about the me-and-Crew part—we've settled into these hangouts where we watch movies...and fuck. *We always fuck.* And laugh though.

If somebody had told me at the start of this that not only would we fuck our anger out but that we'd find an easy comfort with each other, I would've called bullshit.

Crew was cool when we met, but I went from one-night stand to live-in nanny for his dick. So hiccups would've been expected...aggravation...something. But we've been easy breezy outside of pretending to almost say his name when I come just to torture him.

My brows draw together as the thoughts start to compound.

*Oh shit...*we're severely couply.

I pause at the thought. Turning my head to stare at him, I'm suddenly panicked that I used his razor on my legs this morning and that he was using the homemade shave cream I just made on his face.

That's couple shit.

Do I like you...too much?

Oh, I'm going to be pissed if I like him too much.

I clear my throat, smiling tightly as he glances at me before I scrunch my face in worry again.

No, I'm overthinking.

But not one of my personalities believes that.

Wait.

No…I'm fine.

He's Crew. Serial non-monogamist and just that guy I married. We're just friends who fuck…*and also have more fun with each other than we have with other people.*

But I could say that about Millie, and I don't want to date *her.*

Oh, this war in my head is making me actually feel like there are multiple POVs happening upstairs.

I pull out my phone, typing out a quick text.

> Me: What's the non-emergency number because this isn't a 911, but it's still a priority…

> Sami: 311

> Mills: ha ha nerd. She's prefacing, not being literal.

> Me: I think I like the way he likes me, and I want to like him back that way too.

> Sami: Ummmm, what?

> Mills: Our girl has a big-ass crush and is worried she wants a boyfriend.

> Sami: That was inevitable, Elle…you're fucking him. Of course, you like him. But the only reason this feels so strong is because it's got an expiration date. There's no real commitment. You can lower your guard because you know it'll end.

> Mills: Sam's preaching facts. There's comfort in premeditation. *smirk emoji

> Me: Okay, serial killer. But you're right, Sami. I def don't want a boyfriend. I want a salon and Sunday mimosas with besties without anyone having an opinion.

Me: And tbh if this was real, I wouldn't be fucking his friends without any conversation about our feelings.

Mills: WHAT!!!!!

Sami: THAT WASN'T THE LEAD IN?!?!?!?!?!?!

I'm smiling at my phone, feeling relieved. They're right. We're living in a Utopia. What we have isn't real. In real life, Crew and I would be fighting about warring schedules, dreams, and destinations. His life is football. Mine is the salon.

This is a vacation, and everybody wants to move to Italy when they visit.

I look up and realize it's gotten really dark out. As in, no streetlights dark. Whoa. I turn my body toward Crew, doing the thing I'm best at—putting shit out of sight, out of mind.

"So, are you going to tell me what we're doing?"

He smirks as I say it, and the tires hit gravel, making me tear away from his profile to look out the windshield. Unreasonably tall treescapes litter the sky until, as we drive underneath them, I finally see our destination.

"No way," I almost shriek.

"Way..." He grins. "Wanna try to guess what movie we're seeing?"

My eyes volley between the three drive-in movie screens for clues, but I'm coming up empty. I feel like a little kid, leaning forward and looking up through the window. The car slows to a stop, and my eyes are on the back of his head as the teenage girl in the booth smiles back at us.

"Hi, how many?"

"Two for *The Hangover Part II*."

I laugh, patting my knees as he glances over at me.

She nods. "Seventeen dollars."

He hands her a twenty as his eyes meet mine.

"I figured it was time for you to see what happens next."

My teeth find my bottom lip because the grin on my face is hurting my cheeks. But I'm also caught on that last part of his sentence...*what happens next.*

All good things come to an end, so I guess it's not the worst thing to enjoy it while I have it.

twenty-five

. . .

"If I give you an inch...I'll give you eleven back."

crew

"Stop it." She laughs, pushing my hand away from between her legs.

God, she's fucking driving me crazy. We're an hour into this movie, and I couldn't give a fuck less about what's happening. Because I can't concentrate past the way her lips close around that goddamn straw in her fucking drink. And the fact that her legs look way too good in short shorts.

Not to mention we're in the back of this truck I bartered for just so I could fuck her in it under the stars.

"Come on. You're killing me. I'm dying a slow death, and when I'm shipped to the Niners DOA, you're gonna feel bad."

She shovels some popcorn into her mouth and grins, shrugging.

I groan and fall sideways into her lap, nuzzling my face directly into her pussy, growling, and she laughs.

Eleanor tugs my hair, making me look up at her as I hug her waist.

"You have yourself to blame. You brought me to the drive-in.

This is a wholesome place; people don't fuck here. That would be gross. The best I can do is maybe make out with you."

The smirk on her face is irritating because I know she's full of shit. She's torturing me on purpose. I said it the day we failed at divorce. She's a cruel little vixen. *And I like it.*

"I'll beg," I whisper, sticking out my bottom lip.

But she shakes her head, eating more popcorn.

"Fine," I growl. "We make out."

I turn my head back to her pussy and start kissing it, making her squeal and double over, covering me.

She slaps my cheek as I grab her wrist and bite the meaty part of her hand.

She's laughing, looking down at me lying on her lap before we both quiet, and her fingers begin stroking my hair.

Her lips part as we stay connected like she's going to say something, but then it's suddenly gone, so my brows draw together.

"What were you gonna say?"

She shakes her head. "No, if I give you an inch—"

"I'll give you eleven back," I toss out, finishing her sentence and making her smile. "Just say it."

She takes a deep breath and then says, "Hypothetically speaking, if we were alone. One of three cars in a ginormous parking lot…in the dark. Lying in the back of a truck…what would you want to do to me?"

"How about I show you?"

She looks around as I sit up and grab her, dragging her over in between my legs as she laughs.

"Why are you worried?" Her hypothetical was completely accurate. "I parked all the way the fuck out specifically to ensure nobody would see us."

She nestles back against my chest, letting her head rest on it. With one hand, I pop the button on her shorts, hearing her breath catch.

"Just watch the movie. The good part's coming up."

"Oh, I bet it is," she teases back as I lower her zipper.

"Put one knee up," I whisper for absolutely no reason because nobody can even hear us. But she does as I slowly shove my hand down the front of her shorts.

The movie's playing in surround sound on the speakers from the truck, but the only thing I hear is her steady breathing picking up pace as I gently massage her clit, feeling it swell beneath my fingers.

She hums, and it vibrates my chest. With my free hand, I tangle my fingers with hers, holding her hand as I dip inside her wet pussy and draw out her arousal, spreading the wetness over her clit.

My tongue darts out over my lips before I lean in, whispering in her ear. Because I want everything to only be owned by her.

"When we get home, I want you spread out on the bed because I'm gonna lick your pussy until your legs shake so hard that you won't be able to stand for the rest of the fucking night."

She squeezes my hand as her other leg bends, and she locks her thighs together. The soft moan that leaves her lips sounds like heaven and makes my dick pulse.

"The friction feels good, doesn't it?"

She nods as I keep steady circles, kissing her neck and trailing over her jaw and back to her ear.

"And when you're lying there coming down off that high, I'm gonna flip you over and eat you again from behind while I fuck you with my fingers."

Her breath catches as her hips start to rock, pressing into my fingers. My hand moves faster, rubbing her begging clit, feeling her throb for that release.

"Come on, baby. That's it. Let me feel it. I want to hear you begging to come."

Her head falls to the side, her cheek on me as I shove my big hand between the tension in her thighs, rubbing her faster.

"Yes," she pants.

Her hips rock faster as she holds my hand like she wants to break it. Her body has taken over, and she's chasing that sweet release.

She's so fucking wet I want to pull my fingers out and taste her, but I'm not moving or stopping until she comes.

Heavy exhales tumble from her lips, and I watch her nipples harden and bead under her T-shirt.

"Crew," she whispers, catching herself quickly. "That doesn't count. I whispered it."

I don't give a fuck. Because it was enough to make my dick hard.

"Say it again."

But she won't, shaking her head and biting her lip as I grin.

My fingers work magic, never stopping, applying just enough pressure as she grips my thigh and pulls the hand I'm holding to her chest, silently chanting, "I'm coming. I'm coming. I'm coming. I'm..."

"There it is," I praise as her whole body stiffens, and she comes all over my hand. "Good girl. Good fucking girl."

Her hand wraps around my wrist, making sure I don't move as she rides out her pleasure, letting her body quiver until it stops. Her chin raises, upturning her mouth to mine.

So, I kiss her, our lips gliding over each other's and our tongues teasing as I slowly draw my hand away from her pussy.

She gasps, but it's eaten by the kiss.

I pull my hand away from hers, cradling her face as her body shifts, turning to face mine, and she wraps her arms around my neck before straddling me.

She looks around again as I grin and then says, "My turn."

Eleanor reaches inside my basketball shorts, fisting my cock before she pulls it out to join the party.

"I like your turn...a lot." I chuckle.

She winks and brings her hand to her mouth before she spits in it.

"Marry me," I breathe out, teasing.

But she laughs. "I already did."

Her hand glides back over my cock, and my fucking eyes almost roll into the back of my damn head because this girl's hand is operating at expert level. She circles her wrist as she drags up and down the shaft, smiling at me the whole time.

"Fuck," I growl as my body involuntarily jerks.

I hear her chuckle, so I add, "You're too fucking good at this. I'm gonna blow my load like it's the first time someone touched my wiener."

Eleanor laughs, but I'm fucking serious.

She leans in with that diabolical look on her face, pressing her tits against my chest as she jerks me off between us, whispering in my ear, "Blow your load, QB, because trust me, I'll make sure not to spill a drop."

Holy fuck.

I grab the nape of her neck, holding her in place as she strokes me faster and faster, circling that fucking hand, making my cock feel harder than it's ever felt. My ass indents on the sides as I press forward, rocking my hips into her hand, fucking the tight hold she has on me.

She jacks me as I grunt like a fucking animal, until my breath matches the pace.

I can feel it coming. My balls draw up, and my stomach contracts as I picture her pussy on my face. My voice is low, barely above a whisper.

"I'm gonna come. Baby, I'm gonna come. Oh fuck, oh...fuck..."

My body fucking explodes as Eleanor rips from my grasp and seals her mouth over my cock. My fist hits the side of the truck, making a loud thwack as she milks my dick, taking all I have to give.

I fill her mouth with cum. Honestly, it feels like it'll never end, but she does exactly what she said and doesn't spill a drop.

My head dips back to the sky as I try to regain consciousness.

Because I just died and went to heaven. She lets my softening cock go with a pop before sitting up and maneuvering my head back so I look at her.

"Are you good?"

"Never been better," I exhale. "Never better."

She tucks me back inside my shorts and scoots forward, grabbing the tub of popcorn and tossing a few pieces in her mouth before looking quizzically over her shoulder.

"You know what's crazy? Earlier, I thought this popcorn was salty"—she grins—"but now I feel like not as much."

My shoulder shakes before I drag her back up against me, wrapping my arms around her and kissing her neck.

"Shut up and watch that movie, Wild Card."

Jesus Christ. There really is never a dull moment with this girl.

Me: 11k

Me: You're cutting her in. Confess.

Wild Card's sister: sheesh...you'd think the NFL would teach you how to lose.

DJ Mills: Yeah, it looks like the only "deflate-gate scandal" is yo dick.

Me: Ladies, you deserve each other. You're all feral and god help the people who love you.

Me: I got a sweetener for the pot.... I get her to scream my name on the last night, and you two have to change all your socials to my photo for the whole season. Be my biggest fans.

DJ Mills: Sucka. Done.

Wild Card's sister: And if you don't?

Me: I'll publicly say I get my hair cut at Eleanor's salon.

Wild Card's sister: Deal.

twenty-six

. . .

"Next up, I'll be living on a commune, calling some dude named Sunshine Twig my leader."

crew

I took a day off.

And I'm trying to ignore how problematic that is.

I haven't missed a workout since my rookie year. And even then, it was because I broke my throwing arm. But when she walked out in her bikini, showing off every bit of what god gave her, there was no fucking way I wasn't following her straight to this pool.

I glance up, appreciating her ass, before I shoot out a text to the fellas.

> Me: Playing hooky at the pool. Pass through.

> TJ: Nate just told me you had hookers at the pool. I don't think he can read.

> Nate: Fuck you. I glanced at it. We'll be by.

> Nate: Hooky, huh?

I ignore the last text, frowning. *Read the plays on the field, Nate. Not the ones in my life.*

> Me: Shut up. It's not that big of a deal. Claire suggested I take a recovery day.

Complete fucking lie. She actually told me I was her worst client. Which makes me laugh because I'm her only client now that she's transitioning with me to the Niners.

> TJ: Give us like fifteen. We gotta see a cute little blonde to a cab. *wink emoji

> Me: Ever the gentlemen. But do me a favor and take a dip in Clorox before you come here tryna touch my girl.

"Are you texting the guys?" Eleanor throws out from her lounge chair, interrupting my thoughts. As I look at her, she smiles. "Yay. This version of you is way better than the machine."

She says the last part like a bad impersonation of Arnold Schwarzenegger.

"Machine?" I laugh.

She nods, propping herself up on her elbows.

"Yeah. You work hard, but sometimes you gotta play hard too. And you never do that."

My forehead wrinkles. "I just borrowed a car and took you out on a whole drive-in date. And if memory serves, you played with something hard."

She giggles. I've never heard that from her. *Oh fuck, it's cute.*

My phone vibrates, but I choose to ignore those two jackasses because the pool attendant comes to the cabana to take our order, and Eleanor lets out a dramatic celebratory groan in the name of snacks.

"Gil!" she squeals.

My brows draw together.

Who the fuck is Gil? His brother better be named Flounder.

My arm extends, dropping down behind her as Gil starts talking.

"What can I get for the happy couple?" She smiles at him as he adds, "You finally got him down here, huh?"

Finally? The fuck? Who are you, and how do you know where I've been? She's too friendly. No more roaming the casino.

This feels like when I visit TJ's grandma with him, and she makes me do the rounds, saying hi to all her friends. They know me, but I don't know them.

But also…she talks about me?

Eleanor's hand absentmindedly slides up and down my six-pack as she looks at the menu.

"What do you want for later?" she says to just me. "We can put in our order now, and then Gil will bring it then."

How nice of Gil.

"Absolutely," everyone's favorite pool attendant chimes in. "Anything for my favorite resident."

My phone vibrates again, so I glance down, the caps jumping out at me.

> Nate: And now we got a YOUR girl coming at us.

Wait. What? I scroll up, seeing what I last said. Oh shit, why'd I write that?

> Me: It's a typo. You're tripping.

> TJ: We're tripping, but you fell…in love. *heart eyes emoji

> Nate: Wow. And you don't even tell us? Your best friends.

> TJ: Your best men.

Fuck these two. They're never going to let me live that down, even though I didn't mean it like that.

> Nate: Exactly. Of all people, we should know that you fell in love with your wife.

> TJ: Frankly, I feel betrayed.

For fuck's sake, they need to stop. It was a typo. We're not even a real couple, but as I think it, my eyes drop to her hand, still rubbing my stomach.

> Nate: He's not the same guy we used to know. Love's changed him.

> TJ: *GIF of Snoop Dogg pouring out malt liquor

Oh shit. This is *my girl* territory…I'm a boyfriend. No, no, no, no, no. I swallow hard, reading the last text.

> Nate: RIP Crew Matthews' balls. It was a good run, but we're pouring some out for you, homies.

Crew Matthews has left the chat.

I'm still deep in my thoughts. Not thoughts, more like sheer-ass panic. My heart is actually beating too fast. I can feel the flutter. She's not *mine*. I mean, she *is*, but like in an *I can't get rid of her because I'm legally obligated* kind of way.

Right?

I definitely don't have feelings for her. That would be crazy.

Yeah…right.

I mean, there aren't *zero* feelings…but… I wipe my brow, looking at Gil.

"Is it hotter out here? Like more than usual today?"

He shakes his head, staring at me like I'm high.

Just high on the demise of my life, buddy. Fuck.

My throat suddenly feels thick, so I clear it as I squint before running my hands through my hair.

I like her more than I should.

Eleanor's face shifts to mine, her smile peeking out.

"Did I tell you Gil here has a nephew that might get drafted?"

She looks at the attendant and then back to me as I mutter, "Congratulations. That's awesome."

But I'm still staring at her, just shaking my head because of course I didn't know. *But I'm sure you were going to tell me during our weekly trip to Costco before we did some gardening together.*

Holy fuck. We became a couple...like for real. I can't be trusted with my own life decisions. Next up, I'll be living on a commune, calling some dude named Sunshine Twig my leader.

She laughs and raises her brows. "Are you good? Do you want me to just order stuff you'll like?" She looks back to the choices and then points to something I can't see because I'm about to pass out before she adds, "Maybe the French dip. You love that. You eat it like..." She winks. "Like you like it a lot."

I just keep nodding because what am I supposed to say?

Hey, stop acting like my girlfriend and go back to being my fake wife?

This is bad. This is so fucking bad. Without looking at her, I lift her hand as my bullshit excuse to put some space between us tumbles out.

"I'm gonna go for a swim." *And maybe stay underwater for a bit.*

She hums an acknowledgment, setting the menu aside after ordering and lying back to soak up the sun.

The minute I hit the water, I turn around and look at her. I can't help it. And it's like she knows, too, because she pushes up on her elbows again and stares right at me. Even with her sunglasses on, I know her eyes are locked on mine.

Damn, meeting this girl has turned my life upside down.

And apparently, it only took seventeen days to get me used to the view.

I'm doomed.

❦

"HOW DIDN'T I SEE THIS COMING?" I MUTTER TO TJ AS HE TAKES A drink of his beer. "I'm fucking embarrassed to say that I thought we'd just ride out the thirty days fucking and hanging out. In my mind, I was like, we're just gonna high-five when she leaves."

TJ laughs, and so do I. Because what the fuck?

We're sitting on lounge chairs, watching Nate throw Eleanor around in the pool, making her squeal before she tries like hell to dunk him under. It's not happening, but it's cute to watch her try.

"Isn't that why you call her Wild Card, though? Cuz she ain't the thing you saw comin'?"

I shake my hand, gripping the football they brought, tapping it with my other.

"Nah, it was because she was an unexpected opportunity."

I glance over at him as his brows pull together.

"An opportunity for what?"

I exhale, eyes on her as she splashes Nate a couple of times before he almost drowns her in a wave and I grin.

"That night? That was an opportunity for fun. A way to let loose and just be wild. All this contract shit had been wearing me down, and she just felt like a breath of fresh air."

He takes another swig, then looks at me.

"And now?"

"Shit, Teej. I don't know. She's gotten under my skin, you know? But I don't have room in my life for anyone. And honestly, neither does she. We both made that clear."

He scoffs, but both our heads snap to the pool when we hear

Eleanor and Nate calling our names and waving us out to join them.

"Bullshit," he throws out before he takes the ball off my stomach and hurls it toward Nate before adding, "No room? Then build an addition in the house of Crew. You got the cash."

I crack a laugh because that's such a TJ thing to say, but the initial humor dims because the truth isn't as funny.

"Truth?" I don't have to look at him to know he's nodding. "I don't want to. And that's the fucked-up part because I hear myself, dude. But I don't *want* a girlfriend. I don't want to have to think about someone else and how my life affects them... I'm just getting started toward where I want to go. But damn, she makes me feel like I *should*."

I'm waiting for him to call me a dick because I deserve it. But TJ doesn't say anything. We just sit in silence, staring out at the pool as Eleanor laughs and starts calling us out again.

"Damn, you really do like her," he says under his breath.

So I nod. "Yeah. I do. She's kinda the perfect girl, just in the wrong lifetime."

TJ blows out a deep breath before he stands up, rubbing his chest. When we look at each other, my brows raise, and he smiles before delivering his trademark outlandish thoughts.

"This shit's getting too serious for two guys lying next to each other at the pool. Here's what I'm thinking. Scale it back. Just be cool, talk to her like you would us. Don't be like boyfriendy and shit. Definitely don't take her out on drive-in dates."

"Yeah." I chuckle. "In hindsight...you know? I'm a fucking idiot."

He stretches his arms wide, yawning, before Nate throws a shitty pass to him. Doesn't matter though—TJ catches it like it was meant to go where it did.

"And not to be a dick," he adds with a laugh, "but you act like that girl is gonna fall all over herself because you got a boner for her personality. She's *been* pullin'. Ya know?"

We both start laughing. Because he's not wrong. Just because I like her doesn't mean shit. Eleanor is not the girl who's waiting for her prince. Why would she when she's been running the kingdom. Fucking A.

"I just need back on my game," I say resolutely. "No more taking days off and giving in to distractions."

He laughs. I don't, my brows pulling together as I speak.

"We've got two more weeks together. It's not like anybody's falling in love in that time frame. So, I'm hands-off."

He looks at me, surprised, until I specify, "I mean everything but sex." My smirk grows. "A man's gotta eat."

He nods, throwing the ball back to Nate.

"Understandable, sir. I concur."

I smile, watching her splash around like she's doing those old-people water aerobics. Why does she have to be so fucking cute? And why do I want to go out there and wrap her fucking legs around me just so she'll kiss my neck. *Oh, you dumb fuck. Get it together.*

"Plus," I breathe out, selling every fucking word to TJ and myself. "The reality is, even if we decided to be idiots and try dating—"

TJ cuts me off. "You'd definitely make her cry. She'd just end up hatin' you."

I snap my fingers, pointing at him.

"Precisely."

TJ slaps the wet football he just caught on my stomach, gut-checking me as I let out a groan. But he laughs before giving me a double fist tap to my shoulder and jogging out into the water to join them.

I'm spinning the ball around in my hand as I let my thoughts ruminate. This is for the best. I'm doing what's best for me. And I owe that to myself and all the work I've put in.

"Crew!"

Her voice calls my attention again as she waves her hands in the air before she starts dancing to the "YMCA" song.

"It's our song."

I can't help but thunder a laugh because when we got married, they asked us what our "special song" was. Told us they'd play it as she walked down the aisle. Because apparently, the officiant/Elvis only sings during the hours of six to midnight. I let her choose.

"YMCA" is what she strolled down the aisle to, and the entire place joined in at the chorus.

TJ and Nate are laughing, remembering the same memory as TJ lowers his shoulders below the water, and Nate grabs her waist to hoist her up on top.

Every bit of her pearly whites can be seen from the pool to the cabana as she continues spelling out the song with her arms. But a glimmer of something off to the side catches my eye.

I shift my gaze, looking out past her to a guy sitting by staring at her. And my jaw tenses because he's holding up an iPhone, aimed at her. *What the fuck? Is he...*

Is this motherfucker taking pictures of her?

I'm staring for what feels like minutes but probably is only a few seconds as my hand grips the football hard, spinning it around to make it laces up.

Everything in my body calms, and the only pathway I see is from this chair to that motherfucker's face about twenty yards away.

Before reason has time to catch up to action, I yell, "Nate, go long," before I launch the football across the pool, whizzing past Eleanor, dead through that fucking cell phone and directly into that dude's nose.

Two things happen: blood erupts from his broken nose, and Eleanor shrieks in surprise.

Wild Card's already off TJ's shoulders, her hands covering her mouth as her eyes turn into saucers.

But the guys are looking at me, easing her behind them protectively.

I stand, holding up my hands as I walk toward where that dude's sitting, raising my voice.

"Wow. I'm so sorry about that, my guy. The ball really got away from me."

Nate chuckles in the background, but I ignore it, keeping my face on the motherfucker who now has ice and a towel from the pool attendants.

I smirk.

"You should pinch the bridge of your nose...keep your head back."

He glares at me, speaking like he's stuffed up.

"You fucking broke my nose, asshole. I'm going to sue you. I know who you are."

I look down at the ground where his shattered phone is lying before I swipe it up and pocket it.

"Well, if you're going to sue me, then I'll probably have to pay damages. Maybe even fix your phone. So, I'm gonna get a head start and take it with me."

"You can't take my fucking phone," he grits out, shoving more of the towel against his bleeding nose.

But I squat down next to his chair, and glancing over my shoulder, I see the guys have gotten Eleanor out of the pool, and she's now drying off in the cabana.

I look back at him, keeping my voice quiet.

"Do you think I don't know who you are? You think I don't fucking recognize you? I know who you and all your slimy friends are. Out here with cameras all the time, trying to track our every move."

I stand again, looking down at him, watching his whole demeanor change, worry on his brow as I pull out his phone and waggle it in my hand.

"Sneak in here again and try to take another picture of my wife...and I'll break more than just your fucking nose."

I walk away without a worry in the world. Let him sue me. Nobody fucking treats her like that.

Eleanor meets me halfway back around the pool, flanked by TJ and Nate, who look at me with matching smirks.

"What's the game plan?" TJ says slyly.

I throw my arm over Eleanor and look down. What am I doing? This is quite literally the opposite of the plan. But all reason leaves me again as she smiles up at me.

"Did you do that on purpose?" she whispers as we walk toward the hotel entrance.

I press a kiss to her forehead, inhaling the scent of coconut oil and pool.

"Never. See what happens when I skip a day of training? My aim gets so bad."

Just because I like her doesn't mean I have to admit it. And maybe a little fun upstairs will get my head straight.

twenty-seven

. . .

"I think we should share custody of your cock."

eleanor

I don't know what the hell happened at the pool, but what I do know is Crew Matthews is full of shit. That football zoomed past me like a fucking ballistic missile locked onto exactly what it was aiming for.

The nosy part of me wants to know why, but honestly, if he doesn't want to tell me, I'm fine with it. Oddly enough, I trust his judgment. I don't know what that says about me because he just hit a guy in the face with a football, but here we are.

"Waters?" I offer, putting my bag on the edge of the counter as I walk toward the refrigerator.

But a crashing sound immediately spins me around as everything from inside my bag spills out all over the floor.

"Shit," I rush out, as my tanning oil hemorrhages out over the marble floors. I look up, noticing Crew closest to the paper towels. "Hey, grab me some, please."

But instead of jumping into action, he starts chuckling at me because the moment I got down on all fours, my hand slid straight across the floor, leaving me on my belly.

"Look at you…all laid out on the floor. Fellas, take a look at *my*…erm…our girl. If I didn't know any better…"

I cut him off, laughing at myself.

"Shut up." I lift my dry hand for him to help me out, but instead, he takes it and spins me in a circle, making me scream a laugh as the other guys look on, entertained.

"Will someone tell him to stop playing around," I scold playfully, not at all mad.

Neither of the guys says a thing as they walk toward me and Crew.

I let out a quiet breath because there's a shift that's palpable when those two work as a team. And suddenly, I'm pretty sure the goal isn't to get me on my feet. More like onto my back.

My gaze shifts between them. Their eyes are on my body at the same time, drifting over their favorite parts. I smirk before I huff a laugh. Because I've been in a bikini all day in front of these three, but somehow, it's in this moment that I feel half naked. Completely exposed.

Jesus. They're coming on stronger than they ever have.

"Or…" Nate draws out, stopping and looking down at me. "Instead of telling Crew to stop, we could tell him to keep playing around. Right, Crew? I think that's a better plan…"

Crew looks at TJ and then Nate like they've suddenly developed telekinesis before TJ chuckles and squats. He runs one of his hands through the oil before bringing it to my legs and slicking it over my skin.

Oh, helloooo.

I hear Crew let out a quiet growl next to me.

"You know what this reminds me of, darlin'?" TJ grins.

"Not a clue," I whisper before biting my bottom lip.

"Spin the bottle."

I laugh, throwing my head back before I say, "TJ. How does me covered in oil on the floor remind you of spin the bottle?"

But TJ doesn't answer me before he looks at Crew and smirks, taking my hand from him.

"I say we spin Eleanor, and whatever lands in front of us, we kiss. What do you think, Crew? You in?"

I smile, not minding where this is going at all.

Crew steals my hand back, gritting, "I go first."

Oh shit. Here we go. I'm either going to throw up all over the floor, or I'm about to go to sexual heaven. The lord really does giveth and giveth and giveth.

Fucketh the taking away part.

I look up at Crew, then Nate, then TJ, but nobody is looking at me. They're staring at each other. *What is happening?* If this is one of those little competitions again, my pussy may not survive, but the soldier in me wants to try anyway.

"Am I spinning myself?" I tease, biting my bottom lip as I laugh.

But Crew's eyes snap to me, his jaw tense before suddenly, the world whizzes by. He spins me around, making me scream with laughter and land splayed out with my leg next to him.

"You're nuts" tumbles out as he grabs my calf, lifting my shin to his mouth and kissing it softly.

I suck in a quiet breath, my body stilling as our eyes meet and he kisses it again. Something in his eyes has mine locked to him, and I can feel my chest already rising and falling with a heavier rhythm.

My lips begin to tip up into a smile, matching exactly what's happening on his face, but the moment is broken as Nate cuts in.

"Don't bogart *our* girl, Crew..."

Crew grumpily looks away as he moves over, giving Nate barely enough room to take my hand as I sit up before he spins me.

I'm laughing, squealing, "This is insane," as I stop with my back to Nate, so I look up at him as he peers over.

He smirks. "Looks like I got lips."

Nate bends over as he tips my head back further before his lips barely graze mine—graze because Crew's pushing Nate to the side, which makes me fall sideways and causes Crew's foot to catch in some oil. He slips around, too awkward for someone athletic, before grabbing the counter and huffing out his words.

"Noooo...nope. That's not the rule...that's cheating. You have to kiss the back of her head. That's what you got," he rushes out like the sexy spin-the-bottle police.

Crew motions for Nate to do that, and we both start laughing. *Has he lost his mind?*

"Are you okay?" I offer Crew as Nate presses a kiss to the back of my head.

Crew clears his throat and nods, getting his footing. "Yep, right as rain. I'm good. I'mmmm amazing."

He has sun poisoning, for sure.

TJ steps up and winks at me before reaching down and grabbing my ankle.

"Fuck this—someone's gonna break a sixty-million-dollar arm. We're taking this one to the bedroom."

I don't have time to react before TJ starts to drag me like a fucking caveman, sliding me along the floor as I thunder a laugh before I scream his name.

"TJ! You're nuts."

TJ looks over his shoulder directly at Crew, halting our movement.

"Would you look at that...she screamed my name. Does that mean I get on her roster? Or are you paying me thirty-K?"

Oh shit. My face swings to Crew from where I'm lying, my mouth open like I wanna say, "Ooo, burnnnnn."

Except who hasn't frozen is Crew—who is coming right for us.

Holy fuck.

Crew wastes no time hauling me to my feet, his hand squeezing gently around my arm as his giant frame hovers over me, and those ocean-blue eyes meet mine.

"Why am I in trouble?" I grin.

His voice makes me shudder like gravel across my flesh. "What have I told you about flirting with the bench?"

My tongue darts out over my bottom lip because dominant Crew is one of my favorite versions.

"You said not to because you're the starting lineup," I whisper.

"Technically," TJ interjects, leaning in next to me. "I start too."

Crew's face snaps to his, and I try to hide my smile as Crew barks, "Didn't you and Nate fuck some random pussy last night? You could have gonorrhea, syphilis, herpes, fucking crabs—"

My eyes are saucers as Crew looks at me. "Do you want any of those things?"

A laugh tears from me before I shove it back down because, oh fuck, he's serious. And I get the distinct impression now is not the time to mention the various routes of safe sex. So I shake my head because, damn, TJ's in so much trouble for that comment.

Never kick a guy when he's down sixteen thousand.

TJ chuckles and pats Crew's arm. "You're right. Wow, I can't believe *I*...or that *we*—" He motions to Nate, who's leaning up against the counter, smirking with his arms crossed as he nods before TJ continues. "Yeah, that we didn't consider that exact thing. Must still be all the liquor in our systems."

TJ touches my waist, leaning in and kissing my cheek chastely.

"Guess you dodged a bullet."

I'm smiling, but also what? I feel like I'm missing part of the conversation. Nate and TJ take their leave, but as the door closes, I stare at Crew.

"What is going on?"

He shakes his head, hands on my waist, walking me backward toward the bedroom. So I repeat myself.

"No, dude. What is going on?"

He stops in the doorway before he looks over his shoulder and grabs my hand, dragging me over to the couch and lifting me to stand on it.

He's doing that thing again, making us eye to eye. *Why is that so cute?*

Crew cracks his neck. "What's going on is that I want you."

My eyes search his because, for the briefest moment, my heart stops. Is he saying what I think he's saying? But then he continues, and I can breathe again.

"I want you to myself tonight. I think I'm all amped up over that guy taking your pic, and I just—"

"He was taking my picture?" I shriek, but Crew chuckles, pulling out the cracked phone from his pocket and tossing it behind him on the table.

"Problem solved." He frowns before reaching out and touching my stomach, drawing little squiggles in the oil as he speaks. "I want you all to myself. I wanna fuck you bent over this couch again and eat your pussy until you can't speak. I want to desecrate that ass. I want my cum in your mouth and yours on my cock."

His eyes lift back to mine.

"I want your body just for me tonight."

Well, goddamn. I'm not sure there's been a time when I've been wetter. Guys say, "Let's fuck." Crew says, "I want my cum in your mouth and yours on my cock."

For fuck's sake, give a masterclass already.

"Done," I breathe out, hands on his shoulders, already bouncing a little before I throw out my thought, suddenly wanting him to know that I want him to myself too.

Don't do that, dummy. He's a vacation, not a permanent destination. But my lips start moving anyway.

"And truthfully, I don't care if the other night never happens again. TJ and Nate are meant for a good time, not a long time. I don't even want one boyfriend, let alone two additional complications. You know what I mean?"

Crew smirks, holding my waist tighter as he lifts, and my legs wrap around his waist.

His hands are on my ass as he carries me, so I take the opportunity to kiss along his jawline, laughing each time he has to hoist me up because I'm slippery.

The minute we're in the bedroom, he chucks me onto the bed and crawls over me, letting one of his legs slip between mine.

"Where do you want to start on that list of yours," I breathe out huskily.

Crew's fingers ghost my collarbone, then run down over the fabric of my bikini top before he tugs it open and covers his mouth over my nipple.

I suck in a breath, letting my head rub on the bed as I lift my chin. His tongue runs circles over the pebbled flesh as it grows harder between his lips.

He sucks the tender bud, making me jut my breasts toward him and moan.

"Goddamn, that feels good."

Crew releases my nipple with a pop, his eyes meeting mine again as his hand travels further south, leaving goose bumps in its wake.

He doesn't say a thing, just stares into my eyes as he grazes over my stomach, all the way down to my bikini bottoms.

But he doesn't bother to untie them. Instead, Crew slips his hand inside, smirking as my lips part both on my mouth and my pussy as he thrusts between the wetness gathered around my hairs before he massages my clit.

I arch my back off the bed, eyes closing, feeling his lips land on my collarbone.

"I love how wet your pussy gets," he whispers along my skin.

He pulls his finger out, dragging my arousal back up over my stomach to my tit before circling my wetness around my nipple.

I lick my lips, watching him coat me before he seals his mouth over it again.

"Fuck," I cry out, running my hands through his hair and over his muscular back.

Crew kisses my desire off me before abandoning my chest and working his way down the path he left, kissing my body. His tongue glides and dips into my belly button before moving further down until he reaches my bottoms.

His mouth covers the fabric, kissing my cunt deeply and making my body buck.

"Oh god." I exhale harshly, but ever so delicately, Crew slides the fabric aside and runs his tongue straight over my clit.

"Fuck," I moan.

God, his tongue is magic. Crew maneuvers himself between my legs so his arms are hooked under them. He's licking and circling his tongue, humming and growling against my clit as I writhe and pant.

My fingers weave through his hair, holding his face to my pussy, as I grind into him, letting him devour every bit of my wetness.

"Oh my god. I love the way you lick my pussy."

Crew's large hands grip the inside of my legs as he growls, nipping my sensitive throbbing clit before he lifts my ass off the bed and brings me to his face. He feeds on me before dropping me back down and slapping his hands down my thighs, spreading me wider.

I'm panting and moaning because he's made it his mission to make me come. It's so overwhelming that my body's already quaking.

"Oh fuck. Oh my god."

He sucks my clit, and I start crawling backward because I can barely take it. It's too good. I'm too open—he's everywhere on my pussy. I'm throbbing and trembling, grinding into him and simultaneously feeling like I could crawl up the wall.

But Crew doesn't stop, groaning, "More. C'mere," as he follows me, grunting and needing my pussy.

My hand slaps against his back, trying to reach for anything to hold on to as my hips rock against his face.

"Oh god, yes, yes, yes..."

But before I can come, he tears away, rising up to his knees and grabbing my thighs before he jerks me forward flush to him. I'm fumbling, trying to get my bikini bottoms off. But Crew doesn't give a fuck about that. Without hesitating, he rips them aside, pulls out his cock, and thrusts inside of me.

"Oh my god," I gasp, whispering his name. "Crew."

But as I stare at him, gripping the sheets, his chest heaves. He's hammering inside me, pounding over and over, staring down at me.

And he looks like a fucking god.

"Oh, so now you remember my name?"

There's no point in pretending I don't like his arrogance because the way my pussy just got even wetter gives it away.

"That's right," he croons, smirking, his jaw slack as his hips work like a damn machine, never slowing. "I felt that pussy start to cry for me. Because she's my dirty little bitch."

Holy fucking hell. I may die from pleasure overload.

His voice washes over me as I close my eyes.

"I'm not going to punish *her* for not screaming my name…"

My eyes are rolling into the back of my head, and I feel like I can't catch my breath. Crew's fucking me so good that he will be the bar I set until the end of time.

He chuckles, enjoying what he sees as he continues, his voice ragged.

"Why would I punish her? This little slot and me…we understand each other."

Crew brings the back of my legs to his chest, holding them there, my stems flanking his face as he rams inside of me over and over. Our skin slaps each time his dick glides out and in my wet pussy as he grinds his words out.

"She comes when I tell her."

He thrusts harder.

"She takes what I give her."

Crew slaps my tit, making me gasp.

"And she knows whose cock owns her."

I'm breathless, my hands running over my body, brazen and wild as I moan, unable to think as he grunts with each thrust.

My whole body is trembling with need as I whimper.

Crew holds my legs with one arm, and with his other, he brings his hand down to my pussy, his fingers rubbing my clit.

He's literally playing my body like a fucking violin. My breath is shaky at best. And I'm all but screaming as he viciously rubs my clit.

"Ohmygodohmygodohmygod."

My body keeps climbing, contracting and assaulting me with fucking pleasure as I chase my release.

"Are you gonna come for me, baby?" he whispers, staring down at my wet cunt. "You gonna come all over my cock? Are you gonna be my good girl and gush so much that it's gonna drip down your ass so I fuck that too?"

Jesus Christ.

That's all I need. His filthy mouth tips me right over the edge, and I thunder unintelligible words toward the ceiling. My fucking soul leaves my body.

A guttural and deep, visceral cry tears from my lungs as I grip the sheets next to me. My arms spread, body held as he pounds inside me over and over and over, coaxing every ounce of pleasure from my body until I'm suddenly climbing again, hurled into an atomic fucking explosion.

I can't say for sure that I didn't just scream his name, but if I did, neither of us understood it because I'm not sure I was even speaking English.

My lips quiver like I'm cold, but my entire body is warm. I stare up at him, breathless, taking him in as his cock moves slower and slower.

Crew licks the shine off his bottom lip, his eyes hooded as he stares down at me, releasing my legs, and they flop down on either side of him.

He's not done.

Crew pulls his cock out of me, making me gasp before he moves off the side of the bed, standing and stroking himself.

Fuck, he's so sexy, coated in my cum, his eyes drifting over my body. I swallow, catching my breath as he tilts his head.

"I told you I wouldn't punish your pussy." He sucks his bottom lip between his teeth and lets it drag out, taking long draws up and down his cock. "Because it's your goddamn mouth that's the problem."

Crew steps back and crooks his finger, calling me to stand in front of him. Involuntarily, my hips rock because I'm fucking turned on all over again. So, I slink off the bed and stand on weak legs in front of him, inhaling harshly as he runs his hand over my breast and up my neck, forcing my chin and eyes to him.

He leans down and kisses me gently at first before he sucks my bottom lip, then lets it go harshly before whispering his words onto them.

"Put your mouth on my cock."

My eyes close, a rush of pleasure hitting me before I walk my hands down his body and kneel in front of him.

Crew runs the tip of his cock over my lips, letting me taste myself, reminding me of the first time we did this.

"You don't want to scream my name…that's fine. But you're still gonna fucking remember whose mouth this is."

His fingers weave through my hair, gripping it before his dick thrusts past my lips.

The taste of his precum mingles with *me* as I suck and draw circles just under the rim of his dick with my tongue. Crew growls, pressing himself further into my mouth before drawing out and doing it again.

My hands find the sides of his ass, loving the way it indents every time he thrusts forward. And I moan, wanting him to know.

"You like that, baby? You like it when I fuck your face like the little slut you are?"

I nod before deep-throating him.

"Oh fuck." He groans, his breath catching this time. "Your mouth is so good."

Crew kicks into gear fucking my face, owning the rhythm as he uses my mouth. I hollow my cheeks, bobbing my head as he guides me forward deeper and deeper, making me gag on his cock each time he fucks my throat.

"Yes, baby, that's so good. Suck that cock."

Tears spill down the sides of my eyes as he hits my throat again, stealing my breath and then giving it back to me. His deep, heavy pants coming from above spur me on, making me drop my hand back to my pussy and touch myself, wanting to feel this with him.

"Goddamn, I like you dirty."

He pumps faster and faster into my mouth, until his body begins taking over and racing toward the finish line.

Crew tugs me, grinding into my face, chanting, "Fuck, fuck, fuck," until his body tenses and he grips my hair unmercifully hard to hold my head in place.

Warm spurts of cum begin to fill my mouth, but Crew growls, spitting his words like an animal.

"Don't you fucking swallow."

My fingers rub violent circles over my clit as his cum pools in my mouth.

"I fucking mean it—don't you fucking swallow a goddamn drop."

As he finishes, he drags my lips using my hair down his softening shaft, tilting my head back so that I'm staring up at him, still rubbing myself, desperate to come again.

His voice is ragged and deep.

"Open your mouth like a good girl. Let me see my cum inside you."

I've never felt so possessed, so deliciously degraded and fucking owned, until this moment.

I do exactly as I'm told, and I open my mouth to show him

what he's given me. The side of his lip tips up arrogantly as he wipes the back of his hand over his mouth, wiping away the spit on his lips.

"Are you my dirty whore?"

I nod against the force he's holding my hair, rubbing faster.

"Is that pussy mine to do with what I want?"

I nod again, feeling the precipice.

"Does this mouth know who it belongs to now?"

I nod for the last time.

Because Crew tips my head back further as he leans over me and spits into my mouth.

"Now you can fucking swallow."

I come. Hard.

Crew scoops me up off the floor, letting me cling to him as he walks us to the shower, kissing the top of my head and rubbing my back.

He doesn't need a bet to make me delete my roster. His dick just did it for him.

"Hey," I whisper. "Can you call the lawyer tomorrow because I think we should share custody of your cock. At the very least, I get it on holidays."

Crew laughs, and I follow, but honestly, I'm only half kidding.

twenty-eight

. . .

"I fucked her into straight-up REM sleep."

crew

I don't know what time it is. I don't care either.

All I know is that my body feels cold.

My eyes pop open, my head shifting on my pillow and falling to the side. Eleanor's lying on her back, sleeping soundly. Of course she is. I fucked her into straight-up REM sleep.

I was a man possessed because I wanted it to be just me and her. And from now on, it's only going to be me and her.

Me and her. Everything about that is a bad idea...just like it was this morning. Dammit, I made a plan, and I need to stick to it.

Hands off, Crew. Don't fucking do what's in your head right now.

But I already know I've lost that fight because I'm already rolling over, hooking my arm between her legs, and grabbing a handful of ass before I drag her over to my side.

"C'mere," I growl, draping her body over mine as I run my hand down the back of her thigh before wrapping it around her rib cage.

She moans, cuddling closer to me as I press a kiss to her shoulder, our bodies flush as she hugs me just as tight.

Tomorrow…I'll follow my game plan tomorrow.
Tonight, I want her right where she is.

JULY

S M T W T F S

twenty-nine

. . .

"No wife of mine. Not even a fake one."

eleanor

I t's so early that the birds aren't even awake yet. Then again, even if they were, I wouldn't hear them from the penthouse. I pad out mid-yawn, feet halted as my eyebrows raise in surprise.

"What are you doing here? I thought you'd be at practice already."

Crew is standing at the counter in only boxer briefs, with a piece of toast half hanging out of his mouth, holding two cups of coffee.

Oh damn, between his disheveled hair and all that muscle on display, I have to blink a few times to refocus. It doesn't matter how many times I see his body, those veiny forearms and the six-pack with the perfectly sculpted v always make me horny. I just want to lick him and objectify him all day.

He mumbles something, then motions his head toward the windows, drawing my eyes in that direction. Sweet baby Jesus, it's raining.

I didn't notice when I first woke up and walked out here, but the sky is dark gray, littered with angry clouds, and the rain is coming down so hard that it's making those slash marks against the glass.

"No school. Rain day," he mumbles around the toast before I hear a crunch.

I smile, sauntering over to the counter and leaning forward with my forearms pressed against the cool marble before I take my coffee from his hand, feeling playful.

"Look at you. All the other little QBs have to go to class and work hard today." I crane my neck to look at what he's wearing. "And you get to hang out in your underwear all day."

I take a swig of my coffee before pretending I have a microphone in my hand as I hold my fist up to Crew's mouth.

"Tell us, Crew Matthews. What's it like to be God's favorite?"

He laughs, shoving my hand away before finishing off his toast with a giant bite. I chuckle as everything he says is mumbled through his mouthful.

"There are flash flood warnings throughout the entire city, so we're pretty much stuck here for the day."

I look out the windows again as lightning brightens the sky, followed by a clap of thunder. My brows raise as I turn back to his grinning face.

"Did you plan that?"

His shoulders shake. "Obviously. I score touchdowns and manipulate the weather. I had it written into my contract, actually."

God, I have a weakness for Crew like this—half naked and charming. But it's fine. I'm on vacation. He's just my Italy.

"Well then," I breathe out, moving past my thoughts as my palms smack the counter, raising me back to my full height. "There's only one acceptable solution for rainy day boredom."

The look on his face is wary at best. Which is funny because that pretty much confirms that he knows me well.

"And that is?"

I shake my hips, doing a little dance.

"Duh. Spa day."

crew

"Is this going to burn my face?" I grimace, sticking my finger in the bowl before wiping it off.

She's laughing, but I'm fucking serious.

The moment she'd said "spa day," I thought she meant here at the hotel.

So when she ran to the phone and started ordering a bunch of random shit up from the concierge, I stupidly thought it was all just a bunch of snacks because it was, like, blueberries, strawberries, and yogurt.

But once it all arrived, she spent the next thirty minutes mushing it up and putting together all these concoctions while simultaneously talking about everything from reality television to whether I believe the conspiracy theories about Britney Spears.

And I've sat here, on this barstool, hanging on her every word before berating myself and trying to distract myself from how fucking cute she is. Honestly, that's the best description of this week I could ever have.

That's been exactly me since the night we cuddled like fucking koalas—warring with what I want and what I shouldn't take. Because when I'd said to myself I'd follow the game plan tomorrow, it became ten days' worth of them.

Her hair's up on top of her head as she bops around the kitchen, taste testing what she swears will make my pores nonexistent. I didn't even know they showed or weren't supposed to.

"Come on," she directs sweetly, walking past me to the living room.

Her feet hit the blanket she had me set up on the floor in front of the windows so that we could watch the rain.

She sets the bowls down before sitting crisscross on the floor, looking at me like I'm supposed to follow suit. So I do, frowning.

"Let me get this straight. I have to put fruit and yogurt on my face?"

She laughs before putting a finger in front of my mouth, shushing me.

"Yes. It has antioxidants, and it's good for you. I mixed it with some clay stuff I had too, so it'll make your skin glow."

I smirk. "Wow…I've always wanted to glow."

Eleanor rolls her eyes before dipping her fingers into the bowl. She leans forward with some blue slop on them, smiling before gently swiping over my cheek.

My tongue darts out, licking my lips because she may not be looking at me, but I'm fucking looking at her.

Fuck it. Today won't count. I'm rain-checking reason.

I reach out, tugging at her hip as I straighten my legs, guiding her to straddle me before I sink my palms behind me, propping myself up.

She rocks herself over me only once, getting comfortable, but it still makes my dick pay attention.

I'm so fucked. But I don't care.

I just want her on me, her body touching mine.

Her fingers smooth the cream over my face inch by inch as we sit in silence until my tongue darts out again. This time, I get a nasty surprise.

"Don't eat the face cream," she scolds, giggling.

I chuckle, feeling parts of my face already starting to get tight.

"You said it was edible."

"Lies. You started tuning out after I said antioxidants."

My brows draw together as I stick my tongue out, still tasting that shit on the tip of my tongue. She's laughing, looking down at her hands, which are covered in goop, before she leans forward and sucks my tongue clean.

Now I'm completely hard.

She spits what's in her mouth on the towel and puts her eyes back on mine.

"Don't say I never did anything for you."

My hand winds around her neck, gripping the back as I pull her back into a proper kiss. She melts into me, rocking her center against me again as she hums into my mouth.

Fuck… This girl.

I jerk my hips up, making her bounce and laugh as I growl into the kiss. Her palms come to rest on my chest before she pushes, breaking away, breathless as she touches her forehead to mine.

"We need to wash off because if it's burning your face, imagine what it'll feel like on your…"

That makes me grin, but I shake my head. Because, yes, I want to fuck her, but right now, I want to hang out with her more.

"Tell me something," I breathe out, letting her go back to slathering me. "When did you know this was your thing? All the salon and face stuff?"

She takes a deep breath, looking thoughtful, before dipping her fingers into the red concoction and motioning for me to lift my chin.

I do because she makes me a good boy.

"Mmm, I feel like I kind of fell into this. My family is high achieving. My sister started her design company right out of college and exploded. But I was the opposite. I dropped out of college my sophomore year."

I lower my face to hers, but she tsks, so I raise it again, speaking toward the ceiling.

"Are they the 'disappointed in you' kind or the 'find your way' kind of parents?"

She smiles; I can feel it.

"The 'find your way' kind. I'm lucky."

"I've always wondered if I'd been adopted if my life would've gone differently." I exhale because I've also always had the same answer. "And I always think, I hope not. I like the result. The journey was a different story. You know?"

"I get that."

She does. It's not something she's just saying. More goop hits my chest, so I lower my head, eyes back on hers.

"Is this shit going on my whole body?"

She winks.

"If you're lucky."

I give her a wink back and just sit there like a good test dummy as she gets that thoughtful look on her face.

"When I look back on where I was at twenty versus where I am now, I don't even feel like the same person sometimes. I bounced around from thing to thing, from idea to idea. Until one day, I was like, 'it's embarrassing that I don't have a *thing.*' I mean, I had a job. But that's different from a calling. So, one night, over couch sushi and wine with Millie and Sam, I just started making a list of all the things I would want to do with my life if I won the lottery. And bam…skin care, wellness, that was like my thang."

She laughs, and I want to follow suit, but my concentration is currently being stolen by the feel of her fingers sliding down my throat to my chest over and over absentmindedly.

But the words formed tumble out on their own anyway.

"I think it's brave to take the time to figure out what you want. We only get a handful of trips around the sun. Might as well make them epic, right?"

Her eyes bore into mine as if a thousand thoughts are cluttering her head. So, I fill in the silence.

"And for the record, you're good at this. Cuz I really like having your coochie cream on my face every day."

She gives me a little shove, laughing.

"I'm glad you're enjoying the cream, but truth be told, I also like your face in my coochie every day."

Dirty little thing. I fucking love it.

I grab her waist and tickle her, smiling as she screams and wiggles.

"No! Crew!"

She smacks my chest, grinning ear to ear, but I keep tickling her, forcing her sideways until she's lying flat on her back and I'm looking down at her, nestled right between her legs.

"I'll kill you," she exhales a little breathlessly, staring up.

Her eyes are so pretty that I'm starting to wonder if the memory of them will ever do them justice. And before I know what I'm saying, something stupid pops out.

"I want to come to the opening of your salon."

Why the fuck did I say that? No, no, no. I have to take that back.

She stares back at me, unblinking, not saying anything. Because it's one thing for us to play house, but what I just said took us into the real world.

And the one thing both of us have done since the beginning of this has been to dance around what happens *after*. Are we friends? Are we still hooking up? It's something we don't touch.

My lips part to take it back or, if I'm being honest, to confess the truth. *Can we know each other after this?* is on the tip of my tongue. But she smiles just as cold cream hits my face.

I suck in a breath as she smears the handful down over my chest, laughing her words out.

"Okay, but only if you promise to bring the girls you're hooking up with. Because securing all the pussy in the Bay Area would be awesome."

And just like that, the clock is reset.

I reach into the dish behind me, grabbing who knows what.

"Oh…you think that's funny? Because you're so clever? That's right, I'm a big ole whore."

I smush my own handful into her cheek as she screams. And like two responsible adults, we do exactly what we should.

We break out into a full-fledged food mask fight.

Shit's getting slung everywhere as we scramble to the sides of the room, trying to pelt each other with nasty-colored yogurts and whatever else we can find.

She takes off running toward the kitchen for more supplies, but I'm right behind her, hooking my arm around her stomach and lifting her off the ground as I slather her hair in whatever the blueberry stuff was.

"Did you think you were going to get away? Yeah, right. You're a terrible fucking running back. Who runs a straight route?"

She laughs harder as I carry her like a football from the kitchen toward the living room so I can empty the bowls on her.

But she stops me in my tracks as she says, "What the hell is a running back?"

I set her to her feet and look her directly in those yogurt-and-fruit-crusted eyes, unable to hide my shock.

"Did you just ask me what a running back is?"

She shrugs the cutest fucking shrug as she scrunches her nose, countering, "Are they important?"

Are they important? Is she serious? This is a joke.

My head draws back as I huff a laugh and look over my shoulder because I must be hallucinating.

I wag my finger at her, matching her smile as I say, "No wife of mine. No. Wife. Of mine. Not even a fake one."

eleanor

He's insane. He's lost his fucking mind. We're standing in the living room, covered in gunk drying on our bodies, and he picks up a chair and moves it to the left side of the room.

"Okay, baby, so the couch is the offensive line. I stand behind that line. *You* are the defensive end, so you're lined up with the chair."

He motions for me to line up with the chair, so I walk over, chuckling.

"Okay, but so, where's the running back on my side?"

Crew throws his hands in the air, turning in a circle, making me laugh harder before he points at the chair.

"Wild Card, listen to me when I'm on the field. The other team's defense is on the field. Your running back is on the bench."

I squint one eye shut and nod.

"Got it. So you're supposed to throw the ball to me?"

Crew looks like he might give it all up and try punching a hole in the window just so he can jump from the thirtieth floor. But I can't help myself. I refuse to tell him that I was only kidding.

I know exactly what a running back is. I grew up listening to my father TV coach the Niners since I was little.

Now, I may not know who any of the players are because I tap out at watching the game, but that doesn't mean I don't know what a fucking running back is.

His hands smack down on the back of the couch as he lets out a frustrated breath before he stares at me. Shit, this is getting harder to sell. I can't stop smiling.

And the longer we look at each other, the more I start to laugh.

"You. Little. Bullshitter," he barks, standing straight, finally seeing right through me.

I break and start laughing hysterically. Crew walks around the couch, shouting playfully. "It's written all over your face. Son of a bitch. This whole time, you knew exactly what I was talking about."

I shrug, sinking into his arms as he wraps them around me.

"I mean...I'd actually never heard the term *flanker*, so it wasn't a total lie."

His voice gets quieter, but he's still smirking.

"I've been explaining football to you for the last twenty

minutes. When were you going to stop me? Because I was ready to run plays."

"You're a lunatic." I chuckle, picking a dry piece of face mask from his face. "You know that, right?"

He nods and tips his head toward the bedroom, and I follow without hesitation, not even asking why. We walk into the bathroom, but as he heads to the tub, turning it on, I do the same to the shower. Neither of us says a thing; we just follow each other's lead.

I drag my tank over my head, glancing over my shoulder because his hand is already on my waist.

"Rinse here? Soak there?"

I nod as we both step into the massive shower, letting the water rinse off our bodies, making the floor of the shower look like when the rain washes away chalk drawings.

I reach up, wiping my fingers over his smooth neck, and he does the same to me.

Crew and I stand under the warm water beating down on us, silently washing each other off before he runs his hands over my hair, squeezing the water out of it.

"Bath?"

"Yes, please."

The shower cuts off, and his hand slips into mine, our bare bodies walking in step to the tub. I'm helped inside before he lowers himself in, making the water rise almost to the top.

I chuckle, floating my hands over the top of the warmth and staring across at him.

"This is nice."

This, as in all of this...him, me, the last few weeks.

He nods, cupping a handful of water and splashing it over his face before running his hands over my legs and tucking my feet on either side of him.

The thought that's been trying to fucking assault me for the last week finally tumbles out.

"It's crazy to think we have a little less than a week left of this unholy matrimony."

I lay my head back, not wanting to see the look on his face. Because if it's utter relief, that'll sting.

"Yeah. Damn. We survived."

I can't really make out what his voice sounds like. Not that it has to sound like anything. *Ugh, I'm being gross. Shut up, Eleanor.*

"So," he says with my favorite amount of gravel in his voice. "What do you want to do for your final countdown in Crew paradise?"

I laugh and open my eyes, lifting my head as he runs his hands down my legs and sits up.

"Paradise? Someone has good self-esteem. I love that for you. Don't ever give in to what everyone says. You really are almost as cute as Brady."

He jerks me forward, making me squeal and the water splash.

"Almost as cute? Imma hold you under this bathwater."

I laugh as his fingers begin to knead my sides.

"Fine," I whisper, feeling warmer. "You're way cuter. And if I could make a request for my last meal before I'm freed, I'd like—"

To emphasize the filth, I lean in and whisper the details in his ear. His groan is all I need to make me smile as I draw back and look at him.

Crew's eyes dip to the swells of my breasts before lazily making their way back to my face.

"What do you want from me?" I whisper before pressing a kiss to his chin. "The last supper, so to speak."

"Scream my name?"

"Try again."

He reaches down between us, fisting his cock, and grabs my ass with his other hand, lifting me as he says, "Then come to field day. It's my one last thing with the Raiders. That's what I want."

I don't know what it is, but I nod as my chest rises and falls, anticipating what's about to happen. There's no foreplay, no buildup. Crew just stares into my eyes as the tip of his cock presses at my entrance before he slowly slides me down, filling me until he bottoms out.

I gasp, "Oh fuck."

And he groans, running his massive hands up my back.

I wrap my arms around him, rocking my pussy into him, in heaven as he slowly glides in and out.

There are no words, just our breath mingling as we drag our lips over each other's flesh but never kiss.

His hands dip into the water, lifting to wet my hair and slick it back. So I let my head fall back as I ride him, feeling my pussy contract around his cock.

We're just fucking, raw and uninhibited as his palm massages my breast before his mouth closes around my nipple.

I suck in another breath, weaving my fingers through his hair as I rise and fall over and over, pressing my tits against him the moment they're abandoned.

This is exactly what I need at this moment.

To be connected to him. Everywhere.

Crew's hand locks on my hips as he thrusts inside me, taking over. Water splashes around us, but I'm only focused on how good it feels. His cock stretches me, making my breath catch when he hammers inside my tight pussy all the way.

He moans against the curve of my neck, licking my skin and kissing it before his arms lock tightly around me, guiding my body flat against his as he lies back.

Oh fuck. It creates friction on my clit, and he knows it because Crew starts moving me up and down.

Every piece of him fucking me.

I'm panting, picking up the pace as I hold him close to me, my arm wrapped around his neck. God, it feels so fucking good. My swollen clit rubs along his tight stomach as his dick fills me.

Fuck. Yes.

I can feel that twinge, the need. My clit throbs, screaming for more. I wrap my wet arms around him tighter, sliding up and down his body, whimpering as his hands grip my ass, forcing me even closer, grinding my body against him as he fucks my pussy.

Water's slapping between us as our mouths huff hot air.

I grip his neck harder, panting, biting my lip and almost drawing blood as I try to spread my knees wider, wanting my whole pussy dragging over his body.

Stuttered cries fall from my lips as I scream his name in my mind. Building and building, stomach tightening until I press into him, still falling over the edge and feeling my pussy contract around his cock.

"Wild Card," he groans, thrusting hard one last time as we both fall into bliss, coming together.

My body quakes as I hold on to him, goose bumps blooming everywhere.

His lips press to my shoulder as I release my arms. They almost hurt from the tension, but with each deep exhale, they slink away from him until they're by my sides and my head is laid on his chest.

"Damn," he breathes out heavily.

I nod lazily in agreement.

"Want to order burgers?" he adds.

And I laugh.

Goddamn him. I really want to move to Italy.

thirty

. . .

"He's everything I never wanted."

eleanor

"Holy shit, this place is so much bigger than I expected it to be."

Millie laughs on the other end of the phone.

"What do you mean? It's a football stadium."

I laugh too because that's not what I meant, and now I just look like I'm stupid.

"No. I'm at the practice center. Not the stadium." I'm searching over the players warming up in the indoor field. "I don't see him, and it looks like the whole team is here."

"See, you should have gone with the person he sent to pick you up," she says all sassy, like she was there to tell me better.

I step up onto a silver bench, trying for a better vantage point.

"Shush up, Mills. I wanted to get him a present, and I couldn't do that with some rando assistant that might tell him."

I lift my chin, still searching, but to no avail.

"Umm," Millie draws out. "Are we worried about getting surprise gifts for your fake husband who you don't want as your real boyfriend?"

I hop down, fully focused on her.

"We are. But only 'ish.' Listen, we've got four more days together. I'm not throwing it all away for him. You know what I mean? We can relax. It's a goodbye gift."

The only part of that sentence that's true is the fact that we've got four more days together. Because I'm starting to worry that Crew could make me do dumb shit I'd regret later.

Millie starts in with some therapy-grade overanalyzing when some dude I've never seen in my life waves at me, calling me by name. So I interrupt her.

"Mills, I've gotta go. I'll call you later."

Mr. Enthusiasm jogs up, smiling as he greets me.

"Hi, Eleanor, right? I'm Matt." I nod as he continues. "Crew's been waiting for you to get here. But since you didn't come with the driver, I wasn't sure which way you came in. I'm happy I found you."

I smile. "Me too." I glance around again, but Matt shakes his head, motioning toward a golf cart.

"They're not here. This is reserved for the players' practice sessions. Crew, TJ, and Nate are on one of the outdoor fields. How about a ride?"

I follow my new friend to my chariot and try not to feel what I'm feeling...which is giddy. It's impossible not to feel that way, being here where Crew practically lives. It just feels special somehow. We only drive for a few minutes before we're heading down a tunnel.

I'm already laughing because outside of the tunnel sounds like recess in a schoolyard.

"Are there kids out there..." I say, surprised.

I thought he wanted me to come to an exhibition match or something like that.

Matt glances over at me, nodding.

"Yeah, this is what field day is. Crew started it a few years back. He invites kids from low-income neighborhoods through places like the Y—"

My heart stops in my chest. He's shared a lot about how he grew up, and places like that saved him more times than he should have needed.

"These are kids that wouldn't necessarily get the opportunity to do the camps we offer. Anyway, it's really grown over the years and become very popular, so we were really pleased that he pushed for the organization to let him do it one last time before he left."

He pushed. The other night, he played it off like it was just something he had to do. Oh, man. Hot, charming, big dick, and kinky, and now I have to add humble.

Dear Universe, what happened to being a girl's girl? Why are you doing this to me?

The cart slows at the entrance, which is nice because I can already feel the damn heat, and it's 7:00 a.m.

Matt turns toward me. "Between you and me, it's a real shame this organization didn't treat him better. He's a pretty stellar guy."

Yep. Try being married to him, Matt. You'd be an even bigger fan.

I exit the cart, and as soon as we walk out onto the field, my ovaries fucking explode.

Crew is running around shirtless, with a kid tucked under one arm and a ball held above his head in the other. A band of what looks like ten-year-olds are right on his heels, screaming and yelling before he spikes the ball and yells, "Touchdown."

I laugh.

He's adorable. This whole thing is fucking adorable. Maybe I really do just throw it all away. Who needs dreams and accomplishments? Why am I being so this century?

There might be something to the whole barefoot and pregnant road. I laugh to myself because I swear in another life... God.

I'm halfway to the grass when I hear TJ yell, "Crew, your girl is here."

Your girl? Yeah, I'm gonna dine out on that one for weeks.

But all of a sudden, my feet falter, and I stop in my place because tiny head after tiny head turns in my direction. A hundred little sets of eyes on me. It would be a horror movie if it wasn't so cute. All these little people, staring at me like they're so excited I'm here.

Crew lifts both arms in the air and bellows, "Wild Card."

And like a slow clap in an eighties film, my nickname is chanted, loudly, making the smile on my face permanent and my laughter never-ending.

He strolls over to me and smiles down.

"I'd kiss you, but they'd all cringe to death, and the papers would say I did inappropriate things in front of children."

"You already did that..."

His forehead wrinkles in question, so I finish off my joke. "We let TJ and Nate watch."

He chuckles, lifting my hand and pressing a kiss to the top before stepping away, letting his voice carry as he leaves, step by step, his eyes on me.

"Thanks for coming...I put you over in the shade because I know how you feel about the sun." I'm smiling, watching him walk backward and biting my lip. "If you need anything, ask Matt, and make sure you stay out of the splash zone."

"The splash zone?" I yell back, but it's too late.

Before I can duck, water balloons begin flying through the air.

Holy shit.

I squeal, not knowing where to run and somehow, by the grace of god, actually catch one that was launched at me.

I'm staring at it, looking around as Crew yells, "Throw it."

So, I do. And before I know it, I'm running around a football field, laughing and screaming, occasionally being hoisted up and manhandled by my husband as pandemonium erupts around us.

It's perfect. And that scares me to death. Because I'm not

ready for perfect. I don't have room in my life. It's still a mess over here…a work in progress. I'm not ready for company.

But that doesn't change the fact that I'm falling for him, *for real*, at the wrong time. And I need to let the right guy get away.

❦

I'VE BEEN WATCHING FOR ABOUT AN HOUR, DRYING OFF. EVEN though that took about thirteen seconds in this heat. But either way, I've been sitting in my designated seat, watching them play. Sometimes they run routes, and other times, Nate gathers a bunch of kids to show them how to position themselves on the field.

From the looks of it, TJ's job is just to pick people up and throw them around, making prepubescent shrieks sound off around the field, accompanied by "Me next."

"This is a good thing he does," I breathe out, really watching and letting it all sink in.

Before that thought can get any deeper, someone sits down next to me, nabbing my attention. I look to my side, a dark-haired woman with a friendly face staring back, albeit one I don't know.

"Hi," I offer, wondering who the fuck she is.

"Hi, Eleanor." *Knows my name, has to be press.* "Rosanna Marquez. I work for the *Review-Journal*, a newspaper here in Las Vegas. I was just here asking some questions about the kids' annual field day. We like to get the kids' take on what they like and what they don't, and we grab some quotes from the guys. I saw you sitting up here and—"

I smile before cutting in and finishing her sentence.

"And you thought you could get an exclusive from the new and possibly naïve-to-your-tricks wifey?"

"Something like that." She grins, and I don't fault her.

But that doesn't mean I'm stupid enough to answer. "Pass."

"Look," she presses. "You don't have to tell me anything about your wedding. How about you tell me what you think about today? It's a pretty cool thing he does here. A quote from you could get it on the front page."

"Bullshit." I chuckle.

She shrugs. "It was worth a shot. One quote, come on, for the sisterhood."

I scoff, grinning. "Wow, you are good."

My eyes are on him, watching as he smiles, noticing I follow suit. And when he laughs, my shoulders shake quietly. I open my mouth, even though I know I shouldn't, but a piece of me wants us tied somewhere tangible. Like the paper.

I'll buy a hundred copies and keep them, just so I can tell my kids that I was once married to Crew Matthews until I fell madly in love with their father and he stole me away.

It'll only be a little white lie, but my time here will live on.

"I think today is just another example of how life will surprise you when you least expect it. Everyone knows him as their favorite QB or maybe as that jock who does those commercials. But he has so much more to offer outside of that. Crew really is the guy everyone should want to grow up and be like. He was meant to be that dude on the Wheaties box." I glance at her and smile. "Do they even make that cereal anymore?"

She nods, holding her little recorder toward me.

My eyes fall back to him as my thoughts get quiet.

"He's everything I never wanted."

Rosanna's voice slaps me back into reality.

"Sorry, you mean he's everything you've always wanted?"

I frown, looking confused before the realization sets in. *Shit. I said that out loud.*

She clarifies, still staring at me. "Because you said *never*, but you meant *always*. Right?"

I nod vigorously, laughing nervously.

"Yeah. Absolutely, yeah, yep. He's everything I've *always*

wanted." I fan myself. "I think the heat's starting to get to me. Whooo, it really is hot in Vegas."

Suspicious doesn't even cut the look she's giving, but I don't care because I stand, desperate to find an exit.

"I'm gonna go grab some water and maybe get into some cool air. It was...nice?...talking to you."

She smiles as I walk away, not really knowing where I'm going but still chasing distance before I let out a heavy breath and take the stairs down toward the field.

I'm not looking where I'm going, though, because as I turn the corner off the stairs, I run smack into the last person I expected to see.

Josh, Crew's lawyer, and I guess mine too, grabs my shoulders, steadying me.

"Hey, it's my favorite comedian."

"Oh my gosh. What are you doing here? How's the law treating you?"

He smirks and gives me a wink.

"Actually, it's treating me pretty damn good. That's why I'm here today. I was hoping I could catch Crew and let him know that I got that fucking judge recused." He waves an envelope in front of me. "Papers are inside. All you two have to do is sign them, and this nightmare is over."

Well, fuck.

⚓

crew

She bailed during field day, but I'm thinking it's to get ready for tonight since I texted her that I was making good on her request.

I almost got down to business the moment she whispered it in my ear. But delayed gratification will be worth it.

The sound of my duffel hitting the floor echoes through the

penthouse as I toe off my shoes and head for the bedroom. I fling the door open, my voice teasing, "You better be fucking naked in here."

But the room's empty. I look around, walking into the bathroom before retracing my steps back out to the main room.

What the fuck?

My eyes search the space, not necessarily looking for her but because it feels like she hasn't been home. I reach into my pocket to grab my phone, about to call her, when I glance up as I head toward the couch, doing a double take because there are legal papers on the coffee table.

A feeling in the pit of my stomach starts to grow as I get closer. I don't need to look at them because I already know what they are, but I stare at them anyway, plopping down on the couch before I wipe my hand over my mouth.

I'm holding my phone, turning it over and over in my hand, and staring at her signature slashed across the bottom.

Her cheap dice wedding ring sitting next to it.

A deep exhale whooshes from my lungs as I bend forward to swipe the papers. But as I do, I see what's underneath.

Fuck.

It's the goddamn bar napkin from the first time she wrote me a note and snuck out. That thing's been in my nightstand since she left it, and I'd shown it to her the other night, joking about how I was going to frame it.

I drop the papers, swiping up the note and flipping it over.

Here's to chasing dreams not heartbreak.

Thanks for being part of my trip around the sun.

You'll always be epic.

xx Wild Card

I toss the napkin on the table and lie back against the couch, running my hand through my hair before I open up the group text with Millie and her sister.

Me: Technically our girl forfeited by bouncing early. I'm sure you already know that. But I'm a man of my word, and we all know she wasn't caving. So 30k it is.

DJ Mills: Keep your money. It was just for fun.

DJ Mills: *Picture of her Instagram with a Crew Matthews jersey as her profile pic.

Wild Card's sister: Agreed, we don't want it.

Wild Card's sister: *Picture of a sticker on her computer with my new number, 22, next to the words "We love the Niners."

I don't answer because there's nothing to say. I knew this day was coming. We fucking counted down, for fuck's sake. We were always ending, even if it's a few days early. But what really fucking sucks is that it feels like such a goddamn loss.

AUGUST
S M T W T F S
15 16 17 18
20 21 22 23 24 25
27 28 29 30 31
LAS VEGAS NEVADA
77
AUGUST
2 WEEKS
LATER

thirty-one

. . .

"I just got sacked by the tiniest defensive end
I've ever met."

crew

I've shaken more hands today than I can remember shaking all year. Not that I'm complaining because the Niners organization has welcomed me with open arms.

It's everything I ever wanted. *Except why does that sound sarcastic in my head?*

TJ walks by and pats my shoulder as Nate nods his head at me. We've been separated for most of the week with different press obligations. So, I'm happy to finally see them.

"You good, man?" TJ greets, slapping my hand and giving me a dude hug.

The commotion from the press still settling into their seats draws my attention before I look back with an answer.

"Yeah, you know." I run my hands through my hair. "I just hate these things. Especially since the news slow-leaked about the divorce. So it's a matter of time before someone asks. Even when they're not supposed to."

Nate looks at TJ and then back to me. Goddammit, I hate it when they do this. I'd forgotten that this was the perk of not seeing them this week. Because that look was all too familiar.

"Don't start," I warn.

Nate puts his hand on the back of my chair, locking eyes with me.

"Start what? Reminding you of the fact that this will be aired all over the Bay? And maybe a certain area hottie might see it? All right. Sure. Mum's the word."

TJ pretends to be shocked, as if he's sticking up for me.

"Come on, Nate. You act like he fell for the girl. Like maybe when pushed during a friendly game of spin the bottle, he kicked his best friends out of the house. If he did that, then he'd be real dickish, a total pain in the ass. And hooked on the girl. But he's not that…right?"

They both stare at me the same way they've been doing for the last two weeks.

I let out a harsh breath and wrinkle my forehead.

"If you two don't get your asses in your fucking seats and shut the hell up, I'm going to make sure that I tear up my contract so I can go back to the Raiders just for some peace."

They laugh, looking up as things seem to be starting before tapping me on the back as they walk to their seats and sit.

Fuck. They're the biggest pains in my ass because I don't even want to talk about it.

I can't. It feels like Eleanor's consuming my mind more now than she was when we were together. And I need that chick out of my head.

I don't need a distraction like this. Not right now. This is exactly why it doesn't matter if I fell for the girl or if the girl fell for me. She was never a part of the plan. She knew that shit too. Eleanor got it.

Feedback from the microphone makes me jump. That'll be a fucking meme. Great. A woman stands floor level, reaching up and adjusting it.

"Oh gosh, I'm sorry about that. First day on the job. These little buggers can be tricky. Can you do me a favor? Just hold this wire right here."

What? I nod, not knowing what else to do, and hold the wire as she disappears below the table.

Where the fuck did she go? A few chuckles come from the pit, and I join before she pops back up. *Whoa.*

"Sorry again. I dropped the plug. Gosh, this is so embarrassing. I'm not even supposed to talk to you, but I'm a nervous rambler."

Jesus Christ.

She inserts a plug into some port before she sniffs, looking up at me with surprise on her face. I must be looking back at her confused as fuck because she apologizes for the third time.

"Sorry. It's just that I thought I smelled this shave cream that my old esthetician used to make. My sister took me to a salon once, and this angel fixed my skin right up. She's actually opening a new salon. You should tell your wife about it. Didn't you get married? Like last month?"

You've got to be fucking kidding me.

I know the look on my face is bewildered because come the fuck on. How am I being outed by the universe right now? *Fuck you. I'll keep that shave lotion if I want to.*

My face shoots to my left because I can hear TJ laughing. He's eavesdropping on my conversation. So, I discreetly shoot him the middle finger before turning back to the lady, lifting my hand to my cheek to hide what I'm saying.

"Yeah, I bet my wife would love the name of a good salon… what's it called?"

Why are you asking, you fucking masochist.

"Wild Card. Cool name, huh? I think it opens next month… Okay, I'm all good." She gives me a nod. "Have a great press conference."

My hand drops as I nod, swallowing tight, before I put on a smile and look the exact opposite of how I feel—like I just got sacked by the tiniest defensive end I've ever met.

eleanor

"You're officially no fun."

My face lifts to my best friend, who's sitting on my couch, shock and awe marring it. That's a lie—I know I'm not fun right now, but that doesn't mean I won't be fun ever again.

"How dare you? I am so much fun. But I'm also an adult, and I have a ton of work to do before the opening of the salon. We started a whole-ass business, Millie."

"First off, don't act like you've been doing all the work. We split this list down the middle...fifty-fifty."

I hold up a hand, stopping her from talking.

"Second off," I snark. "I don't want to hear the rest of this."

Her hands find her hips as she stares at me like I'm being unreasonable. But what's unreasonable is her undying need to find any reason to point out that I'm miserable.

I get it.

"Too bad," she gripes, following me through my apartment into my kitchen, repeating the same tired list she's lectured me about from the minute I came home.

"You're never going to get over him until you admit what you did."

I spin around, my jaw dropped, eyes wide.

"Millie. It was the right thing to do. You act like he was in love with me. We were fucking and playing house. That's it! It's like Sami said. And frankly, if he wanted to make a move, he has my fucking number."

I lift my phone, swiping it open. "Oh look, no new messages."

I swipe a cup off the counter and dunk it into the sudsy water in the sink.

"But did you tell him how you felt? No, you wrote a note like

269

a Shakespearean Ted Bundy, strangling his heart just so he wouldn't follow. You're so scared. When did you become so scared of falling for someone?"

"Millie." My voice is too loud. So I take a breath, dumping what's in my hand into the sink.

Fuck you, broken dishwasher.

My eyes meet hers, and I speak calmly this time. "Crew and I are the ultimate right-person, wrong-time scenario. I've said this. I'm not afraid. I'm realistic. Did you see his press conference? He's about to accomplish everything he's always wanted. And I'm about to do the same. That takes focus. And relationships steal from you. I like him—yes. I still like him. But it's over."

Her palms smack on the counter as she lets out a growl.

"So then be the right person at the right time."

My hands shoot into the air, carrying suds and water with them.

"I don't control the time, Millie. I'm not the timekeeper of life."

She rolls her eyes, digging her heels in.

"You absolutely control the time. It's your decision. But you know what? Fine, if you want to feel like that, feel like that. But then stop moping around and come out with me tonight."

The answer leaves me before I can catch it.

"Fine."

God, I don't mean it. I just want to shut her up.

"Good. Fine."

FOUR HOURS LATER, I ARRIVE AT THE PINNED LOCATION MILLIE SENT me. But as I open the door to the Irish tavern, I'm assaulted by a sea of red and gold.

"Jesus Christ, is she serious? This has to end. I'm going to kill her."

I navigate through the crowd with more of a bouncer-style quality than I need, finding Millie almost immediately. But before I can say something I might regret, the panic on her face tells me she knew nothing about this.

"Oh god, you're here. You didn't get any of my texts, did you? I didn't know. Everything was fine an hour ago, when you were supposed to be here...and then Niner Nation swarmed this place."

I shake my head. "I didn't get them, but it's okay. Let's go somewhere else though. Preferably somewhere not showing the preseason opener."

She nods, calling the bartender to pay her tab as my eyes drift up and my heart stops.

On the television above the bar is a fleeting picture of us kissing outside the chapel before the camera switches to Crew.

He's in full uniform, smiling and joking with TJ. The camera pans to his number—22. And the whole fucking bar erupts in cheers.

I'm starting to think that I must have fucked the universe's boyfriend. Because payback is really feeling like a bitch.

thirty-two

. . .

"Get your cherry... And put him on top of you."

crew

"**G**oddammit," I shout, hitting my fist on my palm.

Everything about today's practice has been a fucking disaster. I can't throw for shit, my feet feel like fucking lead, and I can't see a fucking pathway to anyone.

Everything's wrong.

I'm thrown another ball so I can try the play again. So I set up, calling it out to the line, and fall back into the pocket, knowing the fucking route, and still, I throw way above TJ's head.

"Fuck," I grind out again, punching the air.

My hands come to my knees as I stare down at the turf, berating myself quietly.

"This is bullshit, Crew. Get your head in the game. You're better than this, you fucking idiot."

I hear my name called as Coach jogs over to where I'm posted and pats my back, so I stand.

"You're being too hard on yourself," he offers. "You're letting all the shit—the press conferences, the news, the divorce...you're letting it get in your head."

If you only fucking knew what I'm really thinking about right now.

"Listen, son. I asked a friend of mine to come and talk to you today. He just got here, and I'd like to introduce you. I think he can help you through this time of transition, and it doesn't hurt that he's a Hall of Fame quarterback."

A v forms between my eyes before I glance over my shoulder, immediately recognizing who's standing about six feet away.

Alec Price walks toward me. The legend himself.

And also one of Eleanor's sister's boyfriends. And I do mean boyfriends because, apparently, she has four.

He extends a hand, and I take it, shaking it as Coach pats both of us on the shoulder and says, "I'll leave you to it."

What he thought he was leaving us to, I'm not sure because neither of us says a thing, choosing to silently size each other up. I'm debating on whether or not it's a power move to speak first when he beats me to the line.

"I've heard a lot about you, Crew Matthews."

I give him a tight smile.

"And I've heard a lot about you."

We stand there staring at each other, tension building until we both break and laugh at the same time. Alec throws an arm over my shoulder as he turns and guides me off the field.

"Are we talking football, or are we talking women?" he says quietly, giving a nod to someone who says his name with admiration.

I look at him, appreciating the frankness, but I shake my head.

"There's only one thing I can talk about. Because the other one's not an option."

He nods, looking thoughtful, and removes his arm as we get to the bench, so I grab my sports bottle and take a drink.

"Well," he finally offers, "if we're talking football, then that's easy. Just do what you know how to do. That's what got you here, and it's what'll keep you here. And maybe if you're lucky, your name will be somewhere around mine in that Hall of Fame."

I nod, and I keep nodding because I heard him, but I'm still thinking about what I really wanted to ask him. And that thought is getting more and more intrusive until I look up and, against my better judgment, say, "How is she?"

He smirks and gives my cheek a pat. "Give me a moment."

Alec pulls out his phone and hits the call button as I frown. *Who the fuck is he calling?* But I don't get a chance to ask before a voice rings out.

"Did he cave already?" *Who the fuck?*

Alec chuckles, covering the phone and whispering, "That's Cole," before he answers the question. "He did. Even before I got to the inspirational shit."

Cole shouts, "Reed, you owe me three hundred dollars."

Jesus Christ, he called the whole damn dick brigade. So now I have to talk to all her sister's boyfriends. Come the fuck on.

"I already gave it to your mom for head," Reed yells back.

Alec hangs up and looks at me.

"Sorry about that, but a bet's a bet. You understand how that is."

I roll my eyes because my girl talks too much—shit, *not my girl*…thought typo.

Alec continues. "And to answer your question, she looks about as good as you."

I take another drink from my water bottle, trying to decide how I'm handling this bullshit. But again, he beats me to the punch.

"You should call her."

"I can't do that, Alec. Simply because she doesn't want me to. I won't pressure her. Why should I? For a chance at love? I don't believe that would make up for giving up who you are. Sometimes people can't have it all, and that just fucking sucks."

Alec crosses his arms, staring back at me for a long, hard few seconds before he takes a deep inhale. But I pipe up first this time.

"Is this gonna be the inspirational part?"

He huffs a laugh, shaking his head.

"No. This is the honest part. I'm assuming you know about my private life?"

I nod.

"Then we're proof that you can have everything you want without sacrificing who you are. We manage that shit daily with five people. Your amateur-hour ass can figure out the two of you. Don't you think?"

I toss my bottle a little harder than necessary, but he's starting to piss me off.

"If I go after her, I'll always wonder if she would have ever eventually chosen that for herself. She wrote the note. She decides for herself. Who the fuck am I to second-guess that?"

"You're the fucking guy that wants to be with her," he presses.

He doesn't get it. "Eleanor isn't there for me to take... That woman is a gift only she can give."

I hear Coach blow the whistle, so I reach out and shake Alec's hand, putting an end to the conversation.

"I appreciate you coming today."

He gives me a tight smile, but as I let go, he holds me in place, his eyes locked on mine.

"Eleanor's a wild card, Crew, but she'll never be able to surprise you if you don't give her the option."

Alec releases my hand, and I take a few steps backward, still staring at him. But as I turn around to head out onto the field, I stop, looking back over my shoulder, and do something I'm scared to death I'll regret.

"Tell her there'll be tickets with her name on them at will call for the season opener. If she wants me, she can come and get me."

eleanor

"Yay, salon opening." Sami cheers, clinking her glass to mine.

I smile and say, "Yay," back before downing the entire flute of champagne I'm holding.

"Whoa," she breathes. "I was assuming the vibe was celebratory, not blackout drunk."

I narrow my eyes at her, aiming for hilarious sarcasm, but instead, I hit too close to home...*mine.*

"Why are you trying to bring up my past?"

Her head draws back as she looks at me like I'm crazy. But before she can say another thing, Millie walks over.

"Oh my gosh. The turnout is amazing, and I'm so excited to see how many bookings we get... hold on a minute." She looks between Samantha and me as her finger shifts between us. "Wait, wait, wait, wait, wait. What's going on here? There are no sister fights at the opening of our salon."

Sami's brows raise as she looks over at Millie.

"Oh, we're not having a sister fight. Your partner in crime and in LLC is losing her shit. She's in a spiral."

I shake my head. "We're not in a spiral... I am not in a fucking spiral. I'm here, being pleasant and shit."

"Babes. Too loud," Millie hisses, hooking my arm as she begins guiding me back to the break room.

But I protest. "What are you doing? I'm not doing this right now."

She keeps her voice low as Samantha follows behind us, grabbing a plate full of hors d'oeuvres.

"Would you please shut up and get in here," Millie rushes out, opening the door to the break room and shoving me inside.

Sami follows before they close the door behind them.

"What are you two doing? You can't trap me in here. I'll gnaw my leg off."

Samantha laughs, shoving the food at me. "Oh my god, eat food, you lightweight. And that only applies to traps…not room, dummy."

"Whatever," I huff, hearing how I sound before I shove a crostini in my mouth.

They're staring at me like two impossibly large, emotionally accountable mountains to bypass. I hate it when they team up on me because then I have to deal with my actual problems. *Just let me bury everything deep down and pay for therapy later, jerks.*

"We should have done this weeks ago," Millie whispers to Sami, who nods.

My shoulders slump as I shove another delicious bite in my mouth with no attempt to be ladylike. Food was definitely needed.

A random thought strikes, suddenly hitting me like lightning, making me feel fried.

He's right. I do eat like an animal.

Sami walks over and slips her hand inside of mine, staring me directly in the eyes.

"I'm going to tell you something that I've been keeping from you. I was waiting to see how you were today. Because if you were great, then you never needed to know. But if you weren't—"

I cut her off, scowling, little pieces of bread flying from my mouth before I cover it.

"What do you mean? What have you been keeping from me?"

Samantha looks at Millie, who starts chewing on her thumbnail, so now I know it's something I'm going to totally fucking hate. I reach out, snatching the water in Millie's hand, and chug it back before wiping my mouth with the back of my hand.

"You two better come clean. Because I don't love the vibes."

Sami takes a deep breath before she dives right in.

"Alec met Crew."

My breath ceases to exist. And I begin blinking too quickly. She did not just say that.

"Is the world spinning?" I whisper. "I think it's spinning."

Samantha grabs my other hand, forcing me to focus on her.

"He still thinks about you."

I'm shaking my head.

"That means nothing, Samantha." I tug my hands from hers and brush past her, needing air. "I still think about him too...but—"

"But nothing, ho," Millie barks, calling my face to hers. She motions around the room. "Is this what you thought having it all would feel like? Be honest. Because you look fucking miserable. And god, you're such a bitch lately." I frown, but she smiles, holding up a hand. "I say that with love. Because I do love you, Mount Elsinore. And I hate that you're depriving yourself."

My chest feels heavy, so I start to rub the spot in the middle as everything I've been feeling hits me hard. God, there's no escaping my truth anymore. Mainly because these bitches won't let me.

But also because I don't want to. I need to say what I'm feeling because I'm not sure he's someone I can just forget about.

"I don't want to get lost in him." I chew the inside of my cheek before I continue. "I spent so much of my life looking for something to complete me. And that can't be a guy." I frown, picking at my nails. "But the shittiest part is that I'm scared I *am* that bitch. None of this feels as good because I want to call him and tell him about it. I want to be his girlfriend. I want to make stupid concoctions and rub them all over his fucking face." My voice is getting louder like a dam has burst, and I'm finally owning my shit. "I want to fuck all night...and I don't even want to fuck his friends. I just want him. I'm supposed to be a bad bitch, a boss babe...and I'm over here wearing these stupid fucking rings because I still want the guy."

I let out a whoosh of air as I pull off the two black bands, one from my thumb and the other from my middle finger. They were supposed to be my surprise for Crew during field day. I had our wedding and divorce dates inscribed to be funny, like a memento.

The metal claps against the counter as I slam them down before I look at Millie and Sam, my chest heaving and my eyes welling with tears.

They rush me, wrapping their damn arms around me, and hug me tight.

Millie speaks first.

"Babe, you're never getting lost in a guy. I wouldn't let you. You wouldn't let you because you've never needed anything to complete you. Even a career. You're amazing."

Sami follows her lead.

"Yeah, and the only reason you want him so badly is because you're ready. You've been a bad bitch since the early 2000s...and you've checked off the list. Accomplishments accomplished. It's time for you to get everything you've always wanted. Get your cherry."

"And put him on top of you," Millie adds, making the three of us laugh.

They set me free from the world's longest hug as we all take a deep breath.

"What if he doesn't want me? I wrote the note. I bailed, knowing he would respect my choice. I fucked up, and now, what if there's no window?"

Sami kisses my cheek before stepping back.

"He left you tickets for the season opener. He told Alec, 'If she wants me, she can come and get me.'"

Millie's face snaps to Samantha's like this is a piece of information she didn't know either. My heart starts racing as I rush out my words.

"When is it? I'll go." I look at Millie. "We'll go?"

She nods enthusiastically as Samantha pulls the information

up on her phone and winces before saying the one thing that I don't want her to.

"It started an hour ago."

There are times in my life when I've thought I love my sister so much it hurt, but right now is not one of those times.

I look between them, feeling my heart start to pump and my nod get bigger and bigger as I speak.

"I'm a boss bitch." Sami nods, her eyes widening. "I *can* have it all." Millie throws her arms in the air as my voice thunders, "I can even leave it with someone to watch and go get the rest of it."

"Yeahhhhh," they both yell back like frat bros until Sami holds up a hand looking confused. "Are you leaving me here with the salon?"

"Yes, Samantha," I exhale harshly, laughing as Millie's already swinging the door open. "But rest assured I will plot your disappearance. Right now, I just have a game to crash."

thirty-three

. . .

"Thanks for finally screaming my name."

eleanor

To say this stadium is loud is an understatement.

It feels like every single person in the Bay Area has shown up today. I couldn't even tell you who the other team is because all anyone can see from section to section is red and gold.

But I genuinely don't care about any of that.

All I know is that without really thinking this through, Millie and I left the salon in Sami's hands, jumped in an Uber, and barely let it slow down before diving out to get our tickets.

Now we're standing in the front row of section 138, wearing heels and cocktail dresses, listening to people grumble that we're down.

"This is stupid. Why am I doing this?" I breathe out, looking at Millie. "This. Is. Stupid."

Millie grabs both of my shoulders, squaring me off to her.

"This is *not* stupid. *You* are fucking epic." She bounces on the balls of her feet, smiling too big. "It's like the ending scene in a romantic comedy. This is your Josie Grossie moment."

I wish I'd never been kissed because I'm fucking dying over here.

"*Orrrr,*" I counter. "It's like a scene in that horror movie with Leonardo DiCaprio where he realizes his reality is all a delusion in his head and he's actually fucking crazy."

I turn away, gripping the railing in front of me, looking down at the empty 49ers bench because it's halftime.

"Oh god. He sat through the first half of the game thinking that I didn't want him. And now I'm supposed to do what? Say 'psych'? Or April-September Fools' Day?"

Fuck.

Millie spreads her arms, looking around.

"How about 'sorry I'm late...'" she says weakly, trying to stay positive.

But I'm fucking sweating, so much. And my mind just keeps vacillating between "this is an atrociously bad idea" to "hell yes, I'm doing this," basically making me want to vomit.

"I think I have heartburn," I say, letting out a whoosh of air and rubbing my chest again. "Can you get heartburn from anxiety?"

She's nodding, suddenly fixing my hair as music starts blaring and the crowd goes wild. It's the most earth-shattering noise I've ever heard. People start chanting, and Millie is fully jumping in place, pointing toward the tunnel.

My head swings in that direction, seeing the team running back onto the field.

Oh my god. It's happening. This is happening.

I feel like I can't breathe.

Millie's smacking my arm, so I slap her hand away, feeling more nervous than I've ever felt in my whole life. I'm searching over a sea of helmets, just trying to look for his number, but I don't see him.

"Where are you, QB?" I whisper to myself.

Suited-up behemoth after behemoth runs out, but he's nowhere to be seen.

Oh my god, did he get injured or something?

"Millie," I rush out, grabbing her hand, still looking at the field. "Google and see if he got injured or something. I don't see him."

But she almost gives me whiplash when she spins my body in the right direction as she yells, "There he is. There's your guy."

Jesus Christ, I'd almost forgotten how fucking gorgeous he is. Crew's running on last and takes my breath away. That's my QB-Wan.

My lips part, wanting to yell something, but then I start to look around because Houston, we have a problem. The bench is packed full of people.

Between cameramen, players, and lots of guys wearing polo shirts, I'm not sure he'll see me, let alone hear me. I'm wringing the hell out of the railing, lifting to my tiptoes, praying to any and all versions of god for Crew to just turn around and see me.

"He'll never see me, Millie."

"Of course he will. Unless…"

My face shoots to hers as she winces and finishes, "Unless he's avoiding looking over here because he doesn't want to be reminded you ghosted him."

Oh god. She's right.

But before I begin to spiral into the abyss of my life and really dig into one of the thirty thousand thoughts I'm having at the same time, I hear Millie's voice ring out into the sky.

"*Crew!*"

The amount of air I suck in as I gasp-speak, "What are you doing?" should suffocate the entire stadium. I took all the air.

But she fucking does it again.

"*Crew!*"

And to make matters worse, some drunk yahoos next to us start yelling it too. Jesus Christ. Millie turns to them, clapping and explaining a mile a minute why we're calling his name.

She tells my whole damn story in fifteen seconds flat, really kicking them into gear as I stand there with my mouth fallen open, drowning in sheer panic. Because like some overly humiliating game of telephone, people start sharing my dumb-ass love story until everyone within a ten-seat radius around me begins chanting his name.

Part of me is wondering how obvious it would be if I just dropped to the ground and crawled along the dirty concrete commando-style until I got to the stairs so I could fucking run.

But the other part is picturing myself on a dirt pitcher's mound with a time clock running down as the music kicks in.

His name is drowned out as whistles blow and the game goes back into full swing.

My heart is racing a mile a minute, almost thumping out of my chest.

"Eleanor," Millie's voice barks, cutting through to me. "This is your fucking moment, bitch. He's right there. Are you going to get him or not?"

I feel a thousand emotions all at once. But the one thing I don't want to feel is regret.

Because Crew Matthews is worth the gamble.

My hands grip the railing again as I turn toward the field, seeing him start to jog out.

The worst idea I've ever had forms in my head. But I don't second-guess it. Not even a little, because today is a day for action.

I'm rolling the fucking dice. I'm betting on red.

My head snaps to Millie as I reach down and take off my heels. "I'm going to get my cherry."

Before she has time to react, I hike a leg over the goddamn railing and launch myself down onto the other side. I want to say I look athletic, but I'll be haunted by that memory.

I hear her scream and the section cheer as I look up, pulling my dress down. Thank god I wore underwear.

Adrenaline is pumping so hard I feel like I could lift a car as my eyes almost pop out of my head.

What the fuck am I doing? Holy shit! I just went over the rail.

It's in that moment that reason uppercuts me in the fucking jaw because reality crashes in.

The whole bench is staring at me. And big, tall men are walking toward me.

Oh fuck. There's security...and they're swarming.

What do I do? Fuck, fuck, fuck.

So I take a deep breath, giving Millie one last look before I do the right thing.

I haul ass.

I'm pushing past players and coaches, hearing *what the fuck* and *who the hell is that* as I whizz past everyone, breaking through the entire 49ers bench as I run straight out onto the goddamn Levi's Stadium field.

I'm gonna die. I'm gonna die. They're gonna take me down and break all my bones. And I'm gonna die.

I glance over my shoulder as my feet move faster than they ever have. Seeing Nate haul one of the security guards up in the air buys me some time, so I scream, "Crew," making him look over his shoulder just as I pounce.

Tackling exactly how he taught me in that penthouse too many months ago.

He topples over, and we roll with me landing on top, straddling him, my hands on his chest pads.

"What the fuck?" he bellows, spitting out his mouth guard.

But the minute he opens his eyes, he's matching my smile.

"I came to get you. Sorry about being late."

He reaches for his helmet, but I don't get to see his face because I'm launched about two feet away, shoved, and carried off by security.

Oh fuck.

There's so much noise that I can't understand what's being yelled at me as two guys hold my arms and start to cart me away. I look over my shoulder, my feet stumbling over each other, seeing a charging Crew, helmet chucked as he barks, "Get your fucking hands off her."

They look confused but listen, just as he spins me around and picks me up. My legs wrap around his waist as his arms wrap around my rib cage.

"You rushed the quarterback," he breathes out, grinning from ear to ear with that black stuff smudged under his eyes.

My palms cradle his face as I start to cry, overwhelmed with emotion because he's the most beautiful goddamn sight I've ever seen. My heart's beating out of my chest as I rush my words out.

"Yeah, I really want him to be my boyfriend." My breath catches as I add, "But only if he wants that too."

Crew's jaw tenses as he stares into my eyes before he starts to laugh, shouting his words to the sky.

"I do."

And just like that, we went full circle. Right back to the two little words that started this.

His lips seal over mine, and I wrap my arms around his neck, kissing the holy fuck out of him. I don't even have to look to know we're on the jumbotron because the crowd is screaming in epic proportions.

I don't know how long he kisses me, but what I do know is that there's a tap on my shoulder as he sets me to my feet. Whistles blow around us, and this time, security motions in the direction I should walk as they reassure a worried Crew.

"Don't worry, she's not going to real jail. Just the holding tank here at the stadium. You can pick her up after the game."

He grips my waist, kissing me one more time, and whispers words into my lips.

"Be a good girl, Wild Card. And thanks for finally screaming my name."

I can't help but start laughing as I'm carted away, glancing back at my hot-as-fuck boyfriend as he watches me go.

I'm not sure if this is the ending Millie's romantic-comedy dream had in mind, but it's good enough for me.

The security guard smiles down at me. "You should wave. They're all cheering for you. For you and Crew."

People always say when luck meets opportunity, that equals success. But I call bullshit. And today is proof. Because even when you get *knot so lucky,* you can still hit a jackpot.

epilogue

. . .

Your lucky numbers: 4, 7, 22, 30

eleanor, march

"**A**re you ready for this?"

"I was born ready for you, Wild Card."

Crew's hand tangles in my hair as he leans down and kisses me gently before rubbing his nose over mine. It feels like the smile on my face has been permanent since he bailed me out of 49er prison camp. Probably because it has.

A soft breath flutters past my lips as I reach up and straighten his bow tie as he presses another kiss to my forehead.

"Hey," he whispers as my eyes meet his again. "Have I told you how beautiful you look today?"

I nod, running my palms over his black lapels, smoothing the fabric of his tux.

"Hmm," he hums. "Then have I told you how perfect you are?"

I nod again, poofing out my '60s vintage white Chanel cocktail dress.

He taps his chin, pretending to think some more, the shine of his Super Bowl ring creating a rainbow on my white dress.

"Then," he draws out, pinching my chin between his fingers

and lifting my face to his. "Have I told you I can't live without you. That every fucking day is better than the one before because of you. Do you know I'd give it all up if you asked me to because there's no better dream than being your husband...*or*...aka I love you."

I stand in silence, drinking him in because I feel the exact same way.

Which is why eight months after we got married, we're back where it all began—the Little White Chapel. Except this time, a hundred of our nearest and dearest are waiting inside to watch us walk down the aisle together and do it all over again.

It's crazy. But so are we.

It's unconventional. But we've never been ordinary.

Plus, who the fuck turns down a Super Bowl–winning quarterback in the middle of the field after the win?

Not this girl.

My palms press to his chest as I lift to my tiptoes, kissing him and speaking my words against his lips.

"I love you too, QB. You'll forever be my number one."

We're lost in the kiss, letting it deepen as we hear, "Get a room," followed by, "But not the one we had before."

Crew chuckles against my lips as we pull away to see Nate and Millie coming from around the corner.

His arms are still around me as I smile at them.

"What's going on?"

Millie holds up my bouquet. "You forgot this."

I roll my eyes at myself, but as I take it, she starts chewing the inside of her cheek. *Uh-oh.*

"What else? Is my dad still mad he's not walking me down the aisle? Because we're doing that at the fancy wedding. I already told him that."

Crew chuckles because it was his idea to have the fancy wedding, all because he's still apologizing for once playing for the Raiders.

She shakes her head and looks at Nate, but he tries to hide his smile as he throws out, "God, you two look a whole lot better than you did the first time."

Crew looks at me, just as skeptical as I am, before he runs a hand over his jaw.

"That's not hard to do when the bar was set to drunk in the club. What the hell is going on?"

Millie motions to Nate like he should speak, and now my eyes are starting to widen.

"Okay," she chuckles as Nate grabs her waist keeping her close. "So here's the thing… He was really excited to surprise you, but I think it's better to know going in."

Millie looks at Nate for help. "Babe—"

"Who's surprising…know what?" I rush out, smiling only because she's smiling.

Nate laughs and shakes his head. "He even made sure the music was perfect…I mean, the guy's a hopeless romantic. Take it from us."

Millie swoons a bit as she adds, "It's so cute," before she looks at Nate, and he winks at her.

Crew and I look at each other, half laughing and fully terrified.

"They mean TJ."

He nods, cradling my face.

"Wild Card, we got two choices: we can jump in that Cadillac that says 'just married' and peel outta here, letting those cans fly in the wind."

"Or?" I interject, starting to laugh harder.

"Or we can just accept that we're never getting rid of our wild and nutty family. And today wouldn't be nearly as fun without them."

I turn, taking his hand as we both face front, side by side, as Millie and Nate each take one of the double doors.

The same ones we burst through all those months ago, getting married on a drunk challenge, not knowing it would change our lives forever.

"We're ready. Open the doors."

Crew kisses my cheek, whispering, "How bad could it be?"

But as they swing open, a four-count beat drops before "YMCA" starts to blare, and our very own Elvis, clad in the white jumpsuit, also known as TJ, throws his hands in the air and yells, "Touchdown. Niners."

If this is the beginning of the rest of our lives, I'd say we're knocking it out of the fucking park.

🎷

Horoscope: Big life changes will alter the road to your happiness.

Your lucky numbers: 4, 7, 22, 30

🎷

NEEDING MILLIE, TJ AND NATE?

Grab **Three Ways to Mend a Broken Heart** or swipe for a sneak peek of their debaucherous origin story.

three ways to mend a broken heart

Sneak Peek

Imagine dating a guy for six months, and then one night, you make him dinner, recreating your first date so you can say "I love you" for the first time.

Romantic, right?

No.

Because when you dress up as dessert, he tells you he'd rather be a party of one.

So now, you're crying in your whipped cream boobs, drinking a bottle of tequila, and debating on cutting bangs.

Rock bottom, you say?

Wrong, again.

Not only does he break up with you, but he shows up to the vacation you'd planned with your friends. So now, here I sit...IN PARADISE..with DJ douchebag and his new girlfriend.

Did I mention she doesn't wear makeup and speaks three languages?

Listen, I don't want him back, but I also don't want to look like the hot mess *before* to their perfect *after*.

So desperate times call for a dirty distraction. A way to keep my mind off everything and maybe even serve up a little payback.

And the universe says there's only one way to do that…

TJ and Nate.

So, I guess that means there are actually *three ways* to mend my broken heart.

Read it now!

sticky wing recipe

sweet spicy sticky sinful wings

These wings are a quadruple threat! They're SWEET, they're SPICY, they're STICKY, and they are SINFULLY good...Kinda like our girl Eleanor and her little Las Vegas rendezvous. These are certain to be the perfect medicine after a night on the strip, where you may or may not have accidentally married a stranger in a drunken stupor. Now, you can choose whether you want to share these wings with him or not, but you should most definitely share them with his two best friends!

Okay, really though, these wings are bomb no matter when, how, or who you enjoy them with.

ingredients:

2.5-3 lbs bone-in chicken wing drums and flats
½ teaspoon salt
½ teaspoon pepper
1 teaspoon crushed red pepper
2 tablespoons avocado oil, divided (or vegetable oil)
2 cloves minced garlic
1 tablespoon minced ginger
1 habanero pepper, seeded, deveined, and minced
2 tablespoons sugar
1 tablespoon rice vinegar
2 tablespoons soy sauce
3 tablespoons gochujang
½ tablespoon toasted sesame seeds
1 green onion, sliced thin

method:

1. Preheat the oven to 450 degrees. Line a large baking sheet with parchment paper. Set aside.
2. Wash wings in cold water and pat dry thoroughly with paper towels. Add the dried wings into a bowl, drizzle with 1 tablespoon oil, and season with salt, pepper, and crushed red pepper. Toss well to coat, then transfer the wings to the prepared baking sheet.
3. Bake for 50 minutes. Remove from the oven.
4. In the meantime, add the remaining oil, garlic, and ginger into a skillet over medium heat, and cook for 2 minutes.
5. Add the minced habanero, and cook for 30 seconds.
6. Add the sugar, rice vinegar, soy sauce, and gochujang. Whisk to combine and cook until the sauce thickens and becomes sticky, about 8-10 minutes, stirring often.
7. Toss the wings with the sauce until the sauce thoroughly coats the wings.
8. Plate the wings and top with toasted sesame seeds and green onion.

Recipe by Bree Dandy
aka @mamacookslowcarb on TikTok and Instagram

THE HOLIDATES SERIES

THE SCANDALOUS SERIES

THE STARCROSSED SERIES

 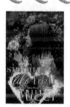 

THE KING BROTHERS SERIES

 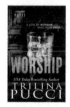 

acknowledgments

Firstly, and in no particular order, thank you—Katie, Kelsey, Sami, and Serena, for listening to me endlessly about the plot and reading and re-reading chapter after chapter. You guys are my lifeline.

Thank you to all the bloggers and influencers, especially my review team and influencer baddies, for all the ways you hype me up and cheer me on. I adore you beyond words! And a special shout out to Bree for the best chicken wings ever!

Big shout-out to my husband for endless amounts of encouragement when life made writing this book an impossible feat. I'm lucky you're always there to remind me that everything is possible if I want it bad enough.

And to my loves, Hoops, Meow—Meow, and Sherlock. The way you never let me give up made this book possible. Thank you for the daily inspirational quotes, the late-night laugh fests, the tangents, and the deep dives on Zillow. The belief you have in me to become a success forces me to believe in myself. If nothing ever gets any better than it is today, I'd be blessed beyond measure because of your friendship.

Finally, thank you, Readers—I literally don't have a job without you. So that makes you my faves.

about the author

#1 Amazon and USA TODAY Best-selling Author, Trilina Pucci, loves cupcakes and bourbon.

When she isn't writing steamy love stories, she can be found devouring Netflix with her husband, Anthony, and their three kiddos. Pucci's journey into writing started impulsively. She wanted to check off a box on her bucket list, but what began as wish fulfillment has become incredibly fulfilling. Now she can't see her life without her characters, her readers, and this amazing indie community.

She's known for being a trope-defier, writing outside the box and creating fictional worlds her readers never want to leave. With every book and each character, she's committed to writing book boyfriends worth binging and smut worth savoring.

Connect with Trilina and stay up to date.

Printed in the USA
CPSIA information can be obtained
at www.ICGtesting.com
LVHW020328281023
762368LV00002B/156